Copyright Dorian Bridges 2024

Exit Note

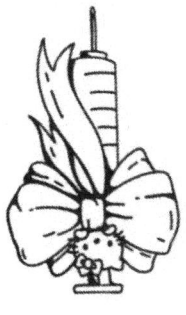

© *Dorian Bridges, 2024*

Copyright Dorian Bridges 2024

Cover art credit to Miss Moon Illustration – scan QR code for Linktree:

(And thanks to my eternal literary inspiration, Poppy Z Brite, from whose gorgeous book Lost Souls *I borrowed my main character's rather unusual name: it was only intended as a placeholder, but it stuck like glue...)*

[handwritten: – basically zihla as a character.]

Copyright Dorian Bridges 2024 [handwritten: em, and zihla's relationship with her.]

Foreword

*'Exit Note' was conceived in 2022, with a singular purpose – to be just that: my posthumous release, and public goodbye to the world, for the day had come. I had no more words with which to fight this country's broken mental health system. All that was left was **'goodbye.'***

*While this tale is, in the main, a work of pure fiction…it is littered and lacerated with copious, blood-stained fragments of truth. The neurodiverse addict is a profoundly misunderstood creature – those few, one-size-fits-all solutions doled out by addiction teams, more often than not **do not work** for us, and when we beg for help, real help, statistically proven **help**, our innate inability to express ourselves in neurotypical language leaves us misunderstood – labelled obnoxious, arrogant drug-seekers, and ultimately, we are left to die.*

*Today, this book is not a death-note, for, despite all efforts and desires to the contrary, **I'm still here**. But I publish this book, in part, in the still-desperate hope that if I filter my words through someone else, they may finally be understood by my doctors, and I will, after **fifteen years** in drug services, **actually be helped**.*

So I dedicate this thing, this plea to the soulless Medical Gods, to all my fellow neurodiverse souls, writhing inside the hell of their own heads, kept afloat by nothing more than grit, fury, and bad ideas.

I hope it gets better – I hope those bastards give you the help you need, and deserve.

And if they don't?

Be loud. Be relentless:

Go down fighting.

Copyright Dorian Bridges 2024

CHAPTER ONE

Zillah:

It's peaceful inside his head – for once.

The peace is rapidly waning…

Somewhere beneath the soft luminescence of heaven, there's a gnawing ache: something's juddering his whole body, shattering his warm cocoon. He clings to it with everything he's got, sinking back to the soothing place where nothing can touch him, where—

A shock of drenching cold shatters the dalliances of his dreams, and he sucks in a breath that feels oddly desperate, as though there hadn't been another in quite some time, and now, like buses, the breaths come all at once, accompanied by a rude assault of noise and daylight.

"Wake up!" yells a familiar voice – the most beloved voice he knows; that voice the whole world has grown used to hearing broadcast through the internet airwaves, entwined with his own. "Zillah, just fucking wake up!"

He tries to rise to the surface, but it's a struggle. The quagmire is too delicious; his eyelids flicker, revealing nothing but a silvery crescent of sclera, then he sinks back down.

"Oh, you *impossible* shit!" Em's voice yells, caught somewhere between panic and heartbreak, and a stinging palm strikes him, hard, across one cheekbone, already wet with the water she's drenched him in. His grey eyes flutter open, but it doesn't stop the assault. Grabbing him by his bony shoulders, she rattles him on the bed, screaming, "I

can't take this anymore, you bloody, *bloody* shit! I thought you'd done it to me again, I thought you were dead, right there in our—"

"'m fine... 'm fine..." he mumbles, his voice rasping with a sleep deeper than any sleep ought to be, hauling himself into a sitting position and drying his face on the duvet. The backs of his heels feel oddly bruised, accompanied by a stiff ache in his lower spine, the result of spending an entire night sedated motionless. "Was that really nec—" He takes in the blazing fury of her expression, and thinks better of it. The adrenaline rush of incoming conflict collides with the dope in his bloodstream, aborting the last velvety tendrils of his dream-state. He rubs his eyes, rerouting to a contrite, "I'm sorry, Em. Do you…want some breakfast? In bed?"

"I'm already up." There's an unnerving sense of distance in her voice – anxiety sparks like a flicked lighter inside his chest. "Do you know why I'm up?"

He gets the strong feeling he'd rather not. She tells him anyway.

"*This*, Zillah." She's holding up an uncapped syringe, pinched between artistically manicured finger and thumb, like it's some alien insect from hell itself. "This repulsive thing stabbed me in the leg, *in our bed,* and now? Now the internet says I need to get tested for hepatitis, HIV for god's sake, and—"

"What?" he says, visibly offended. "HIV from where? You know I'm cleaner with that shit than the average diabetic!"

"Oh hell, that is hardly the point, Zill! When will it get through to you that this is fucked up? I don't want it in my house, I don't want it in my bedroom, and for damn sure I don't want it in my *fucking body!"* Em's voice is enough to shatter crystal – Zillah winces at the volume.

"And then, when I try to confront you, I can't even wake you up – again! Tuesday was—Jesus, man, I still can't get it out of my head – you are not dying in my bloody bed!"

"Em, I'm sorry…" he says, automatically, but his words run dry. He just can't summon it, the fiery eloquence that pays his bills; it's too early…or maybe too late.

"You're not. You're not any kind of sorry, and you damn well know that."

"I am *always* sorry when it upsets you. I hate that I need this shit just to feel ok in my own skin…" He watches her miserably, fighting the childish urge to drag the sodden duvet over his head, and let the residual smack suck him far, far away from this terrifying version of Em, and a day that's defeated him before it's even begun.

"Zill…I need you out. Right now. It's too much, too—"

"No, no, it's my fault; I'll change the bed. Just give me a—"

"Oh – my – god, Zillah, I'm not talking about the bloody bed! I need you *out* – out of this house, out of my life, out of my goddamn head – you can come back for your stuff, but right now, I can't bear another second; I need you *gone*. You almost died three days ago, and you still don't give a shit. You don't care if it kills you, and it *is* – I cannot stand watching this horror show anymore!"

"What the—Em, you know this is only temporary! Things are going to get better as soon as the treatment people *listen to me*, and—"

"That shit will never be the answer, Zill. You're better than this, and you know it."

Copyright Dorian Bridges 2024

He sighs – stares blankly out of the window, half deafened by the thundering of his own anxious blood in his ears. "I try to be better," he says quietly. "I tried 'til it broke me. I know you hate it, but…Christ. You've talked to my friends – you've seen my videos. This has *always*—"

"But that was all in the past…" she says, and there are tears sparkling in her big brown eyes now. "The guy I fell in love with, the guy I *knew,* he was past all that, and I was so bloody proud of him for it. Even when things got rough, last year, you pulled out of it – you always do! I don't understand why you can't just pull out of this goddamn mid—"

"Oh, do *not* say it, Em, just don't. I swear to god, if the words 'midlife crisis' pass your lips one more time, I am going to fucking *vomit.*"

She shakes her head in annoyance, asking,

"How else do you expect me to explain this to myself? How did we, of all people, hundreds of thousands of them telling us every single day how perfect we are together, end up *here?"*

"Oh hell…" he sighs. Every nerve in his body rings with the pain of not touching her – he reaches out, but she doesn't come any closer. He drops his hand, closes his eyes – presses his fingers into them, and the recall is agonising in its perfection. He can hear every word, see every second, from the day their combined fanbase became their matchmaker, 'shipping' them forcefully together until *Emma Lee*, that gorgeous, alien, untouchable creature, came sliding into *his* DMs. When she suggested they meet up – on camera, live, capturing every second of their first-encounter awkwardness, and juicing it for cash – he'd never been so euphoric about an idea that also left him anxious enough to puke. He'd gotten there empty-stomached, lightheaded, got the first of Em's expertly mixed Old Fashioneds inside him...and found there wasn't an ounce of the awkwardness they'd anticipated. Their chemistry was instant, flirtatious, electric, and the camera caught it all, caught it so profoundly, it was barely seven days before a die-hard fan of Em's segued from obsessed, into jealous, into death-threats murderous. The police didn't give a damn – two of those obnoxious social media 'influencers', taking an internet troll seriously? It hardly topped their list of priorities. That was when Zillah moved into Em's spare room, the most anxious bodyguard in history. They couldn't be moving too fast, could they, if her life was in danger? Ten days later, the stalker lobbed a brick through the window, poured petrol through the letterbox, and the police were forced to give a damn. The guy got carted off...but even when the danger had passed, Em didn't want Zillah gone. Six weeks later they broke their leases, and moved into this place, together.

Two years ago. Two fucking years, and she still felt like that glorious alien being – something too bright, too perfect to be a part of his fucked-up life... Even when he'd been truthful about his ongoing struggles, told her the dark awful things almost no one else on Earth knew about him, she hadn't run away screaming. Maybe that made her every bit as mad as he was, but maybe it didn't. Maybe they were just that perfect for each other – wasn't that what everyone said, all those luminous online gossip pages, fawning over them with joy and jealousy? Em was the most—

"Oh *hell*, Zillah! Why do I even bother?" Em's manicured fingers reach out to shake him back to the waking world, and there she is, blue hair and big doe eyes, blazing with palpable fury – too beautiful for this rotten Earth.

"Sorry..." he mumbles, again, jolting back to life. "Shit, I'm sorry, Em, I just need—"

"How did we *get* here?" she repeats, and he wonders if she can see it all, too – their weird, perfect beginnings…or whether all she sees now are his flaws, his fuckups – some of them nearly fatal. "Zill, what went wrong – really?"

He runs his fingers over his eyes. "Don't make me drag it all out again, Em. I tried. I did. Even the shambolic mess of an alcoholic I ended up last year, I was just trying like hell to *avoid* the smack, because I knew how much you hated it. I thought—"

"You're blaming me for this now? You're seriously going to—"

"Ohhh my—*Fuck* no, Em! I'm trying to say you held me together when nothing else could, for nearly a year before things got dark, and if love alone could fix me, or if…if I could *do this thing* fuelled solely by how much I care about you, then this thing would be *fixed*, a thousand times over. But love shouldn't be a band-aid, and it can't fix what's incurable. Because I *am* fucking incurable, Em – unchangeable, can't bash my brains out on the same goddamn wall for another second, *useless*. But you know what could fix me? *Medication.* When I *just* get the—"

"Right, right – when you get that insane, barely-legal script you're never getting anyway, then this shit, right here, can be socially sanctioned too? No. N-O, man. Don't you get why love can't fix you? It's because it never comes from within – you don't love yourself, you don't even *respect* yourself, and I cannot live in your self-destruction warzone anymore! I'm sick of being collateral – Tuesday was literally the worst day of my life, I've never been so scared, and I need you *out!*"

Copyright Dorian Bridges 2024

"Em, I—"

"Oh, *you* do not get to *speak,* right now!" she erupts, fists clenched, tears streaming down her cheeks. Zillah's gnawing the skin of his knuckles hard enough to draw blood, fighting the swelling panic as Em chokes out,

"I wanted *forever* with you, Zill! I could picture the rest of my fucking life with you, and it was so beautiful, but this – now? I'm just meant to stand by, and watch you die? *That's* our life together? I've been waiting and waiting through this downward spiral into hell, every day hoping for my best friend to come back to me, but right now…he is clearly gone. He is clearly fucking *dead.* And I cannot stand looking at the wreckage of him, stumbling round my house for another second, so just…get your stuff, and *get out!"*

It takes a long moment before the gut-punch of her words fades enough for him to utter a single syllable, and even then, all he manages is a very wobbly "Ouch…"

No one's ever had the power to able to render him speechless: Zillah Marsh, winner of every college debate, controversial YouTube wordsmith, and the guy his friends always shove to the front in a confrontation – despite the fact he can't throw a punch to save his life. He's always been able to talk his way out of anything, but…Em? Em knows exactly how to hit him where it hurts – every, fucking, time…

Tentatively, he reaches for her hand, but she whirls away, snatching tissues off the bookshelf. His heart's hammering so hard and fast, only the lingering traces of dope in his bloodstream are keeping him halfway together, as he asks hopelessly,

"Where do you even expect me to go?"

"Tom called," Em mumbles, through tissues and tears, "Last night. I couldn't wake you up. He'll have you."

Zillah buries his head in his shaking hands. "The needle had nothing to do with this, did it? How long have you wanted me gone?"

"*Never,*" she replies, and her chocolate-brown eyes are wide and honest and heartbreaking, spiked with tear-wet lashes. "This is the hardest thing I've ever done, but right now, I'm losing you either way. And if I don't get you out, *right now*, by next week, or next month, they'll be dragging you out in a sodding body-bag, and I can't bear another second. So just get out, Zillah – please? Get out of my fucking house, before I burn this whole place down with you and all our memories still inside it!"

"Since when was it *your*—" he begins, but the door slams, and Em's gone.

> Tom is such a character. he's quite comedic, lightens things ~~whenever still~~

Copyright Dorian Bridges 2024

CHAPTER TWO

> Zillah's friend. I met in colledge.
> → Lucy
> — still friends with Zhilla - seems supportive.

Tom:

Zillah's on my doorstep, slumped on top of a suitcase, looking utterly devastated. It's understandable: what a hefty bloody fall from grace. Here stands social media's favourite fixation, with his pretty face, furious eloquence, and the stunning blogger girlfriend who generally thinks the sun shines directly out of his backside. Now he's back on heroin, dumped, homeless, and I think we all know his career will go up *in smoke* if the internet catches a whiff of this fucking relapse.

"Oh, mate…" I sigh, stepping across the threshold to give him a hug. "I'm sorry. Is Em the antichrist to us now, or is the jury still out?"

He goes from tense to rigid at the mere mention of Em, then pulls away, shaking his head, his eyes locked on the pavement. What worries me more than his visible misery is the fact he also looks shifty, like he's smuggling something very illegal – and he almost certainly is – or possibly like he's about to nick all our valuables and pawn them, which, judging by everything Em hollered at me down the phone last night, might not be too far from the truth either. I figure it might be wise to set some boundaries before I even let him in. As he makes a move for the house, I push him back, put the door on the latch, and close it behind us. He looks bewildered, and wary.

"Zill," I begin, "I've downplayed everything to Lucy, as much as I could. If I told her the truth, about…well, you know, all of it—" Zillah winces, runs his hands through his hair, and starts riffling through his pockets for what I initially think is a roll up, but from the stench of it, turns out to be a joint. We're standing in the middle of *my* street, in broad daylight, he knows full well my neighbours are awful, and now he's blazing up super-skunk. "Not here!" I hiss at him, and he reluctantly grinds it out on a nearby lamppost. He's twitchy as all hell, hands shaky, and I can't tell if he's anxious, withdrawing, or both, but it's not a good sign. "If I told Lucy everything, I have no idea how she'd react – this stuff's over the line, even for her. You're fucking lucky she's not a fan of Em. And you're lucky that I'm a fan of you, 'cause it sounds like Em's been in everyone's ear about you, and I'm not having you sleeping in a gutter, or at a homeless shelter."

"Tom, I'm not broke," he points out, sounding exasperated. "I know everyone thinks my job is a ridiculous non-job and I must be on the perpetual verge of poverty, but I am *not broke*. I just need some time to—"

"Look, I know you're not generally broke – you bought those boots last time the internet unleashed its wrath on you, and the price-tag was eye-watering. I know I could tell you to fuck off, and it'd be fine, but the thing is, it wouldn't be fine, would it? *You* wouldn't be fine. Not on your own, in a hotel, pretending you're a 22-year-old rockstar. How the hell you're not dead already is either a goddamn miracle, or an epic mistake, but I want to keep it that way."

Zillah sighs heavily, and dumps himself down on the nearest garden wall, chewing his nails and peering up at me through eyeliner-smudged eyes. He's lost the final traces of alcoholism weight since I last saw him, and now he's back to an eerie echo of the skinny goth boy I first met at college. How in hell someone who treats his body like a chemical disposal plant still manages to look so young is beyond me, and it's profoundly irritating.

"Does this lecture have a point?" he asks, warily. "Besides the fact I'm too old for this shit, shouldn't be so stupid at my age, and maybe it's a goddamn midlife crisis and I should be in therapy?"

"Hey, you said all of that, I said none. It's not exactly untrue though, is it? Zill, my point is –" I sit down on the wall next to him, and drop my voice to an undertone – "You're not gonna nick anything, are you? I know you've got money in the bank, or on the internet, or however it works, but if the silverware suddenly goes missing, I can't just—"

"Oh, fucking *Jesus*, Tom!" he erupts, shooting to his feet and beginning to pace twitchily back and forth, tugging at his purple hair. "I knew this was a horrible idea! I knew Em'd manage to twist you round her little finger, but I never thought it'd be *this* ridiculous. Look, bad idea, terrible idea, I'll be at the Lion if you need—"

I have to run up the road after him, designer combat boots and spiked leather jacket stomping off ahead of me, before I manage to grab him by one skinny arm, and stop his ongoing flight. When he turns back I realise he's on the verge of tears, and I can't help feeling like the world's biggest arsehole.

"I'm sorry…" I say, lamely. "That was an utterly shitty thing to say. I've known you far, far longer than Em has – I shouldn't have let her get in my head…"

He scrubs at his kohl-smudged eyes, his voice breaking as he says,

"I'm not a fucking *thief*, Tom. How could you even—" He breaks off, sighs, stares up at the sky in despair, and murmurs, "Oh hell. It's all because of that goddamn christening, isn't it? I got high at her niece's

14

christening, and now I'm every dismal stereotype in the book to her, right? Is that it?"

"Oh hell, mate, are you serious? I was hoping the christening fiasco was a gross exaggeration…"

He shakes his head, jaw tense, eyes fixed on the pavement.

"It was an innocent fuckup. Could've happened to anyone. In my defence I refused to hold the baby…'cause I knew I'd only drop it. I never *meant* to," he insists, and when he meets my gaze, his eyes are guarded, but clear, not glassy, not glazed over – he's in there, today. "I'd forgotten all about the bloody christening, so I got high, but it was this new batch – way stronger than I'd anticipated, and I'd had some sodding methadone then forgotten about it; it was the perfect storm. When Em sprung it on me, I figured I'd just sleep it off in the back of the church, but it wasn't like that – we were standing round with all her bloody relatives, they started staring, and it made me so anxious, I—Fuck, you know what I'm like – the anxiety made me sick as a dog. I had to hide out in the bathroom, but I sort of…fell asleep in there. And someone saw my foot poking out under the door, thought I'd dropped dead – I was so high I didn't hear the banging 'til they'd started screaming for help, and I couldn't rein it in, man, the chaos was rolling! I tried telling them I was just tired, that I work late ni—Oh *Tom*, for shit's sake, this is *not funny!* This is my fucking life, not some ridiculous soap opera – you can't just laugh at me while I'm spilling my guts to you!"

He looks furious…but he starts laughing too, after a moment, hiding behind one hand. I hadn't meant to crack up…he's right, none of this is funny, but Jesus, Zillah. Way to ingratiate yourself to Em's family. Anyway, he laughs, just a bit, and thank god – if he didn't, I think he'd be crying, and that would serve no purpose whatsoever. Surely it's over between them, after all this? I just don't know if he realises it yet.

"Are you still hoping to…you know, smooth things over with her?"

The smile's wiped clean off his face. "I don't want to talk about it," he states, avoiding my gaze. "I thought things were salvageable… I really thought we were—Oh, fuck it, man. If she's going round telling my friends to watch out in case I rob them, what am I even meant to say? That's just disgusting. I'm not going back to that." His expression is mulish in the extreme, but I've known him too long to be fooled – it hurts like hell. How could it not?

"Well, thank god we're on the same page about one thing. Nothing worse than tolerating someone in total denial about his corpse of a relationship…"

"Mmm…" he says, blankly. A light breeze ripples through the neighbour's shrubs – Zillah shivers so hard he winces, wrapping his arms tight around his skinny body. Hunched into his jacket like we're in the goddamn arctic circle, he asks, "Am I allowed in yet? It's fucking freezing out here."

I squint up at the sky. It's nearly cloudless blue – sun shining down, the sound of a lawnmower buzzing lazily from a neighbour's place. It's breezy, but I'm in a t-shirt. He's in his heftily spiked leather jacket – shivering violently. Christ. I know he's about half my bodyweight these days, but he's clearly not ok. I don't want to have this conversation with him – I don't want to become his bloody mother, but I also don't want to call an ambulance or a sodding coroner to my house because my dysfunctional tit of a best mate's dead in the spare room.

"Zill…I don't know how to phrase this without you exploding at me, so please just know I care, that's all, it's not an attack, or—"

"Ah hell, Tom," he groans. "What? What the fuck now?" He's shivering and pacing, and looks about five badly placed words away from lamping me.

"Mate…I can tell you're in withdrawal. It is visibly fucking obvious right now, and we all know you don't do withdrawal. Which means, the second I let you through that door, you're going to be—"

"I've got my script," he says rapidly, frowning at the pavement. "All my shit's packed right down in these stupid bags, and Em screwed up my schedule, that's all – I have *got* my script, so just let me in, please, then I can take my crappy medication and in about an hour I'll be better company, alright?"

"Please don't bullshit me, Zill – Em's told me everything."

He growls through gritted teeth, moves to sidestep me, and I have to grab him again.

"Tom!" he snaps, shaking me off with another wince, and resuming his hectic pacing, "Will you lay off it! I feel like fucking death, can't we talk about this inside?"

Tom genuinley cares about his friend - seems acepting.

"In a minute. I need the truth. Look, I offered to put you up not because I want to play Fun Police, but because I actually care about you, and I want to *keep you alive.* So I'm not saying no, never, not under my roof, show me all your stuff right now, like this is a psych ward, 'cause I'm not a bloody moron, Zill – if I stop you using in my house, I know you'll only do it at the train station, and it isn't safe. So just…do what you have to do – alright?"

He stares at me, shocked silent. I can see the addict mathematics spinning in his brain though. *Is this a trick? What the fuck is he playing at?*

"It's not a trick," I tell him, moving closer. This is not a conversation I want Lucy overhearing. "All I care about is getting you through this shitstorm lapse of judgement alive, whatever it takes. So, look, I know what you're about to do, the second we get in there, and while I wish like hell you wouldn't, and I'm here to talk about it, or to take you to rehab *any time,* right now all I'm saying is, you go in the en suite, you do *not* lock the door, I sit on the bed, and we keep talking. When you've done your thing, you come straight out, or I'm coming in after you."

He side-eyes me. "Then what?"

"Then nothing. Aside from the fact you stay out of Lucy's way while you're high. And if you need to use again, you fetch me, and we repeat the exercise. That is the one and only condition of you living here – no using alone."

"And no nicking the silverware, just so we're clear?" he says, smiling slightly. "Tom, d'you even own silverware? Does anyone, in reality?"

"Yes, actually – some of us are legitimate bloody grownups these days, much to our own chagrin."

He shakes his head, laughs, then flings himself at me, jacket-spikes and all, and gives me a hug, saying, "You are genuinely the best person on this planet, Tom. I don't know how someone as useless as me deserves someone like you, but…thank you…" He breaks away, smiling, then shivers himself into another pained wince, and begs,

18

"*Please* can we go inside now, for the love of god? I'm about to throw up all over your street…"

I slap him on the back, and lead the way in, hoping like hell I'm not going to regret this whole stupid affair. It was one thing keeping the secrets of my shambolic best mate when we were in our twenties, but now? Now I have a wife I don't want to lose, now that everyone in the world seems to be gossiping on group WhatsApps – now that Zillah's gone and made himself a fucking public figure, with a vengeful girlfriend bent on airing his dirty laundry? How long before both of us are homeless?

Only time will tell.

Tom is caring however aware that taking care of Zhilla in this way may affect him personally, however, still goes through with this to help his friend. He plays an incredibly supportive role to Zhilla here, even if it may be at the expense of his own personal loss.

> seems like Tom is splitting his life for the sake of his friend, potentially sacreficing his own stability to help his friend get back on track.

Copyright Dorian Bridges 2024

CHAPTER THREE

I manage to hustle Zillah up to the spare room while Lucy's cooking – their paths don't cross. This is fortunate, because he really wasn't exaggerating – by the time we get there, he's gone white as a sheet, dropping his bags like hot coals and barging past me as he flees for the en suite. The tap gets slammed on full blast to minimally mute the sound of him chucking his guts up, and finally he emerges, shuddering and hollow-eyed. I sigh.

"Oh hell, man. What on Earth made going back to it so tempting? I haven't seen you in a state like this in years…"

He opens his mouth to reply, and immediately blanches, groans, and goes dashing back to the bathroom for round two. I shake my head in despair, asking, *while being caring, Tom's trying to help & reduce harm. Even though he is trying his*

"Wouldn't it be less hassle, overall, to just take your sodding methadone? Doesn't it keep you…not-sick, for longer?"

best, his own personal sustration shows.
He finally slumps out of the bathroom, runs his fingers over his bloodshot eyes, and says,

"D'you really think I could keep that awful crap down right now? I'm only this sick because I'm trying to be *responsible*. Em fucked up my schedule, you've been out all sodding day, and I'm not using on top anymore – it's how that stupid OD happened, me taking methadone then doing my usual hit – I never thought the—*Ugh, hell!*" – a violent full-body shudder puts paid to his litany of excuses. He slithers out of his leather jacket, black Joy Division t-shirt drenched with sweat, though he's got goosebumps up both arms, and he's shivering like a wet dog. I get the briefest flash of more needle bruises than I've ever seen on him before, then he's snatched up one of his bags, and he's off into the bathroom like a shot.

"Don't lock it," I remind him. "In fact, keep it ajar. I need to hear you without Lucy wondering why we're yelling."

The door creaks open an inch. There's some clattering about, a bit of rustling, a tap running, then I hear the flick and crackle of a lighter.

"How you doing?" I ask, when silence falls.

"Give me a minute," comes his disembodied voice. I can hear his teeth chattering. "I'm all shaky – it's slowing me down. I'll tell you when I'm starting, but...fuck, Tom – this is *weird*, even for us..."

"Glad the feeling's mutual. Can we do something really normal later, like smoking some of that weed and playing GTA, after Lucy goes to bed?"

"Bring it on. Right…I'm starting. Give me a minute…"

I realise I'm gnawing my lip, heart pounding in my ears. How can he still be playing this mad level of Russian roulette with himself at our age?

"Have you tried this batch before?" I ask, nervously.

"Mm-hmm," comes his muffled reply. "Iff fime…"

"Is that a tourniquet in your mouth, or are you having a fucking stroke?"

Copyright Dorian Bridges 2024

There's a long silence, then, distractedly, "Tom, please just…chill out. You're ruining the best part of my day. Best part of my shitshow life…"

I fall silent. So does he. But I'm watching the second hand on my watch. I give him precisely ninety seconds, then – "Zill? You alive?"

There's another long pause, followed by an incredibly quiet, out-of-it sounding, "Mmmhhhh…"

"Oh bloody hell…" I mutter, hauling myself to my feet. When I knock on the door, he doesn't respond, so I barge straight in. He's still got his trousers on, thank god, but he's passed out with his head on the toilet seat and a needle still uncapped in his lap. He looks alarmingly dead, like some godawful poster-child image splattered across statistics about fentanyl deaths – I move the needle and shake his shoulder, hissing, "Don't you *dare* do this to me in my own fucking house, you cunt! Zillah!"

His eyes flicker vacantly open, and they're glassy grey orbs – pupils nearly non-existent. He gives me this empty smile that just depresses the fuck out of me. We'll be forty in two years' time – assuming he makes it that far – and somehow, here I am, back in the trenches of idiocy with him. I really thought these days were over...

"'m fine…" he mumbles, his voice a slowed-down, rasping slur, like a malfunctioning tape player. Despite this assurance, however, he starts crumpling onto his side on the tiles, looking like he'd happily sleep the afternoon away face-first on my bathroom floor. I have to grab him under the arms, hauling him up and supporting his stumbling carcass back into the bedroom, where he promptly collapses across the bed, and zonks out. Cursing under my breath, I undo his boots, yank them off, and put them down in the corner, then hurry back to the bathroom to tidy his revolting crap away. There's a weird little spoon covered in golden staining, an obvious and rather large drug wrap, a purple rope tourniquet, sachets of Vitamin C for fuck knows what purpose – maybe the secret of his undeserved eternal youth – and a lot of needles, most of which are still in sterile packaging, which is something, I guess. I don't even contemplate flushing the drugs – I've done it before, and what followed was not pretty. If this batch is safe, that's as good as things get while he's being like this. I shove it all back into the Tupperware container it's spilling out of, and return to the bed, resting my hand on his chest to make sure he's still breathing.

"Wha'thfuckyoudoin'?" he mumbles, after a moment. "Izziss about t'get sexual?"

I sigh, and take my hand off him. "Are you ok – seriously? If I leave you now…you'll be ok?"

He grumbles, and rolls lethargically onto his side, then reports, more or less coherently, "'covery position. Couldn' be safer…" When I still don't leave, he sighs, and makes a visible effort to open his eyes, mumbling, "Shit… Sorry'm wasted… S'just…fuckin' Em…" His tone is blank as a whitewashed wall – whatever he was feeling about her before, he doesn't seem to give half a shit now. "Gonna sleep… GTA later…"

He smiles, and his eyes flicker halfway open for another fraction of a second. I've rarely seen anyone look so wholly at peace with the universe, and I have to fight down another wave of despairing déjà vu. No wonder Em's so pissed off with him. She's largely been in a relationship with Functional Zillah, who is, despite his severe anxiety and more-than-occasional belly-flops off the Sobriety Wagon, a bloke

I'm generally proud to call my best mate. I have no idea why the Ghost of Dysfunctional Pasts has come crashing through our lives, and traded that guy for this clattering catastrophe, but I hope I can get to the bottom of it, before he loses his bloody job along with Em and everything else. It takes a special kind of patience to sit amidst the chaos he unleashes, all the while knowing that while we stress about him, he's in his own personal paradise. That's pretty fucking annoying…but then he generally is, when he's in the depths of a life-destroying bender: Zillah's semi-famous for predictable reasons – with a face like his, everything he does looks like an advertisement, and right now, he'd make a pretty convincing model for the drug that'll whisk all your problems away…

* * * * *

Zillah emerges from the bedroom surprisingly soon, looking stressed as all hell in spite of his visible grogginess. He stands there, fidgeting awkwardly about in the kitchen doorway, 'til I follow him back upstairs. As soon as we're out of Lucy's earshot, he whips round and blurts out,

"Help me, Tom! Em's having the world's biggest freakout – what do I do? I just got woken up by all these progressively pissier messages, saying she's sick of the "perfect couple" fangirl shit she gets on Instagram, that she refuses to "lie for me" anymore, and now *I* have to be the one to come out and tell the world we've split, as in, it's over, *finito*…which is—I mean—Is she *serious,* Tom? Is this really *it?* Not just 'on a break', but…*over?* I don't—I can't even—?" He stutters himself into silence, takes a shaky breath, then carries on babbling,

Copyright Dorian Bridges 2024

"Can I not even have five seconds to process things?! We've been broken up less than a day, I'm not okay at *all*, but apparently she's ready to tell the whole world that I'm *dead to her*, meanwhile I've got my sodding manager crawling up my arse 'cause I was meant to do sponsored shit for hair gel or some other *irrelevant tripe,* and I've no idea how I even do that without all my stuff, I don't know what I'm meant to tell *him* about all this, I can't—"

"Mate, take a breath," I say, as he paces back and forth, raking his fingers through his hair. Zillah's ability to freak out completely, even under the influence of enough dope to sedate a rhino, is almost impressive. "Em's upset, that's all – you know she's a spitfire. Give her time. As for your manager, just tell him about the split – for now that'll have to do. I assume this manager is not a trained therapist, so he can't really help you much, can he? There's no reason to cut him in on the whole mess unless you have to. You might get dumped by the agency anyway, if they get wind of—"

"Oh Jesus, Tom!" he groans, "Don't say that – I feel sick, I can't fucking handle this… It's getting worse and worse, and how does anything get worse when you were woken up by the love of your life making you homeless? I—" He breaks off, wincing. I pointedly open the door to the en suite. After a few shaky breaths though, he just starts digging through his pockets, coming out with a handful of dubiously illicit anxiety pills, and gulping them down, dry.

"Tom…" he says, "D'you think she really means it? Are we actually *over* – forever?"

He looks like his whole world's come crashing down around his ears, just…lost – broken. I have no idea what to say – Em sounded furious on the phone, but even so, it was obvious how much she still cared about him. I have no idea which way this thing'll blow – not 'til I've talked to him about it, properly – worked out why he's so hellbent on blowing up his entire universe. All I can do is hedge my bets, and tell him,

"Look, don't stress about it yet. I reckon she's either milking the drama, or she just needs a break from people telling her how lucky she is to have you, while she doesn't actually have you. It's a video, mate – that's all. Money in your pocket. You can take it down if she changes her mind."

"Oh hell," he sighs. "You haven't a clue, Tom. The ripples of this shit don't just vanish when I take it down – people are going to take sides, they're going to mine our socials for gossip, they're going to spin *bullshit* lies and call it 'tea' – you don't know this scummy industry, and what my bloody announcement might unleash…" After staring nervously into space for several seconds, he snaps out of it, asking with a frown, "Do I look ok? Sober, I mean? Can I pass for sober?"

Not really, is all I can think. His pupils are tiny, his eyes are glassy, but equally he's twitchy and stressed enough that the grogginess has become barely noticeable. I tactfully suggest sunglasses, and he just groans, then starts riffling in his bags. He brings out a little blue bottle and liberally squirts eye-drops into both eyes, then he's off round the room, pulling out bits of electronics, until he's set up a weird round light with his camera in the middle, and he's pratting about with his hair, and his eyeliner – I move to go, but he pleads, "Stay, Tom? I know it's weird, but just…stick around for a minute? Give me some moral support 'til these fucking pills kick in? And stop me, ok, if I say something really stupid?"

"Oh Jesus, are you going live? I think that might be—"

He grimaces – "Fuck no. I'm recording the briefest bit of bullshit pseudo-honesty I can muster. You up for it?"

"I'm not going on camera…"

"Not asking you to. Thanks."

He clears his throat, presses a button, swears under his breath a few times, then he just starts talking at the camera like it's a person. It's a bizarre thing to witness, frankly, how fluent he is at pretending this inanimate object is actually a friendly confidante, when in fact it's a portal to every stranger, lover and hater on the planet, and somehow, this act of mass spying doesn't seem to bother him one bit.

"I'm sorry for the weird setup," he's saying, clearly trying to avoid direct eye contact with the camera…which is probably wise. "It might be obvious, but I'm not at home right now. Umm, temporarily, I'm sort of…without one. I'm not broke – I'm not asking for money, it's nothing…awful, like that, but Em and I have been having some…*issues*. Please, *please* no one hassle her over this – don't send her hate, don't bug her for details, don't even mention me – she wants her peace, and she deserves it. All I'm going to say is, no one cheated on anyone, no one abused anyone, and there's still a lot of love between us – we don't need people taking sides. We've just…grown in very different directions, and…something had to give. As of this morning, I've moved out of our place." His voice is shaking – he clears his throat, wrestles himself back under control, and continues, sounding decidedly lacklustre,

"I'll try to keep the content coming, but obviously that might be tough while I'm couch-surfing. Please don't…worry, or anything – I'm ok, Em's…ok, just…give us the space and respect to move on in our own directions, please? I know you want the gory details, but Em deserves better than a huge 'he said, she said' picking apart of our relationship, and our breakup, all scattered with like…saccharine Moving On Positivity that I just can't summon up, 'cause honestly, I'd rather ram a white hot poker through my own *eyeball* right now than—"

"Zill," I intervene, "Keep it factual. I get that it hurts, but the last thing you want to do right now is escalate this shit."

He sighs – runs his hands through his hair, his expression despairing.

"Oh, shit it, Tom, I know, I just— *Ugh…* I'll edit this." He pulls a face, shakes his head and stares into space, looking increasingly anxious. Finally he shivers, takes a deep breath, and rattles off a rapid-fire,

"More positive stuff coming soon. For now, for once, I'm going to filter my mouth. Hugest gratitude to my best friend for letting me stay – moral support doesn't come so easy.

"See you soon, with something happier. I…umm, hope."

With that, he gives the camera a half-hearted wave, stops the recording, and flops abruptly down on his back, looking whiter than the average ghost.

"You alright?" I ask, when he hasn't moved an inch in several seconds.

"You got a bucket?" he says, faintly.

I'm off like a shot, in and out of the bathroom in record time, shoving the plastic bin down by the side of the bed. He's still lying motionless, eyes squeezed shut, as I ask,

Copyright Dorian Bridges 2024

"Should I blame the dope, or your anxiety, for threatening the sanctity of my carpet, right now?"

"Anxiety," he whispers. "My heart's doing something horrible…"

"Mate, this is ridiculous – do you need me to text Em? Tell her to get off your back, stop threatening you with drama-ggedon? Surely she knows what this shit always does to you?"

He just shakes his head. I sit on the bed. It feels like an eternity of his shallow, wobbly breathing before he gets a handle on himself, and cautiously sits up, saying flatly,

"Em knows she can nuke me with a single Tweet, man. Don't poke the bear; she's off her rocker with me this week…"

I sigh, and fetch him a glass of water, praying this won't turn into a giant online mess with half the world involved – he's clearly terrified it will…

Zillah takes another wobbly breath, and digs out his laptop.

I leave him to edit his little speech.

CHAPTER FOUR

Everything feels considerably less tense three hours later, when we're deep into Grand Theft Auto chaos, not bothering with the missions – Zillah's reactions are laughable in a shootout, but he likes driving round with the radio playing, running people over and generally unleashing hell 'til the cops show up and kill us. It always reminds me of the years after uni, when the shift from halls freedom back to our parents' houses was throttling – any form of escapism was welcome. Zillah's place was our preferred location – his mum's a real anything goes type, and his dad had completely given up on him, since he'd come home, for the time being, with no degree. We spent endless hours getting stoned in his room, or rolling back there after nights out, off our faces on Ecstasy. Tonight's a pleasant time-warp, despite the circumstances – it's like some things in life stay a perfect, comforting constant, no matter how old I get. Weed and Zillah are two of those things, and we've both been too busy for each other lately. As we run over gangsters and shoot strippers in the face from within a companionable fug of smoke, he's saying,

"I saw a place earlier – a house, I mean? It's not that far away, actually – looked pretty sweet. I'm gonna phone about a viewing tomorrow."

"Buy or rent?"

"Buy. I mean, why not? I hate the uncertainty of renting, it's fucking awful. After this shit with Em, I want somewhere that's not going to crumble away under my feet…"

"You've seriously got the cash for that? Bearing in mind your current...*expenses*, if you know what I mean?"

He pulls a face. "Dope's not that pricey when you buy in bulk, Tom. Mortgage, obviously, but Em and I had been saving up for a place anyway."

I laugh. "Got it. You figure you'll splash out on her dream house *immediately,* just to show her what she's missing?"

He snorts, conceding, "That is in the back of my mind...but no. It's *my* dream house...or as close to it as I can afford, right now. Screw her, she hates me...what else can I do?"

There's more than a flicker of emotion in his voice – he clears his throat, frowns, and ploughs on,

"Anyway, now I'm out of our place, I could move in just like that. It's kinda perfect..."

I pause the game.

"Zill...I'm not trying to be your mother...but I really feel like you should stay here for a while. And I mean a *while.* You shouldn't be living on your own while you're—"

"Tom," he interrupts, "I love you, but you're paranoid as fuck, man. You've seen way too many dramatic movies about...*certain things...*" he drops his volume, glancing nervously up at the ceiling, and I roll my eyes. It's not like Lucy doesn't know what he's up to, at least generally – they used to be close, she knows he's a disaster, and I had to tell her the partial truth, but it's pretty obvious the last thing he wants right now is another showdown with a furious junkie-hating woman. "I've been at this a long time, on and off, you know that – most of that time I was using alone. I'm fine. I've always *been* fine."

"That is absolute horseshit, and you know it. Em told me about this OD you've been downplaying. It wasn't just going over a bit, it was Naloxone and ambulances – you'd be dead if she hadn't found you – I can't even think about it… You *know* I'm not just going off on one, so don't give me—"

"It was *one time,* Tom, one dodgy batch and the stupid fact I took my methadone first – I learned my lesson. Everything I get now, I test when it's new, and I don't use on top, so it's not going to happen again, is it?"

"You do realise it only takes 'one time' to kill you, you prat? And how do you 'test' these things, anyway? Are we talking sending it to a lab, or using one of those dropper kits, or, fuck, man, enlighten me – what does 'test it' mean?"

He frowns, and starts fiddling with the controller. From his expression alone I can tell I've got him cornered.

"Oh, for fuck's sake, Zillah!" I groan, when he still won't, or can't, reply, "Please tell me 'testing it' doesn't just mean doing a marginally smaller shot than normal? Fentanyl can be the size of—"

"It is *literally* what they advise you to do at the treatment centre! I mean, ok, fine, they tell you to smoke it first, so if it really means that fucking much to you, when I get my new place, I'll do a few noxious lungfuls, just for you. I'm not going to *die* – Christ, man…"

He starts the game back up. I can feel his spiky 'leave it alone' vibes from a mile away – I ignore them.

Copyright Dorian Bridges 2024

"Zill…blunt question coming up, but I saw your arms. This shit is getting excessive, even for you – you've gone way past a little vacation from the wagon this time. Do you honestly care about dying, right now?"

He casts me a dubious side-eye, and after a painfully long hesitation, mutters, "Why does it even matter?"

"Oh *hell*, mate. Of course it matters. Em said you were on a suicide mission, but I thought that was just angry-woman hyperbole. There is no way I can let you move into a house, all by yourself, when you're tiptoeing on the edge of death multiple times a day and now you don't even care if you fall off? That's why you won't smoke it first, isn't it? She's right – you genuinely don't give a damn. Do you even realise how many people would be fucked sideways – like, perhaps, me? – if you died like that?"

"Urghh *hell*, Tom! I told you I'm fine, leave it alone!" He goes back to running people over.

"Ok – so I don't matter. Nice to know. What about the rest of the world? Don't you think you have any responsibility to the kids who follow you? Do you not realise what you'll be doing to hundreds of thousands of fucked-up teens, who look at you as some sort of weird example of…I dunno, maybe I won't be fucked up forever? Do you even give *half* a shit about that, or them?"

Zillah pauses the game, and turns to glare at me like I'm a particularly noxious dog-shit he's just discovered lurking on the sole of his favourite boot.

"If you are trying to help," he says, in a dangerously clipped tone, "You might want to stop harassing me about all this terrifying shit that I *cannot control!"* His voice is rising into a rant that runs the serious risk of waking Lucy, but apparently I've offended him beyond all bounds of giving a toss. "Tom, I never fucking signed up for mass babysitting duty, did I? You know full well I stumbled sideways into this whole social media...*thing*, purely as a result of being an overly opinionated arsehole who can't keep his mouth shut about *anything* online, and I still don't know how I feel about it! But when I watch people, online, I realise they are just fucking *people* – I don't hero-worship them, I don't blindly follow them down stupid paths of—"

"Yeah, 'cause you're not fifteen, are you? Do you even remember being that age, or have you rotted your brains far beyond that point now? Don't you remember how you *felt* about celebrities, back then?"

"Tom, I am *not* a fucking celeb—"

"No, mate – you're *worse.* You're their imaginary best friend, tossing out reams of advice he's clearly incapable of personally sticking to, but they don't see that – they don't see the mess, they just thank you for helping them. Haven't you said it yourself, the way it's beautiful, but daunting, having them write to you, telling you all the stuff you've helped them with, without even knowing it? Do you think *I* want to be your last known address, or Em, hearing from the parents of kids who've got into drugs in the wake of your stupid, preventable, selfish fucking dea—"

Zillah's phone erupts into a volley of pings. He eyes the thing nervously, then ignores it to snap back, "I'm moving out first thing tomorrow, you *sanctimonious* twat! If anything's going to kill me right now, it is your callous, ill-educated *shit-banging*, about problems you've never had, and situations you've never fucking been in! Are you jealous – is that it? Are you really so dissatisfied with your own life that bashing me when I'm down is the most—"

"Honestly, mate? Yes – yes I am pretty fucking jealous. You get to do exactly what you love, on your own schedule, for bloody decent pay, and have people worship at your feet all day…but I'm not stupid enough to think it comes easy – any of it. Trouble is, I think you might be. Like you said, you stumbled into this – you never planned for what would happen if you actually *got* famous, and the messy sides of your faulty personality came to light – I've seen what it does to you, whenever your reputation comes off the tracks a bit, so…shit, Zillah – you need to be careful! I'm not trying to have a go, I'm just saying, there's more riding on this now than just you. You may never have chosen to have kids, but you've got to admit you've accidentally adopted a rather phenomenal number of them…"

He sighs, runs his hands through his hair, and mutters, *"Shit…"*

"Yeah… I'd say that about sums it up."

He relights the joint, exhales, then says quietly, "Are you suggesting I quit? Or like, take a hiatus or something?"

"I think it wouldn't be the worst idea…but equally, you know these people, I don't – if you go silent and Em does flip out, she'll have the whole narrative. And believe me, she's painting you as scum well enough to get in my head, let alone anyone else's."

"The sodding silverware…" he mutters, scowling as he takes a huge drag on the joint. "Talk about an offensive stereotype. I don't even know how you tell silverware from cutlery. And do pawn shops even take that shit now? Isn't it all iPhones and laptops, for fuck's sake?"

He passes me the joint, and I laugh, conceding that point.

"Mate, the best thing for your image, if Em gets gobby, would be to look like you were trying. Take a break, go to rehab. You know the deal."

And there it is – the lamb in the slaughterhouse look. It's guaranteed, every time you say the R-word around Zillah. "Not you *too*, Tom!" he groans, "I've already had Em on my case for weeks – you know full well I can't do rehab! Surely you remember what happened when—"

"Have you actually spoken to someone about it – recently, I mean, not fifteen years ago? Maybe things'd be better now, dealing with your anxiety and all that?"

"*Better,* now?" he repeats, incredulous. "Is anything 'better now', in our thirties, when I've been using on and off for decades and my body's a battered sack of shite? You seriously think withdrawal is gonna go easier on me now than it did as a kid?"

He snatches back the joint, and covetously bogarts it like I'm on some evil mission to rip away every drug in his world.

"Fair point…" I concede. "But they're going to realise that – they'll be careful with you. And you've got the money now, haven't you? Couldn't you afford somewhere halfway decent, somewhere they'd—"

"I have *read the reviews*," he says darkly, "All over the internet. It doesn't matter how private you go, Tom, it's my own worst nightmare. And right now, I'm still on this *evil* dose of methadone half the time, makes me feel like walking brainfog, all in the failed hope of getting rid of my cravings, and even you must know what that means, right? About withdrawal? That it's going to feel like I am *literally dying,* every second of every day, for a straight month? Sleep deprivation 'til I barely know what's real? I can't do it, man. You know I wouldn't survive that shit..." He shivers slightly, and starts fiddling with his hair, looking haunted.

I sigh, torn between agreeing that it's tough, and just telling him to pull his shit together and get through it. Addicts seem to handle withdrawal every day, all over the world, but not Zillah – not ever. If he hasn't got a pocketful of gear to wash it away with, the first hint of serious withdrawal sends him directly off the deep end – in the early days of his addiction, he attempted to detox himself at home, and instead landed himself a week in hospital with an obliterated liver, after trying to kill the hell with over-the-counter codeine pills. When I visited him in that hospital, he told me he'd been inches away from hurling himself off a motorway bridge when the codeine idea had occurred; he'd been trapped in the depths of a withdrawal-induced panic attack that just spiralled up and up, going on for hours and never fading away, until he couldn't bear to go on breathing at all. That was the day we all learned it – Zillah can't do cold turkey: it cranks his already shitty anxiety up beyond all bounds of rational thought and self-preservation – he would genuinely rather die than go through it, and knowing this arsehole inside out, he'd find some way of enacting that scheme, no matter where you locked him up...

"Methadone taper?" I suggest dully, sensing the futility of this discussion. "You said yourself you're on too much..."

"Yeah...too much to function, not enough to stay sane. Stalemate. But I'm looking into something else, Tom; it'd save my life, my reputation, not to men— Oh hell, hang on..." He's finally picked up his erratically pinging phone, and now he's got this look of dawning horror on his face, glowing pale in the light from the screen. I can see the phone starting to shake in his hand.

"What's up?" I ask. "Is it Em?"

"*Shit…*" he whispers, staring wide-eyed at his phone. "Oh Jesus – I can't handle this, Tom! Em's talked to—Christ, I don't even know who, or *how*, but some godforsaken blogger's just spilled fucking…all of it – everything! Now I'm being bombarded with shit about "Is it true? Did you relapse? Did you OD? Did you cheat on Em? Is that why she threw you out?" plus some lovely lines like "Once a junkie, always a liar", or "Don't meet your heroes, they always turn out to be hypocritical failures," and…*fuck,* man! I can't deal with this, this is the fucking *cherry* on the *cake of shit,* and—" He winces, and breaks off, one hand slapped over his mouth. I hurriedly tell him,

"Kitchen sink, Zill – mind the carpet!"

He's already gone, shakily bolting for the kitchen, still clutching his beeping, vibrating hell-phone. To say that internet drama is not Zillah's forte would be the understatement of the millennium – every damn time the online world turns on him, his anxiety goes through the roof, and this is generally the result. When it sounds like he's over the worst, I follow after him. He's standing by the sink, shaking all over, taps still running. His face is ghostly white in the glow of his phone. I lay a hand on his shoulder, asking,

"Can I see what's going on?

Mutely, he clicks and swipes, then passes me the phone, before sinking unsteadily to the ground, head in his hands.

The phone's on Twitter – X – of course it bloody is. If anyone's going to butt into the private life of a person they have no right talking about, then tear them to shreds in the most toxic manner possible, you know you'll find it on Twitter. I'm looking at a large photo of Em and Zillah, laughing together on a livestream, splattered with text that makes me cringe:

"Welcome to today's exclusive tea-spill! YouTubers Zillah Marsh and Emma Lee have broken up, and it isn't pretty. Marsh is, according to a friend of the couple, a 'danger to himself' since relapsing into heroin addiction two months ago. Today he released a video admitting he is now single and homeless, but did not mention the true cause. Rushed to hospital last Tuesday following a near-fatal overdose, Marsh has 'repeatedly' refused all offers of rehab. A 'broken-hearted' Lee felt she had 'no choice' but to end the two-year relationship, and evict him from their shared house. It is not known where he is presently staying – we can only hope it's not a crack den.

"For more steaming hot tea, don't forget to subscribe, and get those notifications – video to follow!"

"Oh, shit…" I murmur, watching Zillah as he sits hunched up like a beaten dog on the floor. I don't even know what to say – he's had his name dragged through the mud before, but never over anything so personal – and never with such bloody awful timing. It feels like the final nail in the coffin of his relationship – let alone this fucking relapse. If we could've just snuck it all under the public's radar, I really thought we'd have ironed everything out in a week or three, but now? Now the whole world knows?

"Who the hell d'you think talked to this son of a bitch?"

Zillah just shakes his head, delving in his pocket for more pills – he's shaking so much he drops one and has to chase it across the linoleum, before getting himself a glass of water and gulping down several of the things. I don't even try to stop him – we'd be in here committing atrocities against my sink for the next month.

"Come on," I say, turning off the taps. I take his arm and try to haul him back to the living room, but he shakes his head, glancing awkwardly towards the sink. I pick up a large bowl and shake it at him – "Mate, we're not sitting on the kitchen floor all night – it's depressing as fuck. C'mon – you'll be fine."

He sighs, takes the bowl, and plods after me, asking,

"What the hell am I going to do? I thought I'd placated Em well enough with that damn video. What more does she *want* from me?"

"I wish I knew, Zill…but who even knows if she's behind it? She was venting to me, maybe she's vented to someone else, too, and they've decided to cash in. Heads will be smashed as soon as we work it out, but…look, it's well past midnight – why not sleep on it, and reply with a clear head in the morning?"

"Oh god, Tom, this shit doesn't *sleep!*" he says, running his fingers over his eyes, "You don't understand how this stuff works, man! Half these fuckers live in America, and it's still the goddamn afternoon there – they will be up *all night* tearing me to shreds if I'm not here to defend myself. This is the part of my job I hate, I despise, I would rather die than deal with!"

"I know," I sigh, his phone still beeping and pinging in my hand. Zillah reaches out to take the thing – I yank it away, closing Twitter and all its vile comments, before I sit down on the sofa beside him,

Copyright Dorian Bridges 2024

and pass it back. He immediately mutes the ghastly piece of technology, but it doesn't stop the speech bubbles popping up on top of the screen – *"Why did you relapse?" "You're single now?" "Never deserved her anyway – LOSER!"*

Then, up pops a text message from Cindy, Zillah's older sister, and he gasps in horror. His shaky breathing's become hyperventilation, hands trembling so much the text on screen becomes a blur of neon tracers to my stoned vision.

"You want me to read it?" I ask. "Just breathe, mate – maybe she's actually got something helpful to say…"

He stiffly shakes his head, closes his eyes, and after taking a few wobbly breaths, he opens Cindy's message. I lean in to read her typically explosive tirade of wrath with him, holding the phone steady.

"Zillah, you better tell me this HORSESHIT online is some kind of twisted stunt! If you're using again, using THAT, I will KICK YOUR ARSE 'til you beg for mercy! If Mum sees this, she'll have a heart attack and blame herself forever – do you even realise that, you selfish little jerkoff?!"

Zillah groans, and starts speed-typing a response with trembling fingers, autocorrect working overtime on his fudged spellings, pounding out an equally hysterical,

"Cindy, shut up, just SHUT UP, ok! DO NOT TELL THE FAMILY – DO YOU UNDERSTAND ME?! You have NO idea what you're on about, and while I have no problem sitting down like ACTUAL ADULTS & explaining my side of the story, suuure, why not keep reading Twatter gossip columns then blowing up in my face like you're an internet troll not my OWN FUCKING SISTER who's meant to be in MY FUCKING CORNER when the rest of the world is lynching me! Are you drunk right now?"

She rapidly comes back with. "Fine, you got me. Just got in from a date, had a few too many. Sorry if that was harsh…but you bloody deserve it. Was that true, about you ODing? Where are you right now – have you got a bed for the night?"

"It's fine. I'm with Tom."

"Can we get brunch – talk this through? I won't bring Mum, I won't even tell Mum – this isn't an intervention…yet. I just need to see you with my own eyes. So don't do anything extra stupid, alright? I do love you, Zill – don't understand you half the time, want to throttle you the other half, but I love you – don't forget that. You matter to a lot of people."

He curses under his breath, tersely agrees to brunch, then dumps the phone down, and says quietly, "Why does all that just sound like guilt-tripping, to me?"

"Probably because your brain has this lethal talent of spinning every kind word into cruel bullshit that convinces you the entire world hates you, thus giving you the perfect excuse to never get clean."

He blinks at me like a flabbergasted owl, then mutters, "Bloody hell, Tom… Since when did weed turn you into a particularly arsey philosophy student?"

"A lot of things change, mate. They do for us normal people, at least – you, less so…"

He sighs. "You're damn right nothing changes. You've never been inside my fucked-up brain – it can't change, it won't – you should know that better than anyone." He picks up the remnants of the joint, relights it, and continues bleakly, "I've said this before, but life's only bearable when I'm high. And no one listened when I said that at twenty-one, but now I'm saying it at thirty-fucking-eight, after giving clean life my all for nearly a decade, surely this shithole planet has to listen? You may hate my maudlin bloody music, but the truest thing I ever wrote was, 'On my gravestone this is what it said: whenever I'm sober I wish that I was dead'. I'm sick of fighting it, Tom – it gets me nowhere. This is who I am, and I'm ok with that. After all these years, I have to be..."

I shake my head. "Mate, that whole speech was number one on the list of shit you had better never, ever utter around anyone that isn't me, 'cause if it comes out publicly, you will be cancelled into a fucking *hole*. You can't just tell your whole sodding audience to embrace relapsing, like it's the solution to—"

"I'm not telling anyone to anything! Why the fucking fuck shouldn't I tell my truth, after all these years of uselessly fighting it? You know how much it *enrages me*, the way people generalise addicts, generalise addiction, and when I said, in that video, all those years ago, that dope was never a disaster for me, that I was functional on it – finally got my degree, even – you know what? People *got it*. People either said, 'Holy shit, same for me!', or they said, 'Well, that's only 'cause you quit when you did', but either way, they listened, they spoke, then they moved the fuck on with their lives. I am not the *Messiah,* Tom – everyone knows I'm about as fixable as Chernobyl!"

I just shake my head at him, wondering how in hell's name someone so intelligent can be so un-self-aware. "Zill…how many followers did

Copyright Dorian Bridges 2024

you have when you posted that ancient video? A few thousand, if that? Things have *changed* for you – don't you see the comments on your own stuff now? People look up to you these days – they even think you're a good influence, as bizarre as we all find that, and I know it galls the hell out of you to realise this, but *you have changed*, and grown, and matured, these past few years – you've had to. The world's been watching. You don't use words you shouldn't, you're not half such a gobby, cocky little prick as you used to be, you're ridiculously switched on about issues I don't know bloody anything about, and you actually come across…fuck. I don't even know how to say this without blowing your top, but these kids see you as the Wise But Cool Grownup, who—"

"I AM MAKING A *MESS OF BEING A GROWNUP!*" he whisper-screams at the floor, fingers clawing the air in exasperation, "And I'm certainly not *wise!* Are these people blind and deaf?! How many stories about my fucked-up youth do I have to tell them before they clock the fact that I'm an irresponsible idiot who shouldn't be listened to by *anyone!*"

"Oh man… What is it about maturity that freaks you out so hard? You are thirty-eight, mate – it happens to us all."

"You don't get it, Tom," he mumbles through yet another joint as he gets it lit, "You just don't fucking get it. I was ok with semi-maturity until I landed myself in the middle of all this – people listening to me. People misconstruing my *every fucking word*, then coming at me with this crazed level of hate over a simple misunderstanding or slip of the tongue. You know I've never wanted any form of responsibility landing on my head, and now you're hammering home the fact I've got more of the stuff than the average parent! And I can't handle that! At all!"

Copyright Dorian Bridges 2024

"Well tough shit, mate – it's happened. And I wouldn't say it's more than the average parent, you grandiose twat…though the way you used to get around, I'm surprised some sixteen-year-old mini-Zillah *hasn't* surfaced by now. That would be scarier, wouldn't it?"

"Terrifying. But what the fuck do I do about this mess, online? Will you stop berating me and just…just tell me what to do? I can't handle an internet shitstorm right now, Tom, I *can't*, without Em, I—" He shivers slightly, visibly on the edge of a complete freakout, and pleads, "*Help me*, man! What do I do!"

"Well…" I take the joint off him, and think about it for a moment. "Look…the beans have been spilled, and that's…unfortunate. I know you've got the whole world bombarding you with questions, but if you jump in too quick, you'll only pre-empt the wrong things and say too much. So, you don't talk to *anyone* tonight – no one, you got me? Don't answer a single DM, comment, email – nothing. And for god's sake don't Google yourself – leave that to me. You go to bed, get some rest, and I'll help you clean up this mess in the morning. Your next statement, as I see it, has to…well, whether you cop to the drugs is up to you, but I think you *need* to cop to being an idiot. Not even specifically, but in general – you.are.an.idiot. Remind everyone that you're just this faulty fucking human with a lot of issues, who fell into his situation sideways, with no preparation, and that ideally, people should see you as a source of entertainment, but not advice. Not right now. Not while you're going through a messy patch."

"What if I'm not 'going through a messy patch'" he mutters, eyes narrowed through the fug of smoke. "What if you actually listened for five seconds, and understood that this is it for me – I am *done* fighting an impossible fight, and I'm embracing the only damn thing that makes me happ—"

"No," I state, slapping a hand over his mouth, "No, no, fucking *no*. None of that. Not ever. 'Messy patch' is what we're calling it. Mate, you know full well you've got the eloquence to sell water to fish, so for Christ's sake, now is the time to use it as a ladder, not a noose."

"Oh what the fuck! How is it not a 'noose' when you're telling me to directly string myself up, you fuckwad? I'm an 'idiot' now?! 'Not even specifically, but *in general'*? Look at me as pure 'entertainment', but for god's sake don't *take me seriously*, like I'm some shit-smeared ape at the zoo, like…like this fucking tragic figure of self-inflicted idiocy, a stumbling, mumbling, screwed-up waste of space who occasionally *shits out* a funny story, or—"

"Oh Jesus, Zill – of course I didn't mean it like that…but it's kind of depressing to me that you think I did – is that really what you see in the mirror? I'm not saying you're intellectually lacking, just…not great with common sense. It wasn't an insult."

"Bloody sounded like one…" he mutters, staring at the floor. "In fact, this whole shitting *day* has been insult piled upon insult. It's no wonder you still have to tolerate me as your best mate after all these years, Tom – you're a fucking *cunt…"*

"Zillah…that is *never* how I mean it. I know it's a sore spot, but I swear to you, no one on this Earth thinks you're stupid – your dad's dead, get him out of your head already. Look, since I've pissed you off so much, I'll finally tell you this – I actually Googled you, a while back, and amidst all the obsessed stans, horny chicks and vicious sniping, I found someone wondering why no one ever picks a fight with you, online, about any of your mad ideas. And you know what the top comment was? It was some kid saying you're such a 'lethal intellectual powerhouse', no one dares go up against you; they know you'd only debate them into an early grave, and they'd come out of it a total laughingstock. It had god knows how many likes – these people genuinely think you're damn near intellectually untouchable among the nutters on that platform. Does that little compliment bandage your ego?"

He's grinning, albeit reluctantly. Knew that'd do it. He can't take a compliment about his looks, Zillah – that's come far too easy for him, all his life, and if anything he takes it as an insult; you're not complimenting him, you're calling him a decorative object. But after the way his dad twisted him up as a kid, refusing to get the ADHD diagnosed or medicated, insisting he was just a lazy, stupid little shit, well, shine even a little sun on his brains and he's pleased as punch. Thank god – he looked ready to bottle me.

"They really called me that? *Seriously?*"

"Well, people say all sorts of shit online, don't they? They've made a nutter like you king of the weirdos, and that says it all. But yes – they really did. *Lethal. Intellectual. Powerhouse.*" Zillah looks like a Labrador with a new ball – you can practically see his tail wagging. This is what happens when your parents don't do praise, I guess – you become an absolute sucker for it, with self-esteem that crumbles like a stale breadstick in the face of criticism…

"However," I continue, "*No one* is going to think that anymore, if you steam ahead with the brutal honesty right now. That whole, 'This is the real me, it always has been, I'm living my best life' shit, when you're talking about dope. You've already been called a 'danger to yourself' – it only takes one more misstep before you become a 'danger to others' too. Please god don't use your 'intellectual powerhouse' to sell an entire generation of disenfranchised brats on smack, with all this 'Oooh, everyone struggling with recovery, come join the Cult of Zillah, where giving up is the way to win, and embracing your inner junkie is the secret to true happiness!' shit. 'Side effects may include a life expectancy of three years, maximum.' 'Cause truly, mate, that is how you sound right now, and it scares me shitless…"

"You know," he says, skinning up again, "If I live for three years, doing this…and then I'm gone, I'd be perfectly happy with that. I'd certainly be happier with it than I would with thirty years sober. That would be the real hell. Unliveable – I mean it."

"I can't even bloody talk to you right now," I state, starting the game back up. "Not about this. You've lost the fucking plot, and we can only hope it doesn't last…"

I hear him sigh, followed by the click of the lighter, and a fresh, billowing cloud of weed smoke. He isn't joining in the game, but that's ok – frankly I'm more use without him. I've almost forgotten, through the haze of weed and blurry pixels, that he's sitting next to me at all, when he says,

"Tom…did you never wonder why I fell off the wagon in the first place? What it was that made—"

"Midlife crisis," I state. "That's Em's take, and I think I agree. You were getting grumpy and finicky about everything, dissatisfied with everything, nothing made you fucking happy, and instead of buying a tacky red sportscar like most blokes our age, you dove headfirst into a mountain of brown powder. If I'm wrong, feel free to enlighten me."

He lets out an exasperated sigh. "How can we be living in the twenty-flipping-twenties, and people around me are still blind and deaf to the symptoms of a friend tumbling into a pit of depression and drowning? What you said, earlier, about me being on a 'suicide mission'? Well, I'm not…but I was. Everything just got…*impossible.* Grey. Bleak. No joy anywhere. That fluffy pink sobriety cloud after I quit the booze, it just *crashed* – I was worse than ever…but apparently I should've been an actor, 'cause I can get two-million-plus views on a video, and no fucker even notices my charade of positivity's a bullshit farce. All Em gave a fuck about was the fact I had no interest in shagging her anymore, which must mean I'm a *misogynistic fat-shaming bastard,* given she's gained eight measly pounds I hadn't even noticed – she never for a second guessed it might be about my malfunctions, not hers… It got so bad I was phoning crisis lines all night, and nothing was helping, and in the end I couldn't take another second of it; I set the date. You know? To just…*do it?* End it all?

"I had everything planned out – every last detail…but then I thought, well, if I'm going, what is there to lose getting high one last time? So I bought the drugs. Didn't have the self-control to wait 'til—" He breaks off sharply, looking uncomfortable. "Doesn't matter. Not telling you my stupid plans… I used the drugs while Em was out pole-dancing, just…tested them out, and you know what happened? It was *wonderful.* There I was – back again. There I fucking was! The world had colour, things interested me, I could *finally* fucking concentrate, I had this safe little place I could curl up in anytime and feel *blissful,* and that's when I knew: I never wanted to die in the first place. I just couldn't live like *that* anymore – sober, miserable, overwhelmed, crushed and terrified by life itself… But like this? Like this I can manage. Some days, I even catch myself feeling happy to be alive."

He passes me the joint, and I smoke it in silence, feeling cold all over, the game long paused. When I regain the power of speech, I ask,

"What was the date? When were you going to do it?"

"28th April," he answers, without hesitation. "It's after all the family birthdays, and I'd get to my cousin's wedding, see everyone one final time, plus it's the same day my old dog died. It's still rung round as 'D-Day', in my calendar…"

I just stare at him. He's so utterly factual, it's like we're discussing the purchase of a new toaster.

"What the fuck, Zill? That was months ago – you never said a thing! You were seriously planning to just…off yourself, and I didn't even get a goodbye?"

He pulls a face, mutters, "Sorry… I was going to record a lot of little video clips – like saying my goodbyes in person, but after the fact. If I've learned anything from all our fucked-up friends, it is to never, ever post a suicidal goodbye on Facebook, or act suspiciously in the days beforehand. Those people always get stopped. And I was *not* being stopped…"

"Oh hell, man. I don't even know what to say… Are you on meds now? Therapy? Anything?"

He blows a defeatist raspberry. "Tried a few pills, tried three sodding therapists, but the pills were a nightmare, and the therapy just made me worse – we went round and round about my shit, shit brain, and all the *shit* in the past – it just dredged up all the old horrors, it intensified my hatred of the present, and in the end I quit before it pushed me into bringing forward D-Day even more..."

I don't even know what to say to him. I just give the stupid bastard a hug, telling him, "You are never going through that shit alone again –

Copyright Dorian Bridges 2024

I want you to swear on that. However bleak it gets, you fucking *tell* me about it, please? I reckon I'm owed that, after all these years. But…are you still thinking like this – honestly? Is there still a…you know – a 'D-Day'?"

He gently pushes me away, and says, "No. There's no D-Day. Not right now. So long as I have enough emotional avoidance powder, I don't need to fantasise about being dead. But that's the truth of it. Living like this is the only way I can bring myself to live at all. Maybe that's why I didn't fight Em over the house – just let her turf me out. I don't really care where I end up, so long as I have the one thing that makes life liveable…"

"Oh Christ, Zill. You do realise what you sound like? This only sounds like logic because you've got shoes on your feet and money in the bank, but I can hear every word of it coming out the mouth of a homeless crackhead with no teeth, and I do not want that bloke to wind up being you… Equally, you've only been back on it for what, two months, right – that's what the Twitter thing said?"

He looks uncomfortable. "Closer to four, actually. April, like I said. Em's not the most astute about this stuff. I flew under the radar quite nicely for a while…"

"Well, fuck, two months, four – it's not that long. Maybe it's just the novelty of being back on it. I reckon, in another six months' time, the ugly side effects are going to get on your tits, and you'll start sticking to your script and tapering that crap. It'll work itself out."

He looks disturbed. "If the 'novelty wears off', and I'm back to where I was pre-relapse, don't expect me to be on this Earth for long. But that's not how it works, Tom, and I should fucking know. You don't get bored with dope. You just fall more and more in love with it the more comfortable it gets…"

His phone's still flashing away, a bizarre electronic soup of concern, fury, love and loathing tumbling through the internet. He reaches out to turn it face down, and I point out,

"This time isn't going to be like any other time you've been on it. Not now you're…*this*. You know – online. Everyone knowing you, everyone judging you. Even when we were younger, you had the sense not to tell almost anyone about it, while you were actively using, but these days you are *literally* famous for being a motor-mouth who splatters his own messy past all over the net. Honesty is your brand…but if you start spouting this 'Dope saved my life, I'm incurably fucked and heroin's the only med that works on me' shit to an audience of teenagers, you will be strung up by your fucking *nuts*. And if you clam up on the whole subject…which you *should*, dear god you *should*, while you're thinking like this, people are going to spin their own damn narratives and Christ only knows what they'll come up with. Using isn't going to be 'comfortable' – not this time. You could lose everything…"

He stares me dead in the eyes for several seconds, with this weird expression that hangs somewhere between exasperation, despair, and pity. Finally he drops his gaze, saying quietly,

"You still don't get it, man. Once you have a D-Day circled in your calendar – once your girlfriend's put you out on the streets, and you've got multiple practice goodbyes recorded in your phone?" He shrugs. "Tom, I've got nothing left to fucking lose…"

Copyright Dorian Bridges 2024

CHAPTER FIVE

By the time we go to bed, I've had to physically restrain Zillah from posting a furious comment rant to some poor internet kid who got too nosy, but after a bit of a scuffle, which just ends in us both giggling ourselves paralytic, he settles down and agrees to switch off his phone 'til morning. Honestly, it's obvious this decision has little to do with pragmatism, and far more to do with the fact he wants to get high as a kite and sleep off the tension of the day. He's eaten a third handful of his not-exactly-legally-sourced anxiety pills, and from past experience – and the glazed-out state of his eyes – I strongly suspect that everything I'm saying is now going directly into a benzo blackout. Despite the fact I'm stoned and half asleep, I insist we repeat the "Junkie Buddy System", as Zillah irritably dubs it when I follow him into the spare room.

"Please don't be a twat about this," I whisper, shutting the door behind us. "Do you think I'm doing it for my own entertainment? Zill, aside from the fact you're mixing copious pills with smack and I am fucking worried about you, I could lose my *marriage* over this – if Lucy found out I was enabling you, she'd—"

"Do *not* use that word with me!" he hisses, whipping round and poking a skinny finger in my face, "Enabling, enabling, Jesus Christ! I've had all that crap from Em, and just like I tell her, it's nothing but a *noxious* bloody buzzword for ableist sociopaths with no empathy whatsoever, this nasty little—"

"Oh mate, shut your fucking face before I shut it for you. I am not in the mood for any more intellectual politics of junkiedom tonight! I'm being serious here. Lucy knows you're using, but she thinks you're trying your absolute best to stick to that script, and that I'm helping you with it, not sitting here while you—" I break off, shaking my head and shoving my clenched fists into my pockets before violence becomes an option – Zillah's in silent fits of stoned giggles at the extent of our deception, and in the end all I can do is flip him off, then gesture at the bathroom like he's a stubborn dog that needs to go out for a shit. Frankly I wish he was – it'd be far, far less hassle. He grabs his bag of poison, and slips into the loo, still laughing under his breath.

"Hilarious," I mutter, just loud enough for him to hear. "You've destroyed your own life, now I'm tossing mine on the line for you too, and you still think it's fucking hilarious. Honestly mate, this midlife crisis of yours is getting less tragic, and more disgusting by the second."

A silent moment passes, then the bathroom door creaks open, and he slinks back out, looking chagrined.

"I'm sorry..." he says, sitting down next to me. "Really, I am. For all of this. If it gets—if *I* get too much, just throw me out. If I have to spend a while in a hotel, dwelling on every shitty little thing I've ruined, I won't...cope very well, but it'll still be worth it to keep you and Lucy as friends. I need you in my corner, man. I haven't spent a night without Em in...god, I don't even know. I'd be going out of my head right now if you'd left me to my own devices..."

He trails off, staring bleakly at the bedroom wall, and I remember the tears in his eyes when he stormed off earlier. He's been putting up a decent front, tonight – all that stuff about buying a house, moving on, but he's obviously more cut up about Em than he wants to admit.

Copyright Dorian Bridges 2024

"Do you miss her enough to seriously give it another shot?" I ask. "D'you reckon she'd go for it, if you really begged forgiveness? You could suggest couples counselling, maybe?"

"Oh fuck…" he whispers, then he's got his head in his hands, mumbling shakily, "I've really shafted this, Tom. Em's—Jesus, man, you *know* how I feel about her, underneath all the shit – it hasn't changed! I don't even need the constant social media circus to remind me how lucky I am – the shit she's seen me through this last year? No one else would've had me. I know she can be bloody…*brutal* when she's angry, but do you even realise how rare it is to find someone, in my job, who isn't shallower than a puddle, or just out to tell awful stories about me for clout? Em's my *Person*, Tom – my one and only. You know I never believed in that sappy romantic shite before I met her, but me and my crap luck, crashing into this impossibly stunning, genuine girl, all sad and alone because she was washed up in an industry full of *vacuous wankers*, and stuck in the same boat as me? Too well-known to date – not famous enough to flap NDAs around?

"We both thought we'd die alone, until the world forced us together, and for once the world wasn't full of shit. She's my *everything*…but she's also driving me to literal bloody suicide because she doesn't *understand me at all!* I have a *solution* to this, but she doesn't care, won't wait, just throws me out like I'm garbage, right when I need her most, and I can't understand her, man, I can't stop it all whirling round my head, like, what if this is forever, what if she cuts me out completely and I never get to tell her—"

"D'you think she still loves you though?" I ask, cutting into his audibly spiralling freakout. "Enough to try again, if you played your cards right? Do you think she'd—"

He sniffs, stumbles to his feet, and goes crashing off into the bathroom, his voice cracking as he pleads, "Just fuck off, Tom! Stop turning my brain inside out, *please!*"

That's a resounding 'I hope so' and 'who knows', then. Bloody hell… I hate silencing myself – I always want to fix people, it's probably how I ended up with Zillah as a best mate in the first place, and I know weed can make me infuriatingly analytical, but it's obvious he's had enough of my advice. And while he's in there with what I imagine is enough dope to kill him five times over, it's clearly not the right time to poke the bear.

"I'm sorry…" I tell him, lamely. "I'm blaming the weed…"

"You're not a fucking psychologist, Tom," he says through the door, and I can hear the tears in his voice. "Can you please, please just act like it, for a couple of hours a day? I know this needs saying – I know it needs fixing, *I* need fixing, but…god*,* I'm exhausted. All this…it's *exhausting.* The internet's about to tear me apart, I miss Em like razor-wire in my chest, I can't bear the thought of sleeping alone tonight, I need to call her and say I'm sorry – would that be a horrible idea? To just say I'm—"

"It's 4am, Zill. Drop her a text – one, really, really well thought out text – then leave it. If you call her at this hour, stoned, you won't be helping your cause."

"*Shit…*" he whispers. The rustling starts up, then the click of a lighter, and I shake my head, pointing out,

"Really might help if you formulate this text semi-sober?"

Copyright Dorian Bridges 2024

There's a long silence, then a very wobbly-sounding, "Tom…I think I'm about to puke my fucking guts up again – will you *please* just drop it?"

I sigh. "Am I stirring the pot, or are you fucking withdrawing? How much of this shit are you—"

"I'm not withdrawing for Christ's sake! I'm just…*ugh*…" I hear him sniff, then, "Tom, I'm fucking homeless, the woman I wanted to be with forever wants nothing more to do with me, I've got the entire *internet* blowing up on me, and—" I hear some creaking about, then he mumbles something wholly incomprehensible through a mouthful of tourniquet. A moment later, his speech clear, but increasingly mumbled, he says quietly, "Knew it was a mistake, delaying D-Day… Now the whole world wants me dead. Even Em, probably. So fuck it. Let'em pick the drama from my decaying bones, fill my grave with selfie sticks 'n stale popcorn, cannibalise my busted-up heart 'til the maggots—" He breaks off with a quiet groan. There's a sudden crash of porcelain, instantly followed by the tile-echoing sound of him gagging himself inside out for the third time today. Swearing under my breath, I wait 'til silence falls, then follow him in to pass the mouthwash. He shakily takes it, gargles mint with a grimace, and slowly slumps into a morose heap by the toilet.

"S'no wonder Em doesn't want me there…" he mumbles, staring dully at the floor. "Deal with stress like a real fuckin' professional, don' I?"

I sigh, and hit the flush. "Zill, you were born with a nervous system wired like a jittery grenade – that's hardly your fault, is it? But…mate, all that shit you just spouted about D-Day – you're not about to do something dumb, are you? If you need me to stay up with you, just…" I trail off – his eyes are closing, head nodding forwards. He's not capable of anything dumb tonight. I crouch down, shake him back to the waking world, and drag him to his feet, saying,

"Come on – bedtime. Bin's still there if you need it. I'll text Em, right now, tell her you miss her, and that you want to talk. In the morning we'll see how everyone feels. Maybe a night apart's all you really needed…"

"I need'm to *listen* to me, Tom," he mumbles, staring through me with half-open eyes. "Why won't they *listen?* No one listens to me…*"*

I just keep frogmarching him into the bedroom. He's still mumbling on, with increasing determination – "I'll do w'ever it takes to make those *fuckin'* bastards listen – they've wrecked m'whole life… Wha've I got to lose now? *Nothin'…*"

"What bastards?" I ask, yawning. God it's late…

"Drug people…" he murmurs. "Evil. Em knows…"

"What, like…dealers? Oh hell, Zill, please tell me you're not in some kind of trouble?"

"Ohhh, no'like that… But, yes. Trouble… Drug people. S'bloody awful. Em knows…"

He flops onto the bed, and just zonks out completely – I can't get another coherent word out of him. I'm unnerved, praying this is nothing more than some surreal half-dream pouring out of Zillah's famed motor-mouth, a 4am nonsense spun together from smack and homesickness, but all the same, once I've wrangled him into the recovery position, provoked a few reassuringly-alive grumbles and left him in the dark, I text Em –

"Zillah misses you. He's safe, but not doing well. Especially after that Twitter shit. Who the hell talked to that arsehole? And he just said something about 'trouble' with 'evil drug people', but won't tell me more than 'Em knows', and now he's asleep. What's up? Should I be worried? Honestly, I'm pretty fucking worried. I do NOT need dealers smashing down my front door, so can you please tell me what the hell's going on?"

I keep the phone next to me as I get ready for bed, but Em's either asleep, or she doesn't care. Possibly both.

CHAPTER SIX

It's an awkward Saturday breakfast. I'd expected Zillah to be comatose 'til noon, but he's up and about at half nine, red-eyed and miserable-looking. Lucy makes him toast – he picks it to pieces, manages half a slice, then admits defeat. She's watching him with a worried frown, repeatedly opening her mouth to speak, then shaking her head and closing it again. They were party buddies back in the day, but she's rarely seen behind the mask before, Zillah's social façade of the gobby, outgoing comic. It's clearly jarring her, seeing him like this, but I told her this morning he didn't want to talk about it, not with her, if possible. It's probably true, but honestly, I was covering my own arse more than anything – if Zillah slipped up about what we'd been doing yesterday, I would be *toast*. So she just lurks round the kitchen, all worry-faced and maternal, then gives up and goes to get dressed. I feel an extra brick add itself to the weight on my shoulders – guilt, anxiety; Lucy's great at making people feel better, and I've gone and gag-ordered her like the world's most controlling arsehole…

Zillah sips disgusting decaf, staring blankly into space – I watch him for a good thirty seconds, and he doesn't even blink. I can't tell if he's high, or catatonically depressed. When I hear the shower start up above us, I ask, "How you doing?"

He blinks back to reality with a heavy sigh, and states in a monotone,

"This is my brain on sobriety…"

"Uh huh? Is that…a positive step towards a greater goal, or just too early for certain things?"

"It's never too early," he says, in the same dead monotone. Jesus. It's flashing me back to how he was when we first met at college – for the first week I thought he didn't have a single living braincell in him, he seemed so flat and dull. Then I got to know him, and realised he actually had this weird, cynical sense of humour, and was the furthest thing from brainless – it was all just buried under a fog of depression thick enough to choke on. That version of Zillah disappeared when he started doing drugs – a lot of speed, old-school Ecstasy pills, weed, obviously; that was when his actual personality came to the surface. He got louder, learned how to fucking smile – went directly from party pooper to party central, and that's basically how he's been ever since, bar the occasional lapse into an intense, nihilistic loathing of the world and everyone in it. Seeing him like this again, it's fucking unnerving.

"Brunch with Cindy…" he continues, slumping back in his chair. "If I turn up high, she'll do something awful. Maybe even get me arrested. Fuck…"

"What time? I can give you a lift…or come too, if you need me?" I know I'm being overbearing – it's a family thing, but Cindy is a force to be reckoned with, and right now, he just seems so breakable. I've seen him go horrifically over the edge before, and even though it was twenty years ago, our first year at uni, there are some sights too disturbing to ever forget…

"Eleven," says Zillah. "Café up the road. I'll walk. No intention of staying long. Come though, please…it'll be awful."

"Ok. Have you said anything online yet?"

He shakes his head, blinks back tears, mumbles, "Can't do it… Got no words. I don't care…"

You bloody obviously do, I think, but I don't say it. "I'll help you, whenever you're up to it. I think the words should be pre-prepared this time, not off the cuff. I'll do all the Googling, work out what people are saying, what needs responding to, or at least turd-polishing a bit, so just…don't look at anything, for now. It'll be ok."

He scrubs at his eyes, and slumps out of the kitchen, still clutching his mug of lukewarm pseudo-coffee.

Zillah's clearly lost without social media. For half an hour he lies on the sofa staring at the ceiling, and his hand keeps drifting to his phone. He repeatedly grabs it, sighs in irritation, and drops it again. Finally he logs himself into the fake Instagram profile he uses whenever drama kicks off, and whiles away twenty minutes staring blankly at puppies and goth models.

Across the room, I'm grimly Googling him. So far the fallout from that damned Twitter exposé could be worse – Em's posted nothing but some bland memes about self-care and tough times; she hasn't taken a steaming dump on him – that's optimistic. Zillah's Instagram is flooded with concerned comments, some of which descend into rumour threads, but it's his own fanbase, and they're largely supportive. Twitter and Reddit have numerous arseholes crowing their little heads off in victory, that after all his 'pompous, saccharine lectures' on mental health, he's just as fucked up as everyone else, probably even more so – "Who the hell is dumb enough to take heroin in their teens? Imagine being forty and still doing it!" I shake my head – Zillah's content is a weird mingling of positivity, chaos, and the disturbing tales of his misspent youth; anyone can tell he's not, and has never really been, ok. The thing that concerns me most is a discussion about not supporting him financially, in any way, while he's using. I have no idea how we spin that one. Or where I even stand on the matter. If his income stream dwindled, he'd be stuck living here, where we could look after him, and I'd feel better about that…but would it really help him, long-term? Wouldn't he just get worse and worse, with zero responsibilities and an almighty wallop to his ego? The last time drama kicked off, he got drunk off his face, slurring on about the fact he should just quit it all, pack up everything and get back on disability, like he was for a while post-uni, be a "Full-time professional nutter again; life was easier, Tom, it was *easier!*". I did my best to remind him how much he loves his job, but he wasn't having it – the only thing that kept him going was the money; the night ended when he blew two grand on designer gothic clothing, then slumped back in his chair, flipped off the screen with both hands, and slurred, "Fuckin' haters can suck on *that,*" before making an attempt at storming graciously off to bed, impeded slightly by crashing into a doorframe.

…so it probably wouldn't do him much good, frankly, if the money dried up. He'd almost certainly quit his tempestuous job, and Zillah in active addiction, with nothing to do but use, and no way to legally fund his habit, does not sound like a good thing…

Em finally deigns to text me back just as it's time to go, but all she says is, "I'm glad he's safe. Don't worry about 'drug people trouble', he's having a stupid argument with his worker about those awful meds. Won't shut up about it – he'll be in your ear eventually." I sigh – typical Zillah. I've had literal nightmares about dealers breaking in to murder Lucy, and this is all he meant? I note, however, that Em has nothing to say about the Twitter shitstorm, or who started it. That speaks volumes, to my mind. Did *she* sell the story – would she really sink that low?

I glance at the time – we've really got to go. Zillah slumps to his feet without a word, drags his jacket on, and stands in the hallway scowling from behind a pair of oversized sunglasses, a black beanie pulled down over his hair. As we head outside, there isn't a ray of sunshine anywhere.

"What are the glasses for?" I ask. "Cindy'll only make you take them off…"

"I know," he mutters, and I realise he's lurking close against my left shoulder, all hunched up like he wants to disappear. "I don't want anyone recognising me…"

"Does that happen much, round here?"

"Happens enough. I'm not risking it."

He says nothing else as we wander up the high street, past a hoarse busker Zillah tosses a quid to, then into the café at the end. Cindy's already there, occupying a reasonably private booth, the loudest thing in the room even before she starts talking, her hair neon orange, her clothes a lurid geometric clash of primary colours, shoes painted up to look like ice-cream cones. Frankly you'd think she was another zany internet personality, but Cindy's the surprisingly sensible one, a nurse by trade. Zillah looks startled, shrinking into his leather jacket and chewing his nails – it's obvious he was expecting at least a minute to acclimatise. Cindy waves at me, ignoring Zillah, who's become conveniently fascinated by a subpar painting of a sailboat on the opposite wall.

I get our coffees, and he follows me over to the table, dragging his heels and sighing as he takes off the hat and sunglasses. I sit down in the little wooden booth, leaving him the aisle seat in case he needs to bolt.

"Howdy Tom," says Cindy. "Well done for getting him here." She stares openly at Zillah while he sits down and takes a sip of his drink, then risks meeting her gaze. The minute he frowns and looks away, she shoots out one large hand, and grabs him by the chin, insisting, "Look me in the eye. Am I talking to you, or that crap?"

Zillah glares at her, finally managing to wriggle free as he grumbles, "Fuck *off*, you psychopath, I haven't had anything!"

"Well, you look like shit. Really, really miserable shit. It's clearly true. What's going on? Why now?"

"You know nothing..." he states dully.

"Yeah? Well maybe you should try telling me something once in a while, instead of pretending you're an island unto yourself. Why do you think I have alerts set up for stuff online about you? That's how I heard – not from you. So tell me – why now? What happened?"

Zillah lets out a weary sigh. "You always want to think that, you bloody medical people. It must've been an *event*. Causation – effect. It wasn't. Of course you didn't see it coming – I had to block you on Facebook years ago, 'cause every time I'm real on there, you alert the whole damn family. I can't trust you with a goddamn thing – you make me live a lie, so don't throw that shit in my face."

"Zill, it's bloody obviously a cry for help, whenever you get 'real' on Facebook, about how you're miserable, or using, or both. You're my little brother – when you say you're about to do something potentially fatal, I'd be breaking all my own principles if I didn't try to stop you. Don't throw it in my face either."

"It is *never* a cry for help!" he protests, dumping a sugar packet out onto the table and irritably poking the granules about. "If I wanted help, I'd fucking outright ask for it! It's a vent of desperation in a broken world. It's a plea for understanding, not bossiness, scorn and judgement. And isn't the definition of madness doing the same thing over and over, and expecting a different result? When are you going to drop it, all these bloody interventions and stern talkings to? Why can't you just accept me for who I am?"

"Probably because I can't accept the fact that my ridiculously intelligent brother's nearly forty and still trying to put his world to rights with Denial Powder. Or that he'd rather choose life as a secretive junkie over being part of our family. Would you rather I gave up? Stopped talking to you altogether?"

Zillah tangles his fingers into his hair, elbows on the table, hiding his face – I can already see his hands trembling. It's eternally bizarre, watching him trying, and failing, at dealing with conflict – fifty percent nervous wreck, fifty percent rent-a-gob from hell...

"Of course I don't want that…" he mutters. "I couldn't stand that. But you don't understand me. None of you even try. This family wouldn't know unconditional love if it bit them."

"Zillah, your privilege is obscene. If you saw some of the addicts I see at the hospital, heard their stories, you would feel like shit about what you just said. You've put us all through hell, over and over, and no one has ever dumped you. No one's ever tossed you out on the street. Until now, apparently. Maybe Emma's got more sense than all of us put together. You clearly need to hit rock bottom, and I'd say you're well on your way."

Zillah takes a deep breath, emerges from behind his hands, and says, "How can you be so brutally backwards about all this, as a medical professional? I've showed you the research on ADHD and addiction, and I *showed you* the research on diamorphine scripts, years ago, the fact they help people like me, because some of us can't quit, we just *can't* – surely you must know that? I came here, to—"

"But you did. You quit. You've been almost completely off it since I don't even know when. So why now?"

"Because I have *barely endured* every godforsaken *fucking* moment, Cindy! Sobriety is burning my *brains out,* and I'm not doing it anymore! And this whole time…you think I've been clean? Are you *serious?* I've either been barely holding it together, or I've been dabbling – it's never, ever been smooth sailing, which you would know if you didn't get so ridiculous every time I'm honest with you! I am fucking *miserable,* I am *exhausted,* I've had *enough,* and it was heroin or death – you should be happy I chose the former!"

She watches him with a matronly frown for several seconds, then asks,

"Did you ever try those meetings? Have you still never been to a single NA—"

"Oh stuff it all right up your arse! A meeting isn't going to fix me! It'd probably kill me dead, twenty other people yearning for drugs like it's not bad enough inside my own head. And you know what I'm like, I'd only end up going on a fucking tirade about how sobriety is *bollocks,* how I've been at it half my life and it's still *bollocks,* it doesn't get any *better*, and twenty minutes later I'd be like the Pied Piper leading half of them off to the nearest dealer. I—"

"How can you know 'til you try?" she asks, with all the unflappability of her trade. Zillah's clutching his hair and losing his shit, he'll be quoting Nietzsche in a minute, but nothing ruffles her feathers. I don't know whether it's admirable or sociopathic, but watching her wind him up is an interesting peek into their childhood dynamic… "How can you know anything 'til you go to a meeting?"

"Because!" he erupts, bringing a fist down on the table and sending the spilled sugar crystals bouncing everywhere, "Because I *see* all those fucking tossers, all over the internet, and they are *brainwashed!* My god, they never stop spouting on about it, the fact they're powerless and unmanageable and only a repeated circle-jerk of bleating addicts can save them from total goddamned *dereliction of the spirit,* when that is just not the case, not for me, not at all, I am not *like them,* I—"

"What, so you're saying your own issues aren't unmanageable, right now? That you never feel powerless to addiction?"

To his credit, Zillah at least considers her words for a couple of seconds, before snapping back,

"Of course I'm powerless to addiction, Cindy, I'm not *blind,* but that's not the root of it, is it? I feel powerless to *life,* far more than addiction. Powerless to my miserable, restless brain and my *bullshit* neurochemistry – no one else gets fucking norovirus from their own thoughts, do they? I've seen more of Tom's toilet than Tom's face, since everything kicked off, just…the level of sheer, crushing anxiety, I can't *stand it* in here. I told you, it was death or heroin, and that was not fucking hyperbole. Do *not* tell Mum this, but I had fully laid out plans to top myself in April. The drugs just came along first…so here we are – I'm still alive…"

"What?" she demands, and I see that unflappability starting to crack. "Why didn't you talk to me? When in April were you thinking like this?"

"Oh god, Cindy, I'd been planning it for months. The 28th was D-Day, as if it even matters. It'd be after everything, that's the point – all the events, so I didn't ruin anyone's birthday, or the wedding, and—"

"You seriously think you wouldn't ruin Charlie's wedding, when she got the news you'd killed yourself during her honeymoon? When she came directly home to your funeral? Zillah…what the actual fuck?"

"Well, there's never a good time to do it, is there? I was trying to be as considerate as I could."

There's a beat of silence. Zillah risks a nervous glance up from under his lashes, still poking sugar crystals about with one skinny finger.

"Oh, you *fucking* nob!" Cindy erupts – Zillah winces, shoulders hunched against the onslaught. "You absolute, *unbelievable* nob! I will never, ever forgive you if you go out like that, without even talking to me first, without trying meetings, or rehab, or inpatient – didn't you say to me once that you'd try literally everything before you ended it all, even spending every penny you had travelling the world, 'cause you can't take it with you anyway? What happened to all that?"

"I got older, Cindy. I got fucking older, and everything got more real. I haven't got the energy to fuck about with some Kerouac-style pre-suicide world tour anymore. Or maybe I'm doing it the best I can right now, and all it consists of is dope." He shrugs. "I'm done with the pretence. Sober life is unending misery. I was so ready to just…to just *go home."*

"'Go home'" she repeats, frowning. "What, to god's big old house? I thought you didn't believe in any of that?"

"Oh, fuck off. I believe in something. That's just the words that always come to me. *Going home.* It's how I felt. People say we choose to come here – to learn, and experience, and I think I agree. But I regret it, Cindy… I regret it so much it *hurts,* coming here to this godforsaken planet. I felt like I'd gone on some awful journey of discovery, gotten lost in the desert for a thousand years, ended up regretting the whole stupid experiment, and now all I want, *all* I fucking want, is to go home. That's how it felt. Like my batteries had expired. Like my soul was past its use-by date. All the shit I've done to myself, Cind – why am I still here? I know so many people who aren't. It isn't fair…"

"On them, or you?"

"Both of us. Fucking both. I've known people who wanted to live die of nothing, and I've wanted to die so many times, and here I still am. At thirty-eight. It's bullshit. Life is *bullshit.* Don't pity the dead – pity the ones still stuck here…"

"You felt this way even before it all went south, with Emma?"

"Long before. It's the—" he hesitates, and his eyes flick warily towards me. "Is this a setup?" he demands. "All these questions? Are you trying to have me sectioned?"

I shake my head, but Cindy lays a hand on his arm, a restraint disguised as a supportive touch, and says, "I'm worried about you – that's all. I came here worried, now I'm even more so. Have you still got these plans?" – it's obvious she's directing that question at both of us. I give her a subtle 'not that I know of' headshake. Zillah says, "No. No fucking plans. I'm fine."

She looks as though she'd have been happier if he'd said 'yes', and she could've had him safely contained.

"You don't look, or sound fine. What about this overdose? The one that awful Twitter thing mentioned? Was it deliberate?"

"No," Zillah sulkily states. "And it won't happen again."

"You can't guarantee that, and you know it – you have no idea what's in the shit you're shovelling into yourself. You're using needles, then?"

He shudders slightly, as though this conversation is getting decidedly too personal, and comes out with an intensely childish-sounding, *"Maybe..."*

I chime in with, "I'm not letting him use alone, while he's at mine…but it's not ideal."

She sighs. "I can get you on a script, Zill. No withdrawal, you don't have to do meetings, just—"

He erupts into a weird little fit of giggles, finally spluttering,

"You really have no clue, do you! I never came *off* my fucking script! I've been on it for well over a decade in the theoretical intention of keeping my shit together, but it clearly hasn't worked, has it?"

"A decade?" Cindy repeats, with a frown. "Had they dropped your dose, recently? Before all this, I mean? You don't think your brain had just—"

"No. They fucking *upped* my dose, when I started drinking myself comatose. The methadone stopped all that nonsense, but it didn't make anything else easier. That horrible shit makes me so groggy and braindead, it's half the reason Em can't stand me anymore…" He trails off, looking dejected, then sighs heavily, and continues, "So no, it's not Post Acute Withdrawal Misery-Syndrome, and I've tried *all* the antidepressants – heroin's the only thing that helps me."

Cindy shakes her head in despair, asking, "Are they going to kick you off this script, now you're using again?"

"I am *sly like a fox,*" he stage-whispers, smirking at the floor. Yup – infant Zillah has been unleashed. Cindy looks like she wants to punch his lights out, and I can't really blame her.

"If you're not being honest with them, Zill, they can't monitor you right, and that OD *will* happen again..."

"I'm not a blithering idiot," he retorts. "I know more about this stuff than you do!"

"Well, what am I meant to tell Mum, Zillah? That you're using again, and you've got nowhere to live, but it'll all be fine 'cause you're an expert in the field, and *sly like a fox?* You sound just like Charlie Sheen, and you know how he ended up? With sodding HIV. So what the hell do I tell Mum?"

Zillah glances up nervously. "Don't tell her anything. She can't help. You'll only worry her, and she won't even tell me that, she'll just pray and pray and pray until her knees drop off. Don't tell her, Cind, for fuck's sake, I can't bear it…"

"She'll know. She always does. She asks me about you, every time, what's 'really going on with you', meaning 'What does the internet say'. I'll have to tell her you and Emma are over, at the very least…assuming that's true – it's fully over?"

Zillah's got his head in his heads at the mere mention of that whole catastrophe. "It's true right now," he says quietly. "I don't want it to be. I want her back. I'd do anything just to—" His voice cracks, and he breaks off, taking a deep breath and mumbling, "Don't even make me talk about it, Cind, it all hurts too fucking much…"

Cindy shakes her head, takes a sip of coffee, and states,

"Well, if you're as bloody immovable with her as you are with me, I can't see why in hell's name she'd have you back in the house. Maybe that's some motivation that'll make sense to you."

"Do you know why I bothered coming here today?" he asks, sitting up and glaring at her. "I thought you could actually help me, with this. I thought you, being *you*, with your job, your contacts, might actually be able to *help me,* with the most important thing I've ever needed in my life."

"Wait, what? My job? You're ready to go into detox? An emergency admiss—"

Zillah growls through gritted teeth, flinging his arms out and exclaiming, "You just don't listen, do you? You never fucking listen to me! Am I speaking alien? Is that it? Am I a goddamn fucking alien, sitting here? Because you make me feel like one! Cindy, I am *not getting clean*, in any way, shape or form. Not now, not tomorrow, not ever again. But I want—I *need* my life to not unravel around my ears! I want Em back, I want to not get sodding well cancelled by torch-wielding armies of internet scumbags who've never been where I've been, I want to know that I'm safe—"

"Zill...how can I change any of that? I'm not a miracle worker, I barely even know Emma, and frankly—"

"*Diamorphine!*" he groans, leaning across the table towards her – grabbing her hands. "Can't you help me plead my case with my workers for a decent script? Intravenous fucking diamorphine – I know it doesn't get handed out often, but it does *happen*, and surely by now – at my age, I mean, with my history...doesn't it make me the ideal candidate? Tom – you said it yourself; it's a miracle I'm still here, and my life expectancy's got to be three years tops, if I keep on doing what I'm doing, and the thing is, *I don't even care!* So...Christ, where is the palliative care for incurable mental illnesses? Where is the prescription of proven-effective medications for *mental pain* – not just physical? Why the *fuck* am I living in such a *backwards-ass* world that won't listen to a word I say, when the medication that helps me function is cheap, old, and easily available, but ohhh no, not to me, not unless I buy it illegally, loathed by society, and risk dying every rotten fucking day of my life!" By the end of this outburst, his eyes are glossed with a sheen of tears, and Cindy sighs, taking his hand and asking,

"Have you talked to your treatment team?"

Zillah runs a hand through his hair, looking exhausted and emotional – I get the strong feeling this is what Em was on about; the thing he 'won't shut up about' – the 'trouble' he's in with the Drug People...

"I wrote them a fucking letter," he says. "You know I do everything better in writing. They dicked me around for months, then they just told me to fuck off. I wrote back, argued some more, pointed out that maybe there's some other opioid, that it doesn't have to be injectable, I'd take fentanyl patches, I'd take anything, but honestly…well…now I'm back on it, aren't I? And the needles are— Oh *hell*, man, I don't want to talk to you about this, but I need it to be *right,* ok*,* and I just know if they don't give me the real thing, I'll still be sneaking around, and that's why I need you to put a word in! I've got a lead on this other place, this other clinic, Brownstown – it's not that far away, and on their website they say they do 'diamorphine assisted treatment', but I can't get a hold of anyone useful – will you please, *please* just…help me with this? Help me get through to them, throw your weight around a bit, tell them—"

"What 'weight', Zillah? I'm an NHS nurse, not a flipping specialist consultant! Trust you to find a legal loophole, even when it comes to intravenous smack. You're a nightmare, you really are…"

"But?" he persists, with feverish desperation. "It's an idea – isn't it? I showed you the studies years ago! It helps people like me – there's never been a study where it's failed! And I told you, didn't I, that when I finally got my degree it was *solely* because I was using – I was calmer, I could fucking *concentrate*, it's the only damn reason I got it; I am *functional* on this shit, or I would be if I was taking something safe, clean, dose-measured, reliable and legal! Cindy, it's the system that's broken – not me!"

She shakes her head, her expression despairing. "You really do believe that, don't you? You genuinely won't cop to a thing – not even when it comes to this stupidity. You just have to be the one-percent of addicts that goes at it so hard for so long, with zero desire to change his life, we have to start looking into mad legal loopholes just to keep you alive. Thirty-eight years old, and you still sound like some fifteen-year-old kid banging on about legalising all drugs!"

"Uh huh? And hasn't the revolution started? Weed – getting legal, Portugal, decriminalising *all* the drugs and watching *every* addiction statistic plummet – we are headed towards a *less stupid* tomorrow, and I don't see why I shouldn't be around to see it, why I should be left to overdose in a ditch, all because the medication I need – which is used in hospitals every minute of every day, with zero negative side effects besides constipation and a bit of nausea – is being barred to me by outdated, obscene fucking *Tory lawmakers!"* He's banging on the table now, really getting into his stride – Cindy's leaning across the table too, retorting,

"It always comes back to the bloody Tories with you, doesn't it? That teacher was right, you know – you should've been a fucking politician, and maybe you could've made a bit of actual, genuine difference in this world, with the way you speak, the things you'd fight to the death for, and instead you chose dope and a career in narcissism. What a *bloody* waste – that's all I'm sitting here thinking. What a bloody, *bloody* waste of your potential!"

"I help people!" he snaps back, "You don't see the messages I get, from kids who've gone through the same awful, miserable shit, and now they know they're not—"

"Zill, you better watch your damn self, exchanging messages with those kids: aside from the fact they almost certainly want to fuck you, and you're old enough to be their dad, you are in *no* position to be giving advice to anyone, right now!"

"Cindy, I am not a moron, I have no desire to become a *paedophile*, and this crap is irrelevant! I get it, you hate my job, you think it's stupid, you always will, and I really don't care. I think your job sounds like mopping up puke and wiping arses for miserable pay, which sometimes makes me wonder if you've got a scat fetish, but there we have it, people vary. Getting back to the subject of saving my life, however – *please?* Will you just…talk to this clinic, get them to give me a ring, or an appointment, or something? I know I'm…a lot sometimes, but if you can't bring yourself to do it for me, then…do it for Mum, Cind? Let her bumble off into retirement knowing I'm finally happy, and safe, and stable. Just one phone-call?"

Cindy huffs out another irritable sigh, and says, "Oh fucking *hell*, Zillah. Have you got their number? And their email, or website?"

"Oh, I *love you!*" he blurts out, flinging himself across the table to hug her, then delving for his phone and passing her the details.

"I'll call on Monday," she says. "But don't get your hopes up. And in the meantime, you're doing something for me, in return."

"What?" Zillah asks, warily.

"Attend a meeting. Tom – go with him, for moral support. Even if it's only one, that's my condition. Just try it."

"Fine," says Zillah, to my intense surprise. "I think it'll help my case with the diamorph script, if I've tried literally everything.*"*

Cindy shakes her head. "You're never going to shut up about this, are you? Zillah, I am telling you, your chances are about one in five thousand here, so…keep the hope in check, ok?"

"Oh, god forbid you give me too much *hope*, Cind. I mean, I just told you I nearly topped myself this spring, but god *fucking* forbid this beastly country lets a useless junkie like me go on living with a single grain of hope in his heart."

She frowns. "This is exactly what I mean. You've got to be realistic, Zill. This world is not perfect, but we are stuck with it, and I'm really, horribly afraid that you're going to pin everything on this script, then when it doesn't come through, which it probably won't, you're going to revisit those plans you had in April. Does that sound…likely?"

"No," says Zillah, far too quickly. "I'm thinking positively, that's all!"

"Zill…you'll tell me, won't you, if you start getting close to the edge again?"

"Look," he says, starting to gather up his belongings, "You know full well where I stand on this. I am not being locked up in our shitty local nutter ward that doesn't even provide psychiatric treatment – it's a sick joke. How in hell's name is that supposed to help me? I'm 'nearly forty', as you so charmingly put it, and I know my own mind. If the fucking world lets me down on this, it'll be the last time it does. But that does *not* mean I'm threatening suicide, I'm just saying I—Oh *Jesus* – you know what, fuck it, it doesn't even matter. Just call that place for me. We're never going to agree about this – I'm going home."

"You haven't got a home."

"Ohh *nice* – you want to kick me in the nuts while I'm down, too?"

Copyright Dorian Bridges 2024

He stands up, yanking his beanie back on, and I have no idea whether to go with him, or whether Cindy'll decapitate me if I move.

"Zillah," she pleads, "you've got your methadone – can you not just knock the using on the head while I speak to these people? Wouldn't it be a good resolution to say, right now, 'no more street gear'?" Seeing his expression, she hastily continues, "Or you could just smoke it? No more needles – can you do that for me?"

"Please just…drop it," he says softly. "Cindy, I wouldn't have been honest with you about any of this if I wasn't at the absolute end of my rope. But I am. And you…making these ultimatums? You're just snatching away more fucking rope. I *need* to do what I'm doing. I do. But I'm going down fighting, aren't I? Trying to get this script?"

"You're not fighting at all. You're a drowning man using his final breaths to declare his love for the ocean, and I can't bear it…"

Zillah sighs. "Can't any of you see this drowning man's legs, kicking like hell beneath the surface? They always have been, Cind. *Always*. If this kills me…I need you to know that. I need you to remember that *I tried*."

He turns to go.

"Zill?"

"What?"

She looks at him for a long moment, then says, "I know you think I don't care, but you'll always be my little brother. And for the record…I hope they give you the damn script."

He raises an eyebrow. "For real? You actually agree with me?"

She shrugs, looking defeated. "We've been through the mangle with this, and you, for decades now, and I can feel you slipping away from us. If it can bring you, and our family, some peace at last, then I can't be against it. Not if it's the only way to save your stupid life. So just…don't be a prat, in the meantime, ok? Be *careful,* 'cause if you turn up in that hospital, ODing again, it's more than I can bear. And if that happens, I couldn't in any good conscience let you go free. Not after everything you've said here today."

Zillah throws me a nervous glance. "What the hell is that supposed to mean?"

"It means, Zill, that if you OD again, you're getting sectioned – no ifs, no buts. I'll be telling the emergency department nurses to be on lookout for you, as a favour to me, and whatever you say, I will override it. You've given me more than enough reason to. If you can't lay off the gear by yourself, until this script comes through, I'll do it for you."

"But the script might *never* come through – you said it yourself!"

"We'll cross that bridge when we come to it. Stay out of trouble, and it's all irrelevant anyway, isn't it?"

He backs away, wide-eyed. "You've gone nuts! That is an absolute abuse of power you've just admitted to, that is *legally* abhorr—"

"Oh would you look at that – my little junkie brother suddenly cares about the law. I wonder who they'll believe though, Zill, you or me – huh? You, or—"

"Oh my god*,* you are a fucking *psychopath!"* he erupts, causing several people to turn and stare – "You seriously wonder why I'm never honest with you? You back me into corners like this, corners you know are my worst fucking fears for *very good reason*, then you expect me not to act like a crazed animal? You are an unhinged sodding psychopath, and I'm reporting you to PALS!"

"What, for a theoretical conversation between a brother and sister in a café? I don't think the NHS patient liaison service covers those."

"Tom, where are the keys? Just give me your *fucking keys* – you told me this wasn't an intervention!"

"I'm coming," I concede – this is clearly going nowhere productive. "Sorry, Cindy."

"I'll be watching you," she says, pointing an accusatory finger at Zillah's chest. "If you must use, you do it as sensibly as you can, *or else*. I wish like hell you wouldn't inject, but I know that ship's long sailed. Tom…take him to a meeting – that's an order. And bloody well feed him up a bit."

Zillah growls through gritted teeth, whips round, and storms out of the café, muttering loudly, "Fucking arseholes, you fucking, *fucking* arseholes!"

"Sorry," I say, to the nearest table. "I'm sorry – bad day. Enjoy your…coffee…" I throw an apologetic glance at Cindy, then chase after Zillah, wondering how in hell's name she's tolerated him this long when they aggravate each other so efficiently. There must have been good times, between the two of them – I know he always goes home for Christmas, I've seen pictures of them smiling together in festive paper hats, but it seems such a flimsy thing to hold together such stark differences…

I find him smoking a joint next to the busker, looking pale and tense, hands visibly shaking. It's a Saturday lunchtime, the high street's bustling, and once again he's blazing up his stinkiest weed in public. The minute he sees me, he starts striding towards home – I have to run to catch him up.

I grab him by the arm, forcing him to slow down as I hiss,

"Mate, will you put that out, for the love of god! We are too old to get arrested for this crap!"

He snorts, and before I can cotton onto what he's about to do, he's whipped up his left sleeve, and petulantly ground the joint out on the back of his own arm, leaving a vile-looking patch of charred-black flesh. I mutter "For fuck's sake, man…" but he just lets out a shaky breath, pockets the reeking remnants of the joint, and moves to head home again. I yank him back, saying,

"I seriously can't let you go home like this."

"Like *what?*" he snaps. "My life is fucking disintegrating! That's hardly news, is it?"

"I just get the feeling…this might have been the straw that broke the camel's back. I'm scared that if you get inside my house, right now, you're going to be so desperate to shut the whole mess out, you're going to do too much again, and it's going to kill you."

"Oh for fuck's *sake*, Tom, you paranoid *wanker* – did you not just hear her? If I OD, I'm getting an instant ticket to crazy-jail, when I'm not even crazy! Is that not crazy, in and of itself? Do you not think *she's* bloody crazy? *God*, I—" He breaks off with an infuriated growl, and starts striding off in the opposite direction.

"Where are you going?" I ask, running to catch up.

He whips round, scowling. "You're right, you're right, you're generally fucking right, and that's why people don't smash your face in even when you ask for it. If I go back to yours, I'm going to do something dumb. I won't mean to, but *god* I just want to wipe out my entire *soul* for as long as possible, and—"

"And that doesn't sound like such a great idea."

"Not with Windy Cindy lurking about like a pompous, flatulent poltergeist…"

"Windy Cindy?" I repeat, trying not to laugh at him while he's so riled up. "Is that really the best you could do?"

He smiles, reluctantly. "It's what I called her when I was little."

"Was she? *Windy*, I mean?"

He laughs, just a bit. "No more than any other girl, but back then I thought farts were reserved for boys, and her loathsome habit of running into my bedroom, cracking one out, then running off again, leaving me with the stink, was *really very uncouth.*"

"Sounds like she had the upper hand, even back then. You had a nickname like 'Windy Cindy', while she was developing biological warfare…"

"Yeah…" he says, eyes narrowing. "She's always had the capacity to be terrifying. Maybe that's why she dresses the way she does. She's like some poisonous creature warning you that eating it would be intensely unwise…"

"Do you think it was worth it though, seeing her today? With that…weird bloody script you're after? What is it, anyway? Like, literally prescription heroin?"

"Pure as the driven snow… You can see why it's hard to get. But it fucking *shouldn't* be – not to proven long-term addicts, or high risk ones; you're not making a junkie, you're saving someone's life, and there are so many studies that back it up, but you know this government, they don't give a shit about anyone, especially not poor people or the mentally ill. And honestly, Tom, I have no idea if Cindy can help me…I just bloody hope so. It's my only chance of getting Em back, *or* keeping my sodding career, not to mention the fact that if my mum finds out I'm on street gear again, it'll put her in her grave. I just don't see why it should be so much to ask, to get a prescription we know'll keep me on an even keel, a drug I'm taking anyway, that would let me live a respectable, law-abiding life. The whole system of this corrupt fucking nation makes me want to *die*."

I let him vent himself out. By now, the speed he's got us walking, we've arrived at the park, the sun just beginning to peek through the clouds. The minute our feet hit grass, Zillah pulls out the half-smoked joint, and relights it, striding over to a fallen tree, and dumping himself down on it, staring blankly at the burn on his arm. When I sit down next to him, he glances across at me, and frowns slightly, like he either knows he's been a bit of a tit, or it just hurts more than he remembered. He yanks his sleeve down over the whole blackened mess.

"Fuck…" he mutters, shaking his head. He passes the joint over – I don't refuse.

"What are your chances though – really?" I ask, as he delves in his pocket, brings out a handful of anxiety pills, and gulps them down with a grimace. "I've never heard of anyone being on that stuff, but then you're the only…uhh…" I trail off, blanking on how to put it tactfully.

"I'm the only junkie you're friends with?" he guesses, with a wry half-smile. "It's ok. You can say it. I don't object to the J-word, in the main. Frankly I hate it less than 'addict'. Eurgh. *Addict*. It sounds so…*pathological*. Whenever I hear that word, I see some disapproving Tory face, like…like Theresa fucking May, announcing that 'All addicts are to be socially cleansed, this Wednesday'. That's what I hear. Whereas 'junkie'? Not so bad. It's the title of a pretty decent book. If you had a book called *Addict* it'd be a Tory propaganda pamphlet about handing out needle exchange packs laced with anthrax…"

"That is…good to know. I can use the right words to introduce you at parties now."

He laughs. "Ah, hi, hi, this is Sam Forbes, trainee accountant, and over here, Zillah Marsh, my favourite homeless junkie YouTuber."

I glance over, and he's frowning into the middle distance. He meets my gaze, shrugs, and takes another drag on the joint, mumbling through the smoke, "S'fucking true. Might as well say it."

"Hopefully not permanently the case…"

"Why, am I getting on your nerves already?" He looks uncomfortable.

"No, god no – of course not. Last night was fun, before all the drama kicked off. It's nice having you here."

He frowns, gazing across the park, eyes narrowed against the sudden sunlight. "To be honest, I think I'm glad I am. Here, I mean, with you, and your paranoid fucking Junkie Buddy System, now Cindy's launched her nukes. I wouldn't make it in that asylum. I just wouldn't…"

"What was it you said, anyway, about our 'shitty local facility' not even giving psychiatric treatment? Is that true, or did you pull it directly out of your arse? That can't be legal, surely?"

"Oh, it's true," he says, taking an enormous drag on the joint, and passing the last of it over. "That place is literally just a jail for crazy people – you only see a shrink once a week, and even then they don't give you treatment, all they do is check whether you're ready for release. I mean, they'll medicate you half to death, but that's it – no therapy, no groups; it's a Victorian sanatorium. And there's these…*screams*. Just screams, and wails, and insane fucking shrieks, echoing off the tiles – the staff don't give a shit, they've seen worse, so it's only the other patients who bother tending to all those dead-eyed, bloated, shrieking guys, rocking backwards and forwards, backwards and forwards, howling and raking their nails down their faces, eyes like the inside of a coffin. It's a burned-out wasteland of hopelessness, a circle of hell time and god forgot…"

"Wow…" is all I can say, stubbing out the roach as I realise I'm far more stoned than I wanted to be. "Are you giving me Edgar Allen Poe here, or is this some urban legend, or what?"

"This is *lived experience*, Tom," he says, looking strangely haunted for a guy who's never, to my knowledge, been inside a nuthouse in his life…despite all odds. "Look…this has never left my family before, 'cause while my dad was alive, he had some bloody dark ideas about what having an asylum inmate for a son would make him look like…but I was *in there*. In that fucking place – *me*. Not for long, but long enough. It was a good few years ago – like I said, Dad was alive – and I was still using daily. I ended up with this dodgy batch, had something in it that made me—*Jesus*, I don't even know how to describe it, but it was *terrifying* – my brain went all echoey, nothing was real, things were talking to me – I could fight it off for a day or two, telling myself no, no, it's just the drugs, you're fine, you're cool, pretend it's acid, ride it out…but it went on and on, and I wasn't sleeping, so the hallucinations got worse and worse, and in the end I got so messed up and scared, I just had to…*confess*. I had no idea what was real anymore. So I spoke to my mum, and—" He winces, shakes his head, and mutters, "Christ, Tom, I'm not even telling you what I said, but you know me – I've got no filter. They put me straight in the nuthouse."

"Damn, Zill…that's a bit much, isn't it? Not even therapy, or meds first? They just drove you straight out to the asylum and dumped you like an unruly dog?"

"No, fuck no, it was the right—the *only* thing to do – why d'you think I've never told you this before? I'm not fucking proud of it – I was very, very, impressively mad. I know you'd like the grisly details, but…I can't – not now, not ever. I try not to think about those weeks at all." He shivers, adding, "Never take your cast-iron brain for granted, man. I've felt mine turn pure, unadulterated evil on me, and I've never been so scared in my life. And my family, they didn't know, see, that it was *that place*. None of us did. We'd had no dealings with inpatient facilities before, nothing more brutal than drug workers and psychiatrists, but…*shit*. A place like that, even when you're only in there for five minutes, it leaves its fucking mark."

He turns to stare at me, asking,

"Do you get it now? Do you understand why I'm so determined to get this script? I've personally *experienced* what dodgy gear can do, that it can turn me legitimately psychotic, have me institutionalised, potentially *forever*, and that's the risk I take, every time I score new stuff? Even ignoring the legal elements – right? And that's only my *worst* dodgy batch story! I am *too old* to live with that uncertainty hanging over me anymore. I know what I need to get me through life, and I know it's available. I'm stopping at nothing to get it." His eyes narrow as he adds, "As proven by the fact I was willing to sit down with my lunatic sister and spill my bloody guts to her. But…hell, Tom, do you see why I freaked out so hard on her, now? She is not *helping*, with this sectioning shit – she knows what it was like for me in there, that I'd rather gut myself like a fish than go back, and she hangs it over my head anyway?"

He scowls, then sighs heavily, and says, like a doom-laden confession,

"Tom…when we get back, I need to give you something. I should've given you it the minute I got here, but I didn't, because I'm an arsehole and I don't much care if I die – sorry. But now…it's not death I've got to fear. It's that place…so I'll do as I'm told, and give you the Naloxone – teach you how to use it…" He looks resigned to some awful sort of fate, but I don't know why –

"Naloxone? The overdose antidote stuff, right? Wrong?"

"Right…"

"And yet, you sound like you're handing over your own personal kryptonite…is it that bad, being dragged back from the dead?"

He shudders. "*Yes.* The reason it stops you ODing, is that it kicks all the opiates out of your brain-cells. That'd be fine for you. Not so fine for me. My brain's been running on that shit in one form or another since the mid-2000s, and it does not take kindly to being opiate-bereft. So I'll come back to life, but do *not* expect me to thank you for it. Worst case scenarios only, please – if you can keep me breathing by repeatedly kneeing me in the balls, I'd take that over Naloxone, every time."

"Oof... That bad – seriously?"

"Like I said – fine for you. I can't even explain what it feels like – they say it wears off fast, but it fucking doesn't, not completely...not for me. You know I can't handle withdrawal... It's not even the puking, or the cramps, or the ice-shards in the marrows of your bones, or the shitting five stone of liquid out in the space of— Sorry, sorry, too much detail – it's not fun, is what I'm saying, but it's the bloody *anxiety,* nothing touches it, no other drug, and Naloxone withdrawal's not like other withdrawal – there's no control over it, doesn't matter what you shovel into your veins, you can't stop the hell..." He shivers again, regarding me with wide, nervous eyes. "I'm trusting you with my entire *sanity* here, Tom, when I hand over that wretched yellow box. Honestly I meant to squirt the stuff straight down the toilet rather than hand it over, but, I got high, and then I forgot."

I sigh, and pat him on the back. "Well, thanks for finally owning up. I'll only use it if you're utterly unrousable..." *Or if you're on the floor and Lucy loses it,* I add, silently, but I don't say it aloud. He looks freaked out enough already – I can't tell if it's the nuthouse memories, the threat of Naloxone, or just the weed...

"Come on," he says, getting up, "I'm sick of this day – it's been horrible to me. I'm erasing it."

I get up too, but point out, "You haven't made that public response yet…"

He stares at me for three silent seconds, then clutches his fists to his forehead, and just yells, *"FUUUCK!"* so loudly a cluster of pigeons shoots into the sky, and a nearby dog walker screams shrilly. "Sorry," says Zillah, "Sorry, sorry – not insane, just…working, on a Saturday, you know? Sorry!" Turning back to me, I can see him weighing up the idea, then he just flaps one hand, turns for home, and starts marching off, declaring, "Don't care, fuck the public, fuck it all, I'm blaming Cindy for this hit. I'll be unconscious, you can be my speech writer. It'll be ready by the time I wake up, right?" He turns back, looking hopeful. "Come on, Tom, I'll pay you! You're a natural at this stuff! Think about all the shit I said last night, and you were like, *no, no, don't say that, you sound like a terrible junkie scumbag, put it like this instead, or just shut the fuck up completely* – you know! Write that down! Put it in a speech. Be my director. It'll be fun!"

"Did you do this to Em?" I ask, smiling slightly. "Is the mythical genius of Zillah Marsh actually one rather diminutive blue-haired woman who always seems to be dressed in a Gir onesie?"

"Urgh, Tom…don't do that to me. Don't make me miss her fucking onesie obsession. It's hardly sexy, but I miss it…" He sighs. "And no. No, I do not make her write anything for me. You are…*the chosen one*. But hurry up, I feel disgusting, this shitty methadone's wearing off…"

"Oh *Zill* – what the fuck?" I groan, "I thought you said it was dangerous to take that shit then do smack on top!"

"That's why I only took a pissy little dose, Tom!" he says, in a singsong voice like I'm stupid, not looking back as he powers up the hill towards my house. "Wasn't going to wind up puking in Cindy's lap, was I? But that's also why I'm starting to feel *really* fucking crappy. Hurry up!"

CHAPTER SEVEN

I spend most of the next three hours talking to myself in the mirror, pretending to be Zillah. It's quite fun, actually – I'm getting the feeling anyone could do this job, or at the very least, everyone would like to – sticking their face in a camera and going off about all their favourite subjects? Who hasn't occasionally pretended they were being interviewed by the NME, while they're driving in to work?

I've monitored Zillah into his intended stupor, after he reluctantly handed over the slim yellow box that held the Naloxone, this little syringe to be stabbed into his thigh, right through his jeans, if he fucks up. "Only if I'm literally turning blue, Tom – I'm serious. And no ambulances," he insists, pointing at the instructions, at the bit where it tells you to call one while the stuff kicks in. He even grabs a biro off the bedside table, and crosses that bit out. I ask why you need an ambulance if you have the antidote anyway – he says, "That's the fucking spirit. It's bullshit. Now put this somewhere Lucy won't find it. She might not follow the rules." Then he was off into the bathroom to do his thing, before I could even ask why those other, "bullshit" rules existed.

He returns to the land of the living mid-afternoon, in full on spiky-haired, eyeliner-smudged rockstar mode, ready to charm the world's population into forgiving him.

"Well?" he says. "Did you manage anything?"

"Yeah…I think so. It was difficult putting myself in your shoes though, honestly, 'cause you can talk 'til you're blue in the face, but I still don't understand why in hell's name you're doing this to

Copyright Dorian Bridges 2024

yourself, besides the fact it clearly feels better than reality. And your reality – prior to all this bollocks – seems pretty enviable, frankly. So why you went—"

"My reality? Reality is *subjective,* Tom. Like…imagine you're on a beach, right? If you're on vacation, having sunscreen rubbed into your back by a busty pornstar, that's a very different reality than if you're part of the D-Day Landings and you've just had your leg blown off, you know, all thigh muscle and tendons dribbling out your torso like crabmeat? Horrible shit. But that's still *you*, on a beach. That is the reality of it, as perceived by the sun, or the sand, or the fish in the sea. So, you cannot tell me what reality is, or is not like, for me personally. Am I on vacation, or am I being blown to bits, inside? You don't know. You've never visited my brain." He dances with his hands, singing, "'*I'll give you my skin, so you can feel how I feel – this is my existence!**' Duh-duh, dun, dun, dun, duh-duh, dun, dun, dun…"

"Christ. I think I feel an Ecstasy flashback coming on. Who the fuck was that, anyway?"

"Icon of Coil, you dementia-riddled fart – *Existence in Progress*. Don't you still have my burned CDs from back in the day rolling round your back seat?"

"No, I have Lucy saying, "Tom, this *literally* says 2005 on it – you can't possibly still need it, can you?" No respect for my memories."

(*With lyrical credit to Andy LaPlegua & Sebastian Komor, of Icon of Coil.)

"Well, apparently you don't remember those memories anyway. Weird that I do, isn't it, considering I never had any restraint whatsoever in the realm of eating disco-biscuits…"

I can't help laughing, remembering with a wince, "Christ, you used to drive us home, too. If I ever have kids, do not expect to be their godfather, Zill."

"That's the nicest thing anyone's ever said to me, Tom. I mean it – I'd leave the country if you bestowed me the dubious honour of Pseudo-Religious Emergency-Babydaddy. Anyway, I got us home safe every time, didn't I? Fuck only knows how – I remember driving back from the club watching the brake lights of the car in front bouncing with the beat, doing literal heartbeat lines as I stared at them, I was so high, but not once did I have a fender bender or close call. I was cut out for this life, me…"

"Aaand we're back in the land of 'Shit Zillah must never, *ever* say online…'"

He pulls a "Duh?" face at me, grins, and leans in to whisper, "*We'll take our secrets to the grave, Tom…*" He pulls back, gives me a nod and a wink, then asks, "Well? What've you got? Show me this wonder of a speech!"

"Umm… So, I don't know that you're going to like it, but that's not really the point. The point is, it keeps you out of trouble. We're creating a shield here, against further drama. Because drama sends you off the deep end, and I really, really don't want to stab you in the leg with that yellow stuff, or knee you in the balls for a straight hour. So just…remember that, and read with an open mind, ok?"

"Sounds bloody ominous…"

He takes the printed words, and starts reading. As I watch, his reactions swing from amusement, to exasperation, to "*Really*, Tom?" and numerous paragraphs getting slashed out, replaced with his own lengthy scribbles on the back, until the thing's barely recognisable as my own work, at which point he reaches grim acceptance.

"The Idiot Speech," he intones, when he's done. "You actually went and wrote me The Idiot Speech."

I shrug. "Like I said – it's a shield against anything they can throw at you. And it doesn't cop to a thing – not specifically. I think that's better, 'cause the fact is, you have some overzealous, obsessive fans, and I know that, because I've been stalking you online all afternoon, trying to understand these people, and I swear to god, if you say you're doing gear, some of the real maniacs will go out and try it, to be more like you. I don't fucking understand why, but they will – so don't cop to anything, when it comes to the drugs." My gaze drops to his arms – he's unconsciously rolled up one sleeve, and if that arm's on camera, it won't matter *what* I write for him. "Umm…mate – you can't go on screen like that. How did you…manage it, anyway? I thought you were right-handed?"

He glances down at the muddle of nasty-looking bruises on his right arm, all carving out the scar-dotted pathways of various veins. He looks uncomfortable, drags his sleeve back down, and states, "I'm ambidextrous. At least, as far as this goes. Gotta be, when you're my age and still at it. Shit…do you think the long sleeves are a giveaway? I feel like they are. It's the middle of August, for fuck's sake… Hang on."

He drags his grungy grey sweater over his head, switching it for a tank top with a rather aggressive but faded slogan on the front, then he pulls out a makeup stick, and starts plastering it over his track marks, and, wincingly, right over the top of the fresh burn. It's been a while since I even noticed his left arm, the mess he made of it during our first year of uni, in the days before he discovered drugs and still relied on rampant self-mutilation. That arm used to be so bad he went everywhere with a black cobweb sleeve over the top, but now the chaotic hashing of cuts has entirely faded to white; it could almost be an impressionistic white-ink tattoo…

"Dermablend!" Zillah declares, rubbing makeup into his skin, needle bruises vanishing like magic, "The saviour of junkies worldwide! If this whole saga really blows up, I'm going to them for a sponsorship deal…"

I genuinely can't tell if he's being serious or what, at this point – he's definitely entering his hyperactive social-slash-recording mode. I just shake my head, and let him get on with setting up his camera, until finally, still clutching my edited bits of paper, he hits the record button, and launches off.

"Hello, world! I've got something important I need to— Yeah, sorry, this is weird, I'm going to be…reading at you, for this one? I know, it's odd, I feel like the news guy or something, but the whole idea is that I don't say anything…too…umm… Uhh? *Fuck,* Tom, this feels ridiculous! Take two? Ok… Hello, world… I hope you don't mind me reading something at you, it's just that this is important, and I need to not totally…dump myself…in it? Argh*,* hell! Not contrite enough, *way* too honest, no honesty today, *contrition, contrition!"*

It takes him at least six more manically hopeless introductions before he hits his pre-speech stride, explaining somewhat more sombrely, that "Things have been difficult, I'm a bit frazzled, and no one wants to watch me sitting here in silence scratching my head and wondering where the hell it all went wrong. So, to address the rumours, here's what I need to say. The important stuff:

"My name is Zillah Marsh, and I am an *idiot*. But then, so are you – no offence. When I say 'idiot', what I really mean is fallible. Human. Prone to fuckups – some of them colossal. I'm older than…not all of you, but a fair few, and by the time you reach my age, you'll have *fucked your life up completely* on at least one occasion. That's more or less guaranteed. Everything ebbs and flows, good stuff, bad stuff, wise decisions, dumb ones. Right now, I'm not in the best bit of the cycle."

He frowns, glances from the camera to me, and mutters,

"Even though I'm just a victim of a shitty system, with a furious girlfriend who's been brainwashed by that system…" He rolls his eyes. "Ahem. Blah blah, best bit of the cycle… What I need to say doesn't just apply to me, it applies to everyone you follow online. All this drama, this escalating cancel culture, it's madness, and that madness stems from the desire to worship false idols, to put ordinary people on pedestals and literally *worship them*, as though they can do no wrong. But they do, and they will – they'll let you down time and time again, because they're only human, and they're under a microscope no normal, flawed being can survive. Age doesn't even matter, in terms of wisdom – young or old, you'll still be a fucking idiot, also known as a human, for the rest of your life, for to be human, ultimately, is to fuck up.

"What I mean by all this, is…please don't do that to me – especially not right now. Don't put me on a pedestal, look to me for advice. I haven't got it in me, lately. I'm not saying I'm quitting, going anywhere, I'm just saying that I'm…fucking up a lot of stuff right now, and while I can still *be here* for you, online, doing…all of this, I'm not the person who should be guiding your life, even in such a small way. In short, come here for the entertainment, if that's what you want to call it, but don't let such an obviously damaged human become your guiding light.

"As far as the details of my life go, right now, that's the other thing. No one online owes you every little piece of themselves, and the ones who do, the ones who pretend to *give you everything,* they're generally the biggest liars of the lot, with their scripted reality TV and pre-prepared blooper reels. For the rest of us, the ones who don't want to be that devious or corny, there have to be boundaries. I'm not saying, like, never will I ever, when it comes to the recent stuff…" He trails off, then goes completely off script – "Actually, there's something I'd *love* to tell you about. Bit of a medical battle I'm currently fighting with…certain powers that be. Needs talking about, because it's so much bigger than just me, and it *matters*, but now's…not the time…" He frowns, finds his mark, and carries on – "When it comes to the recent stuff, I hope someday I can tell you everything, from a better place, with some…maybe not wisdom, but perhaps lessons learned, attached to this whole horrible saga." Then he's racing off script again –

"I'm sorry – I know this sounds like a whole load of waffle with really no substance whatsoever – I *know* you came here for the salacious details, about the breakup, and all the horrible, sordid rumours people are chucking about, and instead I'm giving you another lecture that'll get me called a pompous self-aggrandising windbag twat, or something, but…this is what I need to do, right now. My best mate, Tom, he calls me the Infamous Motor-Mouth, and he's right. And it's not always a good thing. I need to pull back from

Copyright Dorian Bridges 2024

speaking before I think, because trying to be all wise and helpful when you're actually in a bit of a mess, and suddenly there are hundreds of thousands of people listening to you, it's not the cleverest idea. So, I repeat –

"I, Zillah Marsh, am a *fucking idiot*. Don't put me on a pedestal. Ever. Remember that all of us are human, and fallible. Stay cynical, question everything, use your own moral compass. Forgive people's bad days, applaud their good ones, and don't get tangled up in online gossip – it's soul-poison.

"Anyway, this is tangential – I've gone way off the words I was meant to say –" he flings the largely-ignored-or-abridged papers over his head, "But I think that might be for the best. I needed to say it in my own words. I wish I could—" He brings himself up short, suddenly looking utterly depressed. After a moment he sighs, shakes his head, and says softly,

"I wish I could make certain things in my life better. I wish there was more understanding in the world. I wish…*I* was different. More cut out for this place. Sometimes I feel like I was dealt a shitty hand, and other times I feel like I *am* the shitty hand, being dealt to the people I love most. That feeling's even worse. I hope…no one feels like they wasted years of their life on me – *with* me. Those years, with you, were the closest thing to—"

"Zill," I interject, "No Em stuff. You'll only stir the pot. If you need to talk to her, use the phone, ok?"

He sighs, runs his hands through his hair, stares bleakly into space, then after a few moments of muttering "What the fuck was I saying?" he wearily goes with, "People who watch other people, in relationships, online, they always want a storyline, a plot arc, and they think people my age, when we seem happy, have found our happy ending. But there *is* no happy ending – the journey just keeps going up and down and round and round until you die. What you thought of me last week won't be the same this week, or in another three weeks' time, and that's the way it's meant to be. That's the way human life is. So…I don't know... I don't know what I'm trying to say. I'm an idiot, I'm tired…and I want to go home. Thanks for listening…"

"Oh mate, you can't finish it like that!" I protest, as he reaches for the off switch. "Talk about bleak – you look ready to hang yourself!" I wince. "Shit. Oh god, Zill, I'm sorry, that was in truly poor taste. You alright?"

He sighs, turns off the camera, and says, "Don't worry about it. I'll finish this disastrous shit later – editing software exists for a reason. You're right, I need to talk to Em. Over the phone. I miss her like hell, and I can't just dance like a monkey for this thing when I don't want to talk to strangers, I need to talk to *her*. I can't stand her hating me like this…"

"Where does she stand on the whole diamorphine script notion?" I ask. "Does she know there's the possibility of hope on the horizon – however slim?"

He looks morose. "She doesn't get it – doesn't get that I need it, doesn't get how much it matters to me. It's no different, to her, than street gear. I…fuck…maybe I need to tell her about…you know? What I told you, earlier – that dodgy batch I got, what it did to me? I'd rather not, frankly, I have hideous nightmares whenever I think about that shit, but it might help her understand? Or, y'know, not. She can be such a bloody *hypocrite* about—Ugh, whatever. Forget it…" He runs his hands through his hair again, his expression despairing.

"Do you think call, or text? Surely we're not at the 'so estranged we can't call each other without warning' place yet?"

"Just call her," I say. "You're getting all twitchy about it – I know you, if she doesn't text back within three minutes, you'll call her anyway. So just call."

He pulls a face, and calls her. I cross my fingers, and leave him to it.

Five minutes later, he comes thundering down the stairs and into the kitchen, announcing,

"Shit, *shit!* Em's coming round – she wants to talk!"

"That's great news!" I enthuse. "I mean, I think? Lucy – girl's perspective?"

"What, exactly, did she say?" Lucy asks, shutting off the radio.

Zillah smiles. "I said I missed her – she got all wobbly-sounding, said she missed me too. Which is *definitely* good," he adds, with profound self-assurance. "But I did sort of manipulate her into coming over. Said I was running out of clothes. And that my camera battery's on the blink. So, she's bringing me some stuff. Oh *what*, Tom? I've read about these things – neutral territory's better than me going round there, where it feels all presumptuous, and we fall back into our assigned roles of…whatever, but mostly, I need you guys for arbitration, so just…Tom? Will you…*linger,* a bit?"

"When's she getting here?" Lucy asks, dubiously. I can see it in her eyes – she hates Em, and it's not even personal, it's just that she liked Zillah's ex better. When she first met him, he was still dating this guy called Henry, and working in an office, snorting coke and hating the world with this bitter, furious, Bill Hicks-esque passion, and I think

Lucy just...liked that version of Zillah better. She definitely blames Em for him becoming this weird social media *thing* none of us really understand – even though Zillah had already started doing it before Em came along. I guess the social media girlfriend was just the final straw – he became an alien to us. Lucy used to love despising her own office job with Zillah – he was her angsty gay friend, much as I kept telling her he swings in every which direction, and when he swung the other way, she never quite knew what to do with it...

"She's coming over right now," says Zillah, "I knew it wasn't over. I knew it *couldn't* be over..." He's beaming as he rummages through the cupboards, then starts eating a cake bar that doesn't belong to him. He's eaten the last two in the box, staring distractedly into space as he chews, before he freezes, looking awkward, and says, "Oh...shit – I'm sorry, were these...special, to anyone?"

"No," Lucy sighs. "It's fine." It's not fine. She'll have to go back to the shops now, on a Saturday, but it's obvious neither of us can quite bring ourselves to bollock the most malnourished member of the household over actually eating something.

"I'll pay you back," Zillah says, apparently cottoning onto the atmosphere. He delves in his pocket, brings out a rolled up twenty-pound note, and plops it on the table. It curls away, and Lucy catches it, laughing as she asks,

"Has this got coke on it? Wait...have you got any?"

"Lucy!" I protest. "We're ancient – we'd have a fucking heart attack!"

"Oh come on, if *Em's* coming over and I have to bloody arbitrate, why not?"

"Sorry," says Zillah, rather sadly, "No coke. Just gives me panic attacks these days… You know I can't even handle caffeine since I knocked the speed on the head…" He sighs. He really did love uppers, right 'til the point they made him so paranoid, he couldn't enter a room without inspecting the entire place for hidden cameras – at which point we had to stage a mini-intervention. It seemed to go quite well, 'til we realised, weeks later, that he'd just replaced the speed with an increasing number of far more addictive downers…

I eye the rolled-up note with suspicion, wondering what the fuck he *has* been using it for – he's already told me UK heroin isn't snortable.

"Ketamine," he says, following the direction of my gaze. "I thought it might make a…you know, more psychedelic, mind-opening, socially sanctioned alternative? You're right though. We're ancient. Just made me throw up and cry…"

"You used to love that stuff," Lucy says, almost accusingly. "Are you sure it wasn't just dodgy?"

"God knows. But honestly, it's a good thing. Haven't you heard? It destroys your bladder, literally makes you incontinent if you go at it hard enough – no one knew that back in the day, did they? Keep wondering about my old dealer – he must be pissing through a straw by now…"

"Hmm," says Lucy, sounding more than a little disappointed that we aren't about to revisit our misspent youth in some weird, ill-advised Saturday afternoon coke binge. "I'll go for a walk, get some food in. Good luck with Em, Zillah…"

"She's the love of my life, Luce!" he calls after her, as she takes the rolled-up note and walks away, "Please don't pull that face!"

"Let's see if you still think that by the time I get back," says Lucy, flipping him off.

"Oh hell…" Zillah groans, flumping down on Lucy's empty chair, "Is it going to be *awful*? Is Em coming over to be *awful* at me? Does Lucy know something I don't? Female intuition?"

"Don't be daft. It'll be fine. Just don't bullshit her anymore – she'll cotton on. Even you can't run out of clothes within 24 hours…"

"You reckon she saw through that? Hmm. But that means…she *knows!* She knows I just wanted to see her…and she came anyway? That's got to be good, hasn't it? Right?"

"No idea mate. No idea."

Zillah twitches round the kitchen, theorising and poking about in the cupboards, until the doorbell rings, and he's off like a greyhound.

"Em!" I hear him declare, with the energy of twenty unleashed puppies, "Thank god! It's been *awful,* it's been *ages!*"

I hear her laughing, and she comments, "You seem pretty perky, for how awful it's been."

"All you. *All* fucking you…"

I roll my eyes as they descend into the Perfect Couple business the social media world gobbles up with a spoon, Em saying almost too quietly for me to hear, "Wow… You really do seem good. I kinda wish we'd done this at home…"

"I could, you know, right now," he says. Em's giggling – it's bloody obvious what he's on about. I peer round the corner, and she's holding his hand, tentatively smiling up at him, a small figure in black, topped off with a vibrant mane of blue hair. I'm pleasantly surprised by how optimistic it all looks…or maybe it's just easier for them to get physical, lapse into the muscle memory of each other's touch, than it is to talk through the mess they're in. "I really *fuckkking could*," Zillah continues, running his fingers through her hair, "I think I might die if we don't. Take me home, Em? I'll let you do anything you like to me. Literally… *anything…"*

When he moves to kiss her, she lets him, and I have to restrain myself from applauding. All I can do is cross my fingers, and hope this truce survives the conversation that's inevitably coming.

"Wait – wait," says Em, breaking away at last, but she's still holding his hand. "We need to talk about this, Zill – I can't just…pretend everything's fine…"

"But you want to?" he asks, hopefully. "I really—I thought you hated me, after those texts, yesterday, you—"

"No," she says, with a sigh. "Of course I don't hate you. It's been unbelievably shit, since you left. I went over to Mum's… Lisa was there. You know, my cousin – from the christening?"

"Oh god… Oh hell. What did she say?"

"What didn't she. Can I come in?"

He leads the way down the corridor, and heads toward the living room, looking nervous. Apparently Em's moment of affection's made him bold enough to do this without arbitration, though the walls are so thin down here, I'll hear every whisper regardless. Which is good, I reckon, while they're both walking on eggshells – if I need to rein in our resident rent-a-gob, hopefully I can jump in before too much shit hits the fan…

"So…umm…" says Em, sounding every bit as nervous as Zillah looked, and more than a little guilty. "The first thing…is that I need to say sorry – indirectly – for everything that went down on Twitter last night. It was Lisa who sold the bloody story, but Zill, I didn't *know*, I swear, not 'til it was all too late – then I genuinely wanted to throttle her. She dated this guy, with addiction issues, round about three years ago – he turned out to be a terrifying, violent asshole, and seeing you, at that christening, so out of it, it…triggered her, big time. She's been on the warpath with me ever since, saying she wants me safely away from you, and if—"

"Safely—? Oh hell. Please tell me you're joking? 'Cause what you're saying is, it's a miracle I'm not also being painted as a domestic abuser right now – to the *whole world?* She really thinks I could—? *Jesus*, Em! I can't even think about it – the last person I hit was a bully when I was twelve, and I got pulverised! You *know* I'm not violent, and my self-destruction is not the whole world's business – why on Earth do I deserve public humiliation for—"

"You don't; I was *beyond* furious – god knows if I'll ever speak to her again, given she clearly thinks my private life is rich financial pickings these days. It wasn't ok – she knew you were already struggling, and I know what drama does to you – if I hadn't known you were safe with Tom, I'd have called the second I found out. Have you been…remotely ok, or is that just a stupid question?"

Someone – almost certainly Zillah – stops pacing the room and flumps down on the sofa. "No…" he says quietly, his voice unsteady. "You know I can't deal with these crazed online shitstorms, and right now, without you – without a home? The entire world's been ripped out from under my feet in a single day, and now everyone on Earth's laughing about it. I've got nothing stable left, Em, I've had Tom getting all analytical on me – I spent most of yesterday with my head down the fucking toilet. It's too much – all of it. I feel like my brain's going to bloody *rupture* if one more bad thing happens…and you know the internet – it will. I'm scared to death, and I miss you like hell. Can't we just…stop all this?"

There's a long moment of quiet – I can only assume she's hugging him. At last she says,

"If things get bad again, will you call me – please? I know your friends don't get the social media stuff…and I know where your head goes. There is no world in which I'd rather you hurt yourself or ended it all than picked up the phone, ok? Any time, Zill – I mean it. If it helps, I tore Lisa a new asshole – so did Mum. Even *Mum* thinks it was atrocious. But at least you know now, right? It wasn't any of your friends, and no one's going to say anything else publicly. That's…something to hold onto, right?"

I faintly hear him sigh. "What else is there to say? The whole world's weaving its own vile little narratives… But your mum's on my side though? For real?"

"No, Zill. Mum gets what was really up with you at that christening, now, and she is *not* impressed. She doesn't want us living together unless you're at least trying to get clean…and I agree. She doesn't want my career or reputation trashed by gossip sites over this shit, either. She is definitely not 'on your side', right now."

"Bloody hell…" he sighs. "Is that why I got all those texts from you, about making it public? Is *that* why I've uploaded the Hi, I'm

Homeless Now video, shredding every last drop of privacy and dignity I had left? 'Cause if so, that didn't add to the stress at all!"

"They were in my ear all day long, Zill, and I was just—I was still *so* angry with you…but I was wrong to make you do that video, so soon. It's your channel, and your business, but if you want to take it down, maybe that would be…for the best?"

There's a long silence, then he says quizzically,

"Are you saying…you don't want me putting that out there – that it's over? Do you…not want it to be over?"

I hear a sniffle, then a shaky,

"Of course I don't want it to be over, you *impossible* asshole! I can't bear our house without you in it. I want nothing more than to take you home, right now, have make-up sex and pretend everything's fine, but you know I can't – I *cannot* let you back in that house, knowing you might wind up dead there. I couldn't live with myself. Has anything really changed? You being here, with Tom, I mean – has it made you…rethink anything?"

"Rehab, you mean?" he asks, with a muffled weariness that suggests his head's buried in his hands at the mere suggestion of the Dreaded R-Word.

"You've never been. Literally never – I don't understand how you can be so against something you've never even tried. Won't you just try it, give it a few days, for me?"

"I—" he begins, then I hear his boots start pacing the room like a caged animal, which pretty much covers the look in his eyes whenever you bring this shit up with him. "Em, I *can't* – you know that! You've seen what withdrawal does to me, I just—"

"But you got through it," she says, "That night, after the OD – you were freaking out, but we got you home, and you got through it. And that was only with me there – there'd be trained staff, who'd actually know what to say and do, and I really think—"

"Oh Christ, Em! I only 'got through it' because I thought it'd be over in no time, but since you gave me nearly the whole Naloxone *syringe* instead of one dose, I was in hell all bloody night! If you hadn't been there, I…well. Neither would I be, right now. But look, it's not even about that. It isn't. I could taper my methadone and get clean without all that nightmarish shit, but you know why I don't?"

"Because you're fucking *stubborn,* Zill. You are stubborn, and stuck in a rut, and it's time to finally *grow up* and learn to handle your shit without this moronic bloody crutch!"

She seems to have rendered him speechless with that one. After a protracted silence, he mutters,

"*Wow*, Em. That was next level brutality, even for you. That fucking *hurt.* I was, believe it or not, being *rhetorical*, but thank you so very much for your refreshing view. Thank you for once more reminding me that I should be far more advanced in every sphere of life, and instead I'm 'almost forty' and still the world's stupidest fuckup. And now everyone on Earth knows it – *everyone*. Reddit's loving my downfall – even your mum's on their team. That's *exactly* what—"

"Oh Zill, I didn't—"

"Em, don't touch me right now, *please!* It's all too fucking much, with the hatred online, and in here, and the fact I haven't got anywhere left to run – I just—I can't stand still and be touched, right now!"

"I'm sorry…" she says, and the high-speed creaky-pacing restarts.

"Look…I was trying to say that I'm not doing rehab not *just* because I'm a complete wimp about withdrawal and would legitimately lose my mind – it's everything after that. It's the sobriety at the end of the tunnel…I can't do it. *Cannot.* Didn't I try everything, last year, after I kicked the booze? Therapy and pills and hypnotists and bizarre fucking diets and all the wacky shit in the book, and I still—I couldn't take another day of it. Life, I mean." The pacing falls silent, and he says more quietly, "I can't go back to that, Em. I wouldn't last a month…and I don't want to do that to you, or to my mum, but I can't see any other way it'd go."

I hear another sniffle from Em, and Zillah says quietly, "Shit…I'm sorry. I didn't mean to get all heavy on you the minute you walked through the door. I just needed to see you – to say I'm sorry, and I really do mean that. I know I've been a burden – a fucking huge one. If you need a break from me, and all my shit, that is one hundred percent understandable, but I needed to let you know that I don't want this to be over – not if you don't. I'll do anything I'm physically capable of to fix things. And I *am* trying – I sat down with sodding Cindy of all people, told her everything – she's going to help me get that diamorphine script. She even thinks it's a good idea, and she knows her stuff, right? So, things are going to change. They are. They'll be better. *I'll* be better. Less intolerable…I hope?"

He definitely sounds hopeful. But all Em says is,

"Why are you even telling me this? You know how I feel about that shit. It's just another awful drug to turn you into a bloody zombie. I thought—I *really* thought things'd be different today, you know? Like, the fact it's finally made you homeless might've changed things for you? But it's just the same crap, isn't it? Are you still using? You seemed…good, at the door, but—"

He sighs. "You can't even tell, can you? Either that or you won't admit it. And please stop staring at my eyes like I can't even be trusted to own up. I used today, but I am essentially sober – you are talking to the Real Me, whatever the fuck that means. And of course things have changed. I realised how bloody miserable I am without you – even with the dope. I can't visualise any kind of life without you in it, Em… But saying that, right now, it just fucking *hurts*, because I can't be something I'm not, and if you think chucking me out of my own house then making me an internet spectacle's going to do anything but make me binge my feelings away, you clearly don't know me at all. If you'd only *listen*, Em, it's like I keep trying to tell you – heroin's a shorter acting drug than methadone; it doesn't leave me fucked up all day like that awful bloody shit does. I know how much you hate me on this massive script, forgetting everything and nodding out everywhere, but I'm *fine* like this – heroin's just better f—"

"Oh god, man – don't you dare! Do not say heroin is 'better for you'! I've seen your arms, whenever they're not caked in makeup – they look like rotten fruit these days, and if that's what your outsides look like, I can't even bear to think about your insides!"

"Every medication has its side effects, doesn't it? I'd rather have a few bruises than—"

"For fuck's *sake*, Zillah, you nearly died! You nearly fucking *died*, on our living room floor, just last Tuesday, and I reckon I'm traumatised for life, but after you'd spent the night shaking and puking and regretting every decision you'd ever made, you were straight back at it on Wednesday like nothing had ever happened! That isn't *medication*, Zill – it's madness, and the fact you can't admit to that, even now, makes me want to hit you!"

"Who said I can't admit to it? I know I've got problems – I know I'm a rolling clusterfuck, I never said I wasn't, but you just *said it,* didn't you? That I seem good, right, like this? *On* this?"

I hear a growl of annoyance, then, "For the love of god, why's it always gotta be the same with you? You'll take one tiny thing I say, and drag it completely out of context, just because it suits your warped narrative! *You* called me, remember – you chose the time, this tiny window of the day when you're semi-sober, and you've got concealer covering the whole ghastly mess, but I know you well enough to know that you *can* pull it together for the duration of a video, or an afternoon, then be an absolute shambles for the rest of the week. Don't quote me back to myself like I'm an idiot, alright?"

"I'm sorry…" he says, his tone hanging somewhere between misery and sullenness. "I don't want to fight with you…not today. I couldn't sleep without you, the whole world's at war with me – I just want to *disappear*. I just want…" He trails off, sighs – says softly. "I just want you back – more than anything…"

"I know you do. And I wish like hell it was that simple. But I just don't know what more I can do, or say, to help you, when you won't help yourself. I can't—"

"I *am* helping myself," he says, earnestly. "I got Cindy on board with the diamorphine, and—"

"Oh *Christ*, Zillah, you're a one-track record! It's insane, being reliant on injecting yourself with painkillers every day, when you're not even in pain! Why—"

"Don't give me that crap, Em – for one, you've never been inside my head; pain comes in many fucking forms, and for two, medications cannot be oversimplified to a single purpose; Viagra was a heart pill, painkillers stop the runs, blood pressure meds nuke anxiety, Ecstasy helps people with PTSD, and heroin helps me concentrate, calm down, and dodge suicidal thoughts – if you find something that works, you—"

"Oh just *stop it*, man! When are you going to quit treating every conversation like you're on the bloody debate team? You can't info-dump your way out of reality, and I *don't* need another crazy lecture on pharmaceuticals right now! I get it, ok, you know it *all*, and everything's in perfect control, except it's not, is it? I can piece together what Tom meant, last night, when he said he was worried about something you said, but you were so bloody 'asleep' he had to ask me what you were on about. Have you at least given him that Naloxone shit, if you're going to keep pushing it this hard? He's keeping an eye on you, right?"

"Oh, for fuck's sake," Zillah irritably mutters. "*Yes* – Tom has the Naloxone – I'm barely allowed to *urinate* here without a witness. And fine, since you're all ganging up on me, I did do too much yesterday. It was nothing dangerous, nothing *stupid*, but enough to get messy. Again, what the hell do you expect, after your bloody cousin outed me to the entire world, the very same day you made me homeless? If I wasn't coping before, how the *fuck* do you—" His voice cracks, and he breaks off, sighs, then mutters,

"Oh hell, Em – I'm not trying to have a go at you… You had your reasons. Bloody massive ones. I'm intolerable. But just…fucking *hell* I hate this! I don't understand why *you* don't understand. We've never been like this before – on such opposite sides of something. It's awful! But don't you see? If I can *just* get that diamorphine script, last Tuesday will never happen again. No more ODs, no more dodgy batches, no more worries about me dropping dead, and isn't that the thing that freaks you out? Isn't that why you've been so…*off* with me since…you know, it all happened? And I mean, hell, if it was you nearly dying in my arms I'd be…fuck. I'd be furious with you too. But I can't *help* being so—" His voice cracks again, then it's muffled, like his head's in his hands, as he says, "I never wanted to put you through that shitshow, Em – I feel like crawling under a rock whenever I think about it. Cindy's threatening to fucking well section me if I ever OD again, throw me in this awful, awful place, and there's…there's stuff I've never even told you, great big rattling skeletons tumbling out of the closet all over my head, but if I can *just* get that script, the whole nightmare's over. It's *over*. Why can't you get behind that?"

"Because I *miss* you, Zill – the way you used to be, without all this terrifying crap! I miss *you,* and I can't keep on living with a greyed-out zombie version of the man I love – you need to work out why you're like this, why you *need* this – you can't just go through life hurting yourself and everyone around you because you can't handle…whatever it is, in your past."

"I'm thirty-eight, Em…" he says, and he sounds exhausted. "I've been fighting this shit half my life – if therapy and self-awareness were going to fix me, don't you think I'd be at least halfway fixed by now? It's faulty wiring, shoddy ADHD neurochemistry – don't you get that? Haven't you seen the addiction statistics, for those of us no one bothers to diagnose in childhood? If they'd picked up on it in time, maybe I'd have my shit together, but they didn't. It just wasn't happening – not in my family, having a kid with dodgy genetics and a fucked-up head. They wanted me to bury it any way I could, so I *did*. I got my degree on junk, and for the first time in my life, everyone was proud of me. And maybe I *am* that fucked up, 'cause I don't even see it as a bad thing. I was happy, and functional, and if I can just get it legally, safely, I'll be right back to—"

"It won't be better," Em says, miserably. "How can you not see that? You're bad enough on the bloody methadone since they upped your dose, you scare me shitless. Your eyes are just…*dead,* there's no one at home – I can't stand seeing you so messed up!"

"Do you think I *want* to be like that, Em? If you'd have an open mind and just listen to me for five seconds, you'd know that methadone is such a mess because as well as being long-acting, it's not designed to have any positive effects! So they upped and upped and *upped* my dose, all in a uselessly failed attempt to get the effects I need, but all it does is dumb me down for the next 24 hours. It isn't fun. Contrary to your clear beliefs, I am not having *fun* while I'm trying to edit and I can't keep my eyes open, I am not having fun when I can't drive my bloody car because I'm weirdly battered without a single shred of pleasurable feeling, and I *despise it* when I can't get my thoughts and words out straight! Believe me, if you detest me on methadone, join the bloody club. But heroin is *short acting* – that's why it's so much bet—"

"Do *not* make me warn you again, man – you bloody dare say that shit's 'better for you', and I swear to god I'm going to throw something. You just don't see it as a problem at all, do you? It's a *solution* to you, and how am I meant—"

"But heroin *has* been the solution – can't you see that, at all? It is literally the sole reason I *didn't* top myself in April! There've been days, since then, that I've felt the exact same way, and heroin makes those thoughts go away when nothing else can. I'd be dead twenty times over, without it. And don't you remember when I was drinking? When the whole studio was littered with my demented, self-loathing graffiti – when we were at the hospital every other week because I'd fallen down the stairs and concussed myself, or done something stupid and the alcohol was stopping the blood from clotting? Em, I don't even know how you tolerated that pissed-up wanker – you're a living saint. The little I remember of those months makes me want to vaporise myself out of existence, but…things got better, right? Aren't things better, now, than they were?"

She sighs. "They were, Zill. The first six months, when we met, then again after you got sober, they were genuinely the best, most beautiful times of my entire life, and the *only* reason I'm still standing here, fighting for you, is that I am *desperate* to believe that guy is still in there. He's my best friend…and I am so confused, and so angry, about the fact it's come to this. I wanted to be with that guy forever…but I can't live with his ghost, Zill – I won't. You're so gone half the time now, and that christening was such an *utter shitshow,* I've never been so *fucking* embarrassed, right in front of—"

"Oh for fuck's sake," he mutters. "Well now bloody Lisa's spread the whole thing round the internet, karma's bit me right in the arse for that one, hasn't it? Embarrassment multiplied by a thousand, tossed straight back in my face – the perfect revenge. Are you sure you didn't tip her off, just to watch me suffer death by a thousa—"

I hear what sounds decidedly like him getting a right royal slap around the face, as Em snaps,

"Oh that was a *fucking* dickhead comment, and you know it! Lisa got to me when I was upset, and I'd had a few glasses of wine, but I would *never* have any hand in—"

He cuts her off with a humourless laugh. "Right. Of course. We're tearing chunks out of each other because you can't stand the one and only drug that stabilises my head, but you go on your weekly bender, flush my whole reputation down the shitter, and the minute I even mention the subject I get hit in the face. Great. Cool. Which one of us has the drug problem here, Em, 'cause I've genuinely forgotten."

"Oh, and here we go again! Come on, man, let it out – I know there's more; alcohol's the worst poison toxin on Earth, it makes people *ungodly* to be around, and a normal night out with a few pissed-up mates is far more dysfunctional than sleeping with used syringes rolling round the bed – how dare I have a bit of wine and say too much once in while, when instead—"

"Once in a while? Try every damn weekend, Em, watching everyone around me getting trashed, all the while knowing how *easy* it would be to just join in, and wind up back in the dismal pits of alcoholism – excuse the fuck out of me for trying to reroute my cravings, and save both of us from the Return of the Drunken Wanker…"

"Wow," she says, at length. "Man, you are far gone. I've heard some unbelievable *shit* come out of your mouth lately, but this really takes the cake. Are you *seriously* trying to flog me the idea that you doing smack is this grand saviour move, because it's so much better that you mainline dodgy street filth than learn how to make a decent mocktail at the weekends? Where do you get *off* with these insane justifications! I can't talk to you about anything these days – everything has to get political, everything's a debate, it's like—"

"Well, some things, like trying to stay alive, are worth debating, and *everything* is political."

"Love isn't, Zill. Love *fucking isn't!*"

There's a brief silence, then, "You're gonna put that on merch, aren't you? I bet you do, you know. What colour t-shirt, d'you think? White, for taking the high road, or black because our love is *dark* and *final* and *over*, or—"

"Ohh *shut – up,* you *flaming* prick! Can't you just read the room and shut the *fuck* up, for once in your life! Zill, you're getting more delusional by the day, and that bloody christening was the most embarrassing shit I've had to live through since *high school,* all because you couldn't rein it in for just one day, one special occasion, for me! I don't *know* this version of you, man! How can you possibly expect me to be in a relationship where I – and my whole family – come second to…to fucking *heroin?"*

There's a despairing sigh – the pacing resumes.

"Em, you know it was a mistake – you know I despise myself for it, I've apologised on my fucking *knees* to you, but it's like you just see me as scum now, isn't it? I'm just this stereotypical sack of worthless junkie scum – that's all I am! I know what you said to Tom, by the way, about the godforsaken 'silverware' – there's literally nothing I wouldn't sink to in your eyes now, is there! But dear god, I am *trying,* Em – I am *still in here,* I am still *me,* and I am trying fucking everything I can possibly think of to keep the wheels on, with you, with work, with…staying alive – you're at least half the reason I'm going after that bloody script so hard. I *know* I've fucked up in every conceivable way, I *know* I deserve the hatred off your mum, off…everyone in that church, you especially, but none of it would've

Copyright Dorian Bridges 2024

happened if it was diamorphine, don't you see? For the *millionth time*, the gear I used was a new batch – I didn't know it'd be double the strength of the last one, because I would *never* intentionally humiliate you in front of *anyone*…" He sighs, adding bleakly, "I can't even tell you how sick I am of running this fucking gamble, every day, never knowing when it'll be too weak to keep me sane, too strong to function at all…"

"Then quit," she says, softly – pleadingly. "Zill…can't you just try it, for a single week – for me?"

"Please don't do that," he mumbles, voice muffled. "Don't make it a test of my love for you. If I could do it for anyone, it would be you, and it would be so, so easy, but right now, I just…*can't*. I'm holding on by my bloodied fingernails, Em, and I don't understand what more you want from me. I've already told the whole world our business, on your insistence, then your sodding cousin's gone and told them all what a fuckup I am, and now here's you determined to watch me fail at shit I'm just not ready for. I'm *sorry* if my justifications sound insane to you, but I am just…*flailing* in desperation to be understood here, to get *across* to you that I cannot do this thing called life without it! I've been fighting this war for *half my life*, Em, I am bloody *exhausted*, and I just need you to be patient with me – to trust in the fact that I know myself, and what I need to—"

"You want me to *trust you?* Right now? With anything – particularly your own health? Zill…you are clearly not thinking straight, and I cannot sit here being 'patient' when I know how much danger you're putting yourself in! That overdose, I just—I can't get it out of my head. You were blue, you were *dead*, and now I keep reading about…about oxygen deprivation, and the damage it does to a person's brain, and I wonder if—if the things you *say*, and do sometimes, are from all the times you've—"

"All the—FUCKING HELL, Emma, you think I'm BRAIN DAMAGED now!?" he yells, sounding a thousand miles beyond offended. Oh Jesus…she actually went there. We've all wondered it, from time to time, whether the daft shit he's done to himself over the years has anything to do with the way he gets at times, but dear god, you don't say it out loud – not to Zillah, whose intellect matters more to him than anything else he possesses. "I—Wait, *all* the times I've gone over? Precisely *when* did you come up with this theory? *When* did you look into my eyes, and think, 'Fuck me, he's not all there, is he! He's pickled his grey matter completely – now he's just this drooling, dead-eyed, incompetent *fuckwit of disaster* – I'd better run quick before he starts *flinging faecal matter around like a fucking monkey,* 'cause his IQ must be in the—'"

"Zill, that is *not* what I am saying! You're the smartest guy I know, and yet you do this stupid, *stupid* stuff, and there's no other explanation for—I mean, *Jesus*, man, I watched some of your old videos, yesterday…'cause I missed you. The *old* you. And I saw this one about…blood clots? About the way you'd been so desperate for a fix once, you took all these old bits of rotten blood out of a load of ancient needles, and you shot it all up, and…Zill…that is not *normal*. That's not…*sane,* or safe, or—"

There's a growl of exasperation, then he demands, "Do you even know what a mental illness is, Em? You get that we look like people and talk like people, pretty fucking intelligent people, sometimes, but there's a pretty big part of us that is *actually completely crazy?* I mean, what would you prefer? You know what I did, as a teenager, before I found drugs – do you want to be back there, sitting round in hospitals while I get my arms stitched back together, everyone knowing it's utterly futile and I'll be right back at it again tomorrow? Is that *preferable?* I am *not ok* without this shit, Em, and as far as anyone can tell, I was *born this way*, so if I'm BRAIN DAMAGED then blame my FUCKING MOTHER! I don't know what deceived you into thinking I ever was, or could be 'normal', but this is me, warts, track-marks and all. I thought you stood for that. I thought you stood for self-care, for taking damaged people as they are, and—"

"Oh, 'cause heroin is 'self-care' now?! Dear god, the shit you come out with makes me sick!"

"Compared to butchering myself? I'd say yeah, actually. Yeah, it is. 'Cause I'm not still crying my eyes out and thinking about suicide once it's done. Generally…"

There's a pause, then, "Generally? Zill… You're not back to…y'know…?"

"I—Fuck, I…don't even want to talk about it. It doesn't matter anyway, I'm brain damaged and I make you sick – I guess I'm better off dead."

"No, I want to talk about this, I do – if you're thinking that way again, we *need* to talk about it…but I can see I'm just winding you up. Do you want me to leave, or d'you want to have a smoke, then talk properly?"

"*Why?*" he says, petulantly. "What's the fucking point? You're not hearing a word I say."

"The point is, I need you to be ok. Whether it's over or not, Zill, I will always care about you, and I *need* you to be ok!"

"Sure. Right. I guess you do, don't you? Given how fucking *brain damaged* I am, I might say anything at all in that suicide note – you'd better not let this *nauseating moron* loose on the world with all the shit he could say about you and your fucked up—"

I walk into the room, clearing my throat loudly – he took Em's slap with more grace than I would've done, but that 'brain damage' comment was clearly the final straw – our resident rent-a-gob's gone full kamikaze, and someone needs to shut him down before the damage is irreversible. Zillah swears, and hurls himself towards the stairs, but I block him, saying in an undertone, "No – we're going for a walk, just like earlier. Not safe. Not right now."

He rolls his eyes at me, whips round, and strides out of the front door with an explosive *"FUCK!"*. Em's got mascara tears all over the place, and looks even tinier than usual as she shakes her head at me, then rockets out of the house after him, jumps straight into her little blue car, and goes skidding off without another word.

Zillah's sitting on the curb, head in his hands, and as I get out there he produces a joint that I have to snatch out of his fingers before it gets lit in the middle of my damn street again.

"No!" he snaps, immediately, "No, no, fucking *no!*" He's on his feet, ducking round me, then he goes shooting back into the house, yelling, "ENOUGH with this fucking babysitting SHIT!"

"Zillah!" I yell after him, but the fucker's fast – he's up the stairs and into the spare room before I can grab him, snatching up a bag, then the bathroom door slams in my face, lock clicking into place. "Mate, don't be a twat! I swear to god, I will kick this door down and Naloxone you just for the fun of it!"

These words provoke a screamed "JUST FUCK OFF, TOM!" – almost immediately followed by what sounds like him punching the living daylights out of my bathroom wall. I just shake my head, and take a few cautionary steps back. Christ... Between this and yesterday's endless anxiety-puking, I haven't seen him in this much of a head-fucked mess in years. Em can, admittedly, have a sharp tongue at times, but even she should've realised what that comment would unleash...

Finally, the thunderous crashing goes silent, the door opens, and he stalks out white as a sheet, shaking all over, both fists bloodied.

"You'll pay for it?" I suggest, not even wanting to *look* at the sodding bathroom.

He just dumps himself down in the middle of the floor, buries his head in his knees, and after a rather tense silence, mumbles,

"I picked up the wrong bag. Sorry about the wall..."

I sigh. "It's fine. I mean, it's not, but I'd rather get a plasterer than a coroner. Are you...shit...that looks bad..."

His right hand's trickling blood onto his jeans, the skin of his knuckles torn and tattered, already bruising blue-black in places, bloodless white in others. He slowly sits up, regarding his mangled hand with eyes so flat and shut-down I'm not sure he's seeing it at all.

"I can't handle this..." he murmurs, and his voice is every bit as spaced-out as his eyes. "Sorry. I just can't..."

Expressionless, he stumbles to his feet, picks up the bag in the corner, and plods toward the bathroom. I know I should stop him. I also know, at this point, that short of knocking him out cold, it's a feat well beyond me.

"Please be careful? The Naloxone awaits. And don't even think about locking that door."

"I know," he says, in the same vague voice. He half-heartedly moves to flip me off, then inhales sharply, glancing down at his hand. "Shit," he mutters, but apparently that's all he can muster. We'll probably have to take him to hospital later, make sure he hasn't broken anything. Then I remember Cindy, and wonder if she'll consider it a sectionable offence. Probably – it looks like he got seriously violent on someone. No hospital then – not unless his arm swells up like a sodding balloon. He'll have to tolerate me pouring booze over the wounds – I guess the dope'll help with that...

I hear the front door slam, and breathe a sigh of relief. I'm about to call Lucy up here, but quickly decide some conversations are best done silently.

"Colossal fuckup," I text her. "Upstairs, now, please?"

I hear her phone twinkle – a minute later she's jogging up the stairs, looking apprehensive.

"Zillah?" I say, walking over to the bathroom door. "You alright in there?"

"No!" comes his incredibly terse response. "My hand is…it's *fucked*, Tom, it's— No, no! Don't come in here! I've got two hands for a reason, get the fuck out!"

I back out of the bathroom, but not before catching him wincing as he yanks a repulsive brown-gunk-filled syringe out of the depths of his arm, looking infuriated. I feel slightly dizzy – the whole thing's gruesome. As I shut the door and sit down on the bed, Lucy walks in, mouthing, *"What the hell's going on?"* at me. I pull out my phone again, and type,

"Didn't go well. She called him brain damaged. And slapped him. He trashed the bathroom. Sorry."

She shakes her head in despair, and finally says out loud, "Would a cake bar help anyone?"

There's a deathly silence, then I hear Zillah laugh, just a bit, though it's a wobbly sound.

"Fuck that girl," says Lucy. "How long have I been telling you she wasn't the one?"

There's no response. I call his name – still nothing. Holding my breath, I open the bathroom door. He's slowly slithering into a heap next to the toilet, zonked out cold, a used needle slipping from his marginally less battered left hand.

Lucy stares at me, then blurts out, "How the—? Did you know he was doing that, in there?"

CHAPTER EIGHT

I have rather a lot of explaining to do. Lucy takes it surprisingly well – I end up feeling like a prize prat for not letting her help sooner; she's angry about the lies, but eventually accepts that my heart was, mostly, in the right place. I agree to never shut her out like this again, accept a week's worth of solo washing-up in penance, and we move on.

Once we've assessed that Zillah's alright – breathing, demi-coherent, all that good stuff – I go and get the vodka from the kitchen, and we use cotton pads dipped in the stuff to wash off his hands. Even through the dope haze it makes him wince, swear, and nearly thwack me in the face, but once it's done, he seems alright. There's something dodgy going on with one knuckle, his right wrist's clearly painful, everything's a bashed-up mess, but nothing's swelling to an obscene degree; Google seems to suggest he'll survive. In the end we bandage him up with some frozen peas, frogmarch him over to the bed, and leave him in the recovery position, one of us returning to check on him every ten minutes, until, on Lucy's watch, he wakes up and concedes to come downstairs. She's already teasing him – I don't know how wise that is, but right now all ground seems equally shaky.

"That's some seriously toxic masculine shit, Zill," she's saying, as he wincingly detaches himself from the largely melted peas. "I told you the straight life didn't suit you." He just shakes his head – mumbles another apology for the bathroom.

"Ah, it's ugly wallpaper anyway," she says. "You know it needed redecorating. You didn't have to take the job on yourself though, let alone with so much enthusiasm."

He flops down on the sofa, and says quietly,

"What the actual fuck is wrong with me?"

"It's been a hell of a day, mate," I sympathise. "Tomorrow we'll do whatever you like – drive to Brighton, maybe, stick your toes in the sea. Things'll get better, you'll see."

"Em's what's wrong with you," says Lucy, rather more bluntly, and when I give her a warning glance, she justifies, "I just mean, you know yourself, we know you, and I have *never* seen you pull this Demolition Man shit before. I know I wasn't here, but you were actually in a really great mood before that bloody woman came over."

"Tom's seen it before," Zillah says flatly. "If there'd been razorblades in your bathroom cabinet, you don't even want to know what you'd be dealing with…"

"I've seen the photos," says Lucy, unruffled. "And everyone's seen your arm. I can put two and two together. You're not that daft anymore, Zill – not without serious provocation. You know it doesn't help."

"Photos of what?" he asks, frowning.

"Your uni accommodation, turned into a murder site a la *you*. You told Tom to snap a few before he cleaned it all up – apparently you were so looped out on vodka and antidepressants, you considered it artwork. You know, for a skinny guy, you've got an impressive amount of blood in you…"

"Vampire's wet dream…" he says, without much humour.

I suppress a shudder as I try not to picture that night – the moment I walked into our halls kitchen for a 3am snack, only to find the entire place gleaming red with fresh gore, blood spattered and smeared across every inch of the floor, clotted handprints marking weird scarlet shapes on cupboard doors, and Zillah's pale skinny figure crouched in the midst of it all, wearing nothing but a pair of black jeans, his arm repeatedly slashed open, vodka bottle rolling empty next to him, head in a bucket as he groaned in nausea, misery, or outright confusion.

His dad had been round earlier, heaping yet more familial pressure on him – Zillah responded by drinking half a bottle of vodka, not remembering that his antidepressants weren't meant to be drunk on at all, and the self-destructive frenzy that resulted was fucking horrifying; I was terrified by the state of him, his dilated, vacant eyes, the warped humour he found in the whole situation, actively proud of the 'death-scene' he'd made of that kitchen – it looked like a massive amount of blood-loss, and the drive to hospital was nothing but a blur of panic for me. Then, when we got there, they had no psych ward beds – Zillah had pulled himself together just enough to insist he wasn't suicidal, just drunk…and that was that – they didn't bother helping him, beyond putting him on a six-month-long waiting list for therapy – they just stitched him up and sent him packing. I was only a kid; I didn't have the first fucking clue what to do with him, other than to not let him out of my sight.

It took me 'til nearly 10am to clean up the unspeakable gore-shock he'd made of that kitchen, and after giggling weirdly and requesting those damn photographs, Zillah just sat limply at the table, wrapped in bandages, staring blankly through me and saying nothing at all, as though the whole thing was nothing more than a surreal dream. It was exam season, in the years before he found drugs – the pressure to succeed cracked him completely, and there was still no help available. So he struggled on, wrapped in endless bloodied bandages beneath long black sleeves, 'til he found club drugs, and the self-medication began. And that's been a messy bloody rollercoaster, but it was *never* as ungodly as the fucking slaughterhouse I walked into that night at uni…

I snap back to the present as Zillah turns to me and asks, "Did I fuck up, Tom? Did I say something totally stupid? I just keep going over and over what I said – I don't understand why she wasn't *hearing me,* why it all fucking kicked off like that… I know I should've been more patient, taken a breather instead of going off on one, but I just couldn't *understand*—"

"Mate, I was listening the whole time. You…I mean, you were *you*, you got pretty damn argumentative, and I definitely stopped you for a reason, but before that, you… Well, I could tell you were trying. And she'd have had you back, too – but only on her own terms, and frankly you're on different planets about this stuff. Unless you do a massive U-turn on the dope – which I really bloody wish you would – I think you need to accept that it's never going to happen with Em. I'd tell you to seriously think about that, while you still have half a chance, but after everything you said last night, if it's between Em or the dope, I don't think you even need to bother answering that question…"

"Ah Tom, for fuck's sake don't *put it* like that!" he pleads, and he sounds genuinely hurt. "Just don't! It's not like that! If they'd give me that fucking script, you'd see it as medication, not 'dope', and you wouldn't all be treating me like I'm a piece of shit over the fact that I need it! God, you make me feel like scum. All of you! Like this…*soulless* lump of junkie scum who'd sell his dog for a hit. And I wouldn't. I would *not*."

"Well, your hypothetical dog is, I'm sure, intensely reassured. Maybe don't get a real one just yet?" I sigh, adding, "For the record, Zill, I'm sorry – no one's trying to make you feel like shit. I'd never even heard of prescription heroin before today. It sounds…extreme, honestly, but if you reckon you need it this badly, then…you know I'm in your corner – always."

"Ugh…" he says, flopping back against the sofa, and pulling out yet another joint like some ganja Houdini. "You still don't get it," he mumbles through the smoke as he gets it lit. "I know you're trying, Tom, but you just don't. I don't think you ever will…I'm staying in bed forever. I'm going to upload the Idiot Speech, then I'm just staying in bed 'til I hear from Cindy about that script. That is *literally* all that matters, in my entire world…"

"Uh huh?" I say, dubiously. "And if it's bad news?"

"It won't be. I mean…it can't. It just fucking *can't*."

As I try to formulate something useful, he takes another drag on the joint, and says,

"Christ…it's all too real now. I mean it – nothing else matters, Tom, my whole life rests on this – don't you see? Em, my career, my *sanity*, the whole—It *matters,* ok? And in two days' time, my phone might ring, and my last chance might just say, fuck off. Nah…you know? Just *fuck off*. No script. Not for fucking *you*. Despite all the evidence, despite everything you've ever been through, just…just fuck off. Get the *hell* off this planet, you *vile* lump of smackhead trash – you don't belong here, you never have, you've always been so *fucking*—" His

Copyright Dorian Bridges 2024

words choke into a sob, and he abruptly curls into a shuddering ball, then he's hyperventilating like the whole world's crumbling round his ears. Lucy's over there in a flash, hugging him tight, telling him it'll be ok, trying to get him to breathe. I don't even know what to say – is this weekend's madness going to end with us breaking into a hospital and holding everyone at knifepoint to get the bloody medication he needs?

I begin to realise how ridiculous it all must seem, from Zillah's perspective; how eye-gougingly frustrating. The one and only drug that actually mellows his anxiety out and makes him want to live – and by god has he tried them all – and there it is, in all these hospitals, all over the country, but he simply can't have it. None for him, not ever, because the government, his eternal Public Enemy Number One, have decided it's simply too naughty for him to consume. Even though he's buying it off the streets every day regardless, funding god knows what criminal awfulness. And all that anti-logic, because of some irrelevant bit of paper, signed largely by Americans, long before any of us were even born.

Sighing, I get up, and go over to the sofa to hug him too.

Copyright Dorian Bridges 2024

CHAPTER NINE

Zillah:

He spends the rest of the weekend in Tom's spare room, editing and uploading his Idiot Speech, floating through opiate dreams. He only leaves the room once, late on Sunday morning, to score his essentials, a risky chore that always makes him anxious. As usual, he tones down his look, puts on a suit-jacket and glasses – anything that makes him look like the kind of upstanding citizen who'd never be found lugging a quarter ounce each of smack and weed, and a bag of dodgily pressed valiums around the city. His dealer finds the 'businessman look' hilarious, as always, a jarring clash with his usual clientele, but Zillah lets him get on with the mockery – he hasn't got it in him today. He buys extra valium – a lot of it – then drops into two pharmacies to max out his sleeping pill allowance. He hopes like hell he won't have to use it, but having it around makes him feel less like he's drowning, the uncertain guillotine blade of that horrifying last-chance phone call looming heavy above his head.

Tom and Lucy have been orbiting his room, popping their heads in, bringing him tea and toast, Tom still insisting on watching over every shot of gear…or the ones he knows about, at least. Caught between the stresses of Cindy, Em, Twitter, and Monday's looming phone call, Zillah does it six times on Sunday, and out of curiosity, he attempts three of them alone and unsupervised – no one comes to stop him. No one hears. That's good: another vital piece of comfort clicking into place. Tom's head doesn't poke round the door 'til bedtime, at which point he clearly knows there's a shot in the offing. Zillah decides it'd be impolite to refuse, and makes it seven.

"Last one of the day, please?" says Tom, peering at his eyes. "You look…beyond wasted…"

"Jus' stoned. Whole point of a 24-hour bed in, isn'it?" Zillah mumbles, as he slips away from Tom's prying gaze into the bathroom. It now sports three large holes in the wall, and a few more bloodied dents – he wishes he knew how to fix them. He wishes he didn't trash everything he touched.

It feels like the clocks have stopped, everything waiting for that one awful, or transcendent phone call. When Tom and Lucy are there, he can't bear the weight of their eyes on him, the tug of societal expectation, the need to participate, perform – pretend to be ok. He cringes every time he remembers falling to pieces like that on Saturday night, crying so hard he couldn't breathe – it's fucking embarrassing; it's not who he wants to be, not in front of people he likes too much to ghost on. But whenever they leave him alone, it hurts just as much – the staleness of the Em-less silence, the alien feeling of no place to call home. He puts his dope playlist on shuffle, a weird gumbo consisting largely of Massive Attack, The Cure, Creux Lies, Lil Peep, Nirvana, Cigarettes After Sex, Digital Daggers, and a few of his own songs, written and recorded while high off his face during a brief but intense relapse six years ago. Those songs got him through a lot of dead time, *sober* time – they were the amber-droplet capsules of past highs, preserved for all eternity. He can still feel the drugs in the fucked-up rhythm of his guitar playing, the way it slows whenever he loses focus, the slurred mumble of lyrics that weren't anywhere close to his best, but that somehow said it all anyway.

And when he dreams, he dreams of Em, wakes with tears still wet on his cheeks. Her words keep echoing through his head, along with every promise they ever made each other – *I wanted forever with you,*

Zill – I could picture the rest of my fucking life with you, and it was so beautiful...

The rest of their lives – his mythical happy ending...they came so close. If he wasn't such a fuckup, he could've been planning proposals right now, not suicides.

Everything rests on Cindy, now. He's never been more grateful for the forcefulness of his older sister. If anyone can still save him, it has to be her...

And then, at long-dreaded last, it's Monday lunchtime.

He's dozing in bed, just emerging from a dope nap, when his phone bursts into life. His eyes flick open, and before it can get out four beats of The Editors' *Papillon*, he has it to his ear, dragging the duvet over his head for extra privacy, and saying,

"Cindy?"

"Hiii, Zillah!" she says, and his heart sinks so rapidly there's a weird buzzing in his ears – he has to lie flat on his back before his stomach rejects the last cup of tea he gagged down. She doesn't need to say another word – it's right there in the forced jollity of her easy-breezy nurse tone. "How are you?"

"Just...get on with it, Cind. What happened? What did they say?"

"Zill—" She hesitates. *Too obvious,* he thinks, *Too fucking obvious. Play along, or she'll lock you up! Stop panicking, and play along!*

"Well?" he says, in the chirpiest voice he can manage, while his heart's thudding up his throat like a drunken pinball, and every breath wants to rip itself in and out at hyper-speed 'til the whole world sparkles and turns black. "Look, Cind, I'm still talking to my own treatment team – it's not like my every hope rests on this."

"I... I thought...? I mean, that's great, Zill – that is really, really great." The relief in her voice is palpable – he knows he can't keep it up for long...but he also knows he should've been a fucking actor. "'Cause honestly, these people? They have a shiny website, they promise you the moon, but it's just not happening. I tried my best, I genuinely bloody did – they were so sick to death of me by the end, I pushed it home with two different workers and a doctor, but...look...it just doesn't work like this. You can't transfer across from another treatment agency with the sole goal of getting diamorphine. It's drug seeking behaviour, and—"

He forces back the tears that prickle behind his squeezed-shut eyelids, as he points out, "How is asking for the right medication 'drug seeking'? And doesn't it kind of come with the territory? Maybe they shouldn't fucking advertise it online if they don't want junkies to make a beeline for them!"

"I know, Zill...I know. Look, do you want me to help with your current treatment—"

"No, no – it's in hand. They know me. I do it all through letters so they can't whip me up into a tizzy or anything. I'm waiting for them to come back to me. It's ok. Thanks for trying."

"Zill, you *are* ok, aren't you? Are you still at Tom's place?"

"Mm-hmm," he says, digging his fingernails into the wounds on his right knuckles 'til he feels slippery blood begin to spill. The pain makes him feel sick, but sick is better than sectioned.

Copyright Dorian Bridges 2024

"Ok… Is he in?"

"Working. Downstairs. I'm actually in the middle of some editing, Cind, can we talk later?"

"Well, sure, if you're positive you're—"

"Have a great day!" he blurts out, and hangs up the phone.

He sits in the silence that follows – stares blankly at the wall. It takes him exactly ten seconds to wrack his brain for an alternative – a new avenue…and just three more to know with a cold, bleak finality, he's been everywhere. He's tried everything. This was the final item on a checklist he's been whittling down for the better part of a year. As the realisation sinks in, he feels something snap, deep inside him.

He knows exactly what it is – it's the final thread, holding him to Earth.

He doesn't grieve, or lash out. In a way, he almost feels relieved.

The anxiety and nausea are fading away, overpowered by something so much bigger: a perfect numbness he's never encountered, in his entire stressed-out life.

He feels like a cloud, like a machine…like a ghost.

All his battles are over, now.

CHAPTER TEN

Tom:

I love an excuse to work from home – sweatpants on, top quality snacks, my own playlist blasting everything from the Beastie Boys to Scooter to the Ramones; it's a sunny day, and if I can't be out in it, I'm bloody well making a racket – it doesn't feel like working at all. Lucy stays, too – we agreed last night things with Zillah felt too perilous to risk either one of us leaving him on Monday Phone Call Day.

Trouble is, we're working, the music's blasting…and the time just slips away – I forget all about him. It's gone four thirty when I finally glance at my phone, and see Cindy's text. It says nothing more than, "Is he really ok?"

For several seconds I don't cotton on – it's just normal sisterly concern, isn't it? I decide I'll call her in an hour, after work, but the second I put the phone back down, this icy wave of panic just blasts me in the guts, and understanding clicks into place. I haven't seen Zillah since I dropped him in his breakfast. Now it's bloody obvious what Cindy means. His dreaded phone call came and went…and it wasn't good news. If he didn't immediately come to tell me, to vent his frustrations, or even to get high, I know what it has to mean.

I get up so fast I nearly knock the whole desk over, running up the stairs two at a time, 'til I'm in the spare room, uselessly rattling the handle of the bathroom door.

"Zillah!" I try, banging on the wall. "Open the fuck up!"

Copyright Dorian Bridges 2024

I can hear some faint burbling, as though his phone's playing a video in there, but he doesn't respond. That freezing blast of terror hits me again – I take a step back, give the door a knee-jarring kick. It takes two more before the lock breaks off, goes flying across the room with a sharp ping, and the minute I see the hellscape that's inside, I'm yelling for Lucy.

It's not just the dead-grey colour of his skin, or the fact he's topless and covered in blood, his chest sliced and slashed with a blade from a shattered safety razor, it's the shakily written sign lying in his lap. It's the video of himself playing on his upturned phone – I don't catch a word of it, but I remember everything he said: it's all on his phone. His little goodbye videos.

I race into our bedroom for the Naloxone, Lucy already sprinting up the stairs as I yell at her,

"Call an ambulance – get him breathing!"

Her eyes widen, and she's off like a shot. I'm back with the Naloxone, and thank god the instructions are fresh in my mind. The sign in Zillah's lap says "DO NOT RESUSCITATE, UNDER ANY CIRCUMSTANCE!!!" with three exclamation marks, but I highly doubt it counts as a binding legal document. I yank out the little syringe, stab him in the leg and shove the plunger down a notch. Lucy's rattling him on the bathroom tiles, but there's no response, no breathing, nothing – in the end I shove her out of the way, force open his mouth like you see on TV, and attempt to blow him up like a Lilo – that's genuinely what it feels like; it's eerie, too intimate, then I'm slamming away on his blood-stickied ribcage while Lucy dials 999.

I have no idea what I'm doing. How and why the *fuck* do I have no idea how to do CPR? Why isn't this taught in schools? All I'm doing is imitating the movies, 'til Lucy puts the phone on speaker, and they start talking me through it, counting the heartbeats, telling me the actual placement and how hard to go. I don't even know why he's got his top off and all these cuts across his body – I feel a sickening wet crack as one of his ribs breaks under my pounding hands, and I jump back, horrified, but they just tell me to keep on going. Lucy's got both hands over her mouth, tears running rivers down her cheeks – I'm pretty sure we both realise the same thing.

He's dead.

He has to be. No one can be this colour and not be dead. His skin still feels warm, but it's the middle of summer – everything's warm.

Even when they have me hit him with a second dose of Naloxone, nothing happens. Walloping away at his dead chest is getting exhausting, and creepy, like I'm abusing a corpse, like I'm beating up his remains when all I want to do is lie down next to him and cry. Lucy takes over, allowing me to dissolve until we hear the sirens, then I'm off down the stairs, the whole world ringing in my ears.

When the ambulance crew get to him, they force a tube down his throat, start puffing his lungs up with a bag – I can't even stand to watch. I leave the room, sit down on the bed, trying to hold my shit together, until they come swooping out with Zillah on a stretcher. They're not respecting the unofficial nature of his wishes either, the paper 'do not resuscitate' sign kicked around the floor. Trust Zillah to try though, to debate-team the sanctity of his own body from beyond the grave…

They don't give us time to discuss who's riding in the ambulance – they just screech off, leaving Lucy and I to pile into the car. I drive like a maniac in their distant wake, but when we get there it's chaos;

we get separated by the necessity to park the car, and once we find him, it's not good news. Somehow, I'd hoped he'd be miraculously revived and furious by now, everything he said to me about Naloxone, but he's not. He's in the ICU, intubated, wires everywhere, heart monitor beeping slow. Turns out he didn't just have a wild, impulsive stab at killing himself, he really went for it – it's increasingly obvious that he took far more than just heroin; that's why the Naloxone didn't work. They eventually realise there's a whole cocktail of downers in his system, some prescription, some not. They're gradually increasing the dose of some benzodiazepine antidote, but apparently he's been prescribed the things for years on end, and I confirm he takes even more off the street – if they go too hard too fast with the antidote, he could have a fatal seizure. The heroin and methadone alone should've been enough to kill him – they keep having to re-antidote him every time his heartbeat drops below a certain point. Between all of it, and the unknown period he was lying there turning blue, starving his brain of oxygen, his ever regaining consciousness – let alone in a functional, non-vegetative state – seems like an overly ambitious goal.

At last they toss around the words 'stable, but critical', and it just echoes in my head, a crazed oxymoron. In essence, his battered body's being supported artificially – he's alive in the technical sense – but no one can tell us if his mind's ever coming back; whether Em's ghoulish comments about brain damage are about to become a dark premonition. A woman with a clipboard's getting very interested in his organ donor status. I have to leave her with Lucy – the adrenaline that got us here in one piece is making me shaky and surreal, and the last thing I can deal with is the idea of someone cutting him open for his fucking organs.

There's nothing to do now but wait. Lucy grabbed Zillah's phone on the dash out of the door – he'd left it unlocked, his goodbye video open; it was running on a loop. When they throw us out of his cubicle to clean up the worst of the self-inflicted cuts on his chest, which look like words, but I can't make them out, it's just nonsense, we sit down in a corner of the fluorescent-glaring waiting room, and open his suicide note. I'm hesitant – I tell Lucy I think we should leave it 'til the day they certify his death…but she's determined. Much as I don't buy it, in her world he's coming back, and he's coming back whole. If he does, we need to know why he did this, every little bit of his reasoning – we have to be able to fix it.

Wincing, I hit play.

The multitude of cuts on his chest immediately make a horrible kind of sense – it's written backwards, carved in the mirror, or in the flipped image on his phone's front camera; Zillah decided, in typically dark flamboyant fashion, to brand himself *"DRUG WAR MARTYR"*, right across his chest. I feel sick – all that time he was up there, intricately butchering himself, and I was right downstairs, music on, forgetting about him altogether. But there he sits, in the video, on our bathroom floor, blood trickling down the pale skin of his slim torso, as he says,

"If you're seeing this…then I'm dead." And then he just cracks up – starts laughing his head off like it's the best joke in the world. "I'm *dead?!*" he repeats, half disbelief, half laughter, flinging his arms out. He keeps the volume down – he obviously didn't want anyone hearing his little recording session, but it's a crow of victory all the same. "I'm finally off this rotten *fucking* planet, man! I'm living out of a suitcase, so all I'll be leaving behind is this goddamn meat-wagon. Life takes everything from you in the end, so, I marked it up a bit –" He indicates the cuts on his chest. "Made sure there's no ignoring this corpse, out of all the endless, uncaring murders our government commits."

The image flickers slightly – trust Zillah to bloody well video-edit his own suicide note – he looks a little more contrite now, saying, "Tom, Lucy, Em, Cindy, Mum – everyone who'll be there after the end, I'm lumping you in together, and I'm…I'm sorry for that, but there isn't time. There just isn't… All I want is to be gone. It's like my brain's fucking flatlined. I'm scraping every word out of my guts. It's unbearable." He runs his battered hands through his hair, and continues flatly,

"I'm sorry for this… I know what you'll think of me. That I was weak…that I overreacted, got hysterical, did a stupid thing…but you don't know what's inside. Don't assume. This has been coming a long, long time. I started the checklist nearly a year ago. Today I ticked off the very last thing. I'm prepared… My only regret is that you couldn't be. I don't talk to people enough, I know I don't. Only Em, and –" he sighs, "I'm sorry, Em. I put too much on you – it was too much for one person. It's too much for me. And today – the diamorphine script? That was the final straw, the last fucking gut-punch, for me. It's hit me like a ten-tonne truck and I just…I can't do it anymore. I guess that's fairly obvious." There's the tiniest flicker of warped humour, but it doesn't last.

"Ask Em," he says, in that same flat voice, "She'll tell you what I couldn't. I tried not to say too much, to anyone, about the shit going on in my head, but she knows. *Everything* was resting on that script – this treatment agency was my last chance, and they knew that. I sent them an email weeks ago, told them everything – what I was planning, all of it. Maybe they didn't get it, but I reckon they did – they just didn't bother to open it. Another mad tirade from that obnoxiously verbose junkie – what's the fucking point? That's how little I mattered… It was stupid, me convincing myself I ever had the chance of a normal, happy life. All I needed was that fucking script, and I fit every one of the government's criteria for eligibility, but it was still too much to ask from this fucked-up world…" He stares blankly at the wall for a moment, then, with more intensity, more typical, recognisable Zillah-ness, says, "Tom – tell the others that story, about the place they sent me to? *That* is the state of mental health treatment in Tory Britain. That's the consequence of living, *surviving,* like I do, and it's—No. It's too much. It's all *been* too much."

He sighs, hangs his head back, stares up at the ceiling as he says, "Maybe I'm just being a stubborn cunt, man. Maybe I could beat the odds, go on for another decade, using like this. You know – illegally, shunned by society, unwanted, alone, my whole career screwed, my friends looking at me like I'm scum, but…frankly, I doubt it? No one realises it's *just* medication – that's all it is. Haven't I proved that? Weren't the most functional years of my life on gear? No one gets furious with someone who finds their miracle depression cure if it's Prozac. This is no fucking different! If you're better on the drug than you are off it, that's not even addiction, it's just being appropriately medicated.

"You all treat me like I'm a fucking idiot, man, too weak and dumb to face his own problems – all of you, the look in your eyes these days, it's just…*disappointment.* Failure. I can't take it anymore – the fucking *distrust* from my best friends, the total lack of understanding, the—Ugh. Whatever. Who even cares, now…" He tugs at a strand of his hair, visibly holding back on a tirade against at least one of us, then he just shakes his head, continuing,

"Whenever I talk to the fuckers at the drug clinic, it's all *about* drugs as a problem, but they never were my bloody problem, were they? My *brain* was the problem, and drugs were the fix, fucking…*Tom?* You know the score – right? You met me before. Was I ever happy? Was I *me*, before I found drugs? And Em…Christ. How do you not see it? How do you not see the *vacuum* I was in, sober, then the goddamn pits of depression when I tried the socially sanctioned thing and drank…but you said it yourself, on Saturday. You said how good I seemed – didn't you? That was, what…three hours after doing a shot? You *said, how good, I seemed!*"

There's another flicker, something else he's edited out. Now he just looks emotionless, staring towards the window as he says,

"Life is a terminal condition. Sometimes it's more terminal than others. I wish I could leave you with something scorching and furious and eloquent, some torch to go marching up Downing Street with and burn it all to fucking rubble, but I just…" he sighs, draws his knees up to his bloodied chest, gestures defeat with one hand. "I don't. I can't… It isn't in me, anymore, all that. They cut it right out of me, and all it took was one word. Just…*no*. That's it. Every fucking study and statistic I know, every argument I've ever made, and all it took was two letters to gut me. *No*." He shakes his head, his expression wry, then blank.

"I loved you all," he says, looking directly at the camera now, but there's barely any emotion there. He looks so fucking worn down, like this speech really is dragging every last ounce of life out of him. "I loved you all, to bits. If any part of me remains, which it will, I'll be loving you from the other side. Don't forget me. I was never right for this place… I hate to say it, but this was always in the mail…and I think Em knew that. Mum – I think you knew it, too. I know neither of you accepted it, but I hope, deep down, you were a little bit prepared. You all deserve to be happy – happier than I could ever make you." He sighs, runs his fingers over his eyes. His voice is just the tiniest bit unsteady, the closest thing to any real emotion he's yet shown. Frowning at the floor, he says quietly,

"Em…find someone who isn't broken, next time. He's out there – he has to be. And don't feel guilty, ever, for moving on. It's a joyous thing. It is. My funeral is a *joyous occasion,* a setting free – I hope you can feel…I don't know, some echo of that? I won't be locked inside this godawful, misfiring torture chamber of a meat-suit anymore. I'll still be me, but…better. No more suffering. More wisdom. Less bullshit. More peace. That's what I believe. It's what I believe *in*. Maybe it's amazing that I still believe in anything, after this fucking life." He shifts position, points at the words on his chest again, and sighs.

"Anyway. That's it, I guess. That's goodbye. I know I should go into the minutiae of my possessions and arrangements, but…I'm sorry. Just let me go. Let me rest in fucking peace – that's goodbye. God, it feels— Umm…no… It feels alright, actually. I've tried this before, you know – saying goodbye? I was always in bits, sobbing my guts out. Now I haven't got a single tear to shed. That's how you know, I think, that it's right. If you're not crying, then you're ready.

"And I am. I am so, so ready.

"I'll see you again, you know – somewhere better. Look after each other. If you have to hate me, to get through this…that's ok. No guilt, alright? Not ever. And Mum…don't blame yourself – this was never on you. Pray as much as you like, but don't get all guilty. Your god loves you, if he's got any sense. And I love you the most…

Copyright Dorian Bridges 2024

"All of you – until the next life."

He shapes a heart with his fingers.

The recording cuts out.

Copyright Dorian Bridges 2024

CHAPTER ELEVEN

I've never had a period of my life be so crystal clear, yet so blurred over, all at once. His battered body's slowly stabilising, but no one seems willing to tell us how much of him's left in there. I've watched his goodbye video six times over. Every time, he sounds more done in, more final, more *relieved* to be going, and now? We've got him hooked up to breathing tubes and drips and catheters, and what if he does come back? Even if, by some utter miracle, he's not brain damaged, or paralysed, or unable to speak – what the fuck do we say to him?

Lucy and Cindy are coping via the medium of fury. They're on the phone to drug treatment teams, both the one Cindy spoke to, and the one Zillah's under. Lucy storms up and down the car park, venting every graphic detail of what he did to himself with that razorblade – she's determined that Zillah's waking up, and when he does, she wants hope there for him, right away. She wants to be able to say, *It worked, you fucking psycho. You got your script. You can still live on this planet – be glad we brought you back.* Cindy rages down the phone through her tears – now she's the one threatening to report everyone to PALS; the family resemblance is at last clear.

Em comes to the hospital clutching a box of chocolates – I don't know what the fuck Lucy said on the phone, I've been too catatonic to deal with it, but I think an act of spite may have been committed. Em's clearly expecting him alive, and conscious. When she walks in and all you can hear is the whoosh of the ventilator, the slow beep-beeping of his heart, and there he is like some awful sci-fi experiment covered in wires, she drops the chocolates, and a nurse has to grab her before she faints. She spends the next ten minutes holding his hand, still scabbed up from his fight with our bathroom wall, whispering, "What did I do? What the fuck did I *do?*" until even Lucy can't bear it anymore, and all three girls disappear to the cafeteria for a pep talk.

Zillah's mum…fuck. She comes in, briefly. I've never seen anyone look so— Christ. It was awful. I went and hid in the car. How could I not? He was in *my* house – I was meant to be looking after him. I've known Zill's mum since we were teenagers – she's great, used to buy me an Easter egg every year and everything, basically became my own second mother. Now she looks about a hundred years old, but when I slink back in to face the music, she won't hear my apology. "You tried," she says, and I can see she means it. We have a blame-off, for a while; she's going on about his childhood, about his dad, his dad was too strict with him, nothing he ever did was good enough, she should've stepped in more – I just dodge that whole mess, and tell her she was perfect; "Zillah adored you, you know he did". I use the past tense without even realising it. She starts crying. Cindy takes her home. It's hellish.

But then the shit really hits the fan.

We should've realised. One of us, *one of us*, should've seen this coming. He'd edited his suicide note, for Christ's sake – wasn't that a bit weird? Did it really matter if it had a few 'umms' and awkward silences in it? Well, it turned out he did all that, 'cause he'd made more than one.

I guess he really did care about the kids that follow him, after all. Because the lunatic made *them* a goodbye, too. He'd scheduled it, on YouTube, to automatically upload 48 hours after he did it – I guess he assumed he'd be safely gone by then, and if not, revived enough to cancel it...so unbeknownst to any of us, Zillah's close to a million subscribers get hit with a video simply, tantalisingly, entitled, "Goodbye. I'm sorry..."

It isn't the same thing he gave us. Or, well – bits of it are. That stupid, *stupid* intro; turns out there was even more of it than we saw. For a good three minutes he's just laughing and joking about how he's always wanted to do the, 'If you're seeing this, I'm *dead!*' thing – it's in bloody revolting taste, even by Zillah's standards. But then he gets going. Tells them everything – how he's a "hypocrite and a liar" who's never been able to cope with sober life – "you call me an inspiration, and I die inside, 'cause it's never, *ever* been true". Staring fixedly at the floor, he finally cops to the fact that he's never been truly clean, that he's been a chronic dabbler on an increasingly high-dose methadone script the entirety of his social media career, and the latter's been fucking him six ways to Sunday, causing Em to dump him, in part, because he's always so out of it on the stuff.

"But it's not her fault," he says wearily, "So please, please don't go after Em – none of you. She tried her best... Em's not the problem – it's the *fucking* laws, and the *fucking* treatment centres that wouldn't know help if it swallowed them whole. 'Cause look, right now – look at me. I'm not nodding out, I'm not a zombie. I'm functional. Tom told me the other day that I got called a goddamn 'intellectual powerhouse' by one of you guys, and... Wow... Thank you? That means the whole world to me, stupid and insecure as it sounds. But d'you know how I achieved that? The *right medication*. For me, that means opiates. *Please* don't misconstrue me – I'm not saying go out and do this, for fuck's sake I am *not* – if you don't already have this problem, don't fucking create it – d'you see where it's gotten me? But, look...I am *stupid as shit*, ok? I told you that already – I tried everything when I was younger...and when I found heroin, it fixed

Copyright Dorian Bridges 2024

my stupid fucking broken brain. Everything wrong with me, just...*fixed.*"

He's on bloody shaky ground, morally speaking, but he gets rolling onto the diamorphine script, all the studies that say it saves lives, the fact that when it's clean and dose-measured it's actually far safer than alcohol, safer than antidepressants even, and that you can get heroin legally, *safely,* ethically – if someone'll only let you. To his intense fucking credit, he even spills the beans about that asylum stay, the dodgy batch he got, and it's even darker than what he told me –

"This is what can happen to you, buying dope off the street. I was nearly diagnosed with paranoid schizophrenia – those were my symptoms, and it took me two full weeks to truly find, and believe in, reality again. It is not *safe,* street heroin, don't fucking touch it. I still can't walk into a church without being terrified of Jesus and Lucifer – terrified of them both, equally, 'cause for those two weeks I was trapped between them, and they were every bit as calculating – as evil. They wanted—" He breaks off, mutters, "Shit... Should I even admit to this?", but after chewing his lip for a nervous moment, he quietly confesses,

"This is the definition of insanity...and those voices got me there, in the space of that unrelenting first week. They wanted me to take a...a fucking...claw hammer...to my own mother. I repeat, I was told by those—" He winces, runs his fingers over his eyes, saying – "I can't *explain it*, man – I can't ever make you understand how they got me there, how they twisted me up inside to that point. It scares me too much. Even now, all these years later, those hallucinations burned themselves so deep in my brain, I still half believe they could get to me, get to her, any time, any place..."

Copyright Dorian Bridges 2024

He talks about the fact he knew he'd be cancelled, online, if anyone found out he was using again – "even though it's a fucking *mental illness!* That's all it is! Everyone says they support you, stand up for the mentally ill, until you have symptoms they find personally repugnant, and mine are apparently *gross*. And *stupid* – can't forget that one, can we? But all I needed, *all I needed*, man, was *one* fucking doctor to listen to me, and I'd be fine. I wouldn't be inflicting this hurt on the people I love most in the world – I *hate* that I'm doing this to them – to all of you, but I just—I can't *do this* anymore! I am *not* saying give smack to anyone who asks for it, I'm just saying…*shit*, man, when there's no other option, just show some fucking humanity! Have some basic bloody empathy for someone who's dragged themselves across the hot coals of their own neurodiverse screwed-up psyche day in day out for nearly four decades."

"But they didn't." He snorts, starts laughing. "They *didn't!* Jesus, why is that even funny to me? I don't know. Maybe it actually makes me happy. Maybe I'm really that done for."

He manages to dredge up a brief lecture on not following in his footsteps, not doing anything stupid with their grief, if they have any, but you can tell his heart's not really in it, this obligatory moral admin – he actually looks at his watch at one point, then catches himself doing it, and laughs, asking, "Who the fuck am I keeping time with now?" He shrugs, then, with the very last spark of fight he's got in him, he tells them exactly who the treatment teams that turned him down were. Gives out the addresses, the emails – but tells them not to use the phone – "Addicts need that phone-line. People like me. I'm not trying to hurt anyone else, so don't block up their phones. Don't do that in my name. But they are endangering people every goddamn day with their shit, so, *don't* get violent, don't get arrested, don't do anything dumb. Just please, please, use your words. Use your stories…use mine. Make sure this never happens to another soul. That's all we are. Souls…and we deserve better. If you want to do an amazing thing, write to your MP. Tell them why diamorphine scripts are needed, and that the prejudice has to end. Give a homeless guy a quid, no matter what he's going to spend it on. Do whatever you can to make this world less shitty for all the other fuckups like me…if you can, if it's not too much of a strain on your heart and your mind and your soul.

"'Cause it's been too big a strain on mine…" He shakes his head, staring out of the window, a flicker of frustration crossing his face, then fading back into blankness. "I never like taking a dump on anyone's day, especially if you generally come here to be cheered up, but you deserved the truth, in this, not dead air and rumours. We've all got an expiration date. Today is mine – I'm at peace with that. If you've supported me on Patreon, thank you, seriously – funerals are expensive shit, and you'll be helping my mum and Em out. After the dust settles, even if it takes a year, I've got a lot of clothes and CDs…I mean, a lot. It's obscene. And you guys have been a huge part of my life. So, if Em's ok with it, if she can handle it, I hope there can be a club-night, or something – all the proceeds going to a drug charity, and if someone can just bring my stuff for you guys to scavenge through and fuck off with, I think that'd be…I dunno. It might just bring a bit of joy to all this, for someone, maybe? Even if it's solely Em, getting rid of my dreadful Doom Pile situation…"

He sits there in silence for so long it's eerie. Finally he raises an imaginary glass to the camera, and says, "Anyway. Here's to you, wherever you are – I wish you the best, in all things, always. My friend, Tom, cracked a horrible joke the other day, about me adopting hundreds of thousands of teenagers, and I truly hope it doesn't feel that way to you, 'cause I don't want to hurt anyone like that, but…I'm too far gone. I can't feel anything anymore – all this? It's muscle memory. I know what I should say, and I'm saying it…but my soul's already gone. Maybe you can feel it…

"But fight on, ok? Go down swinging, and I *don't* mean like this." He points at the words on his chest, and rolls his eyes, admitting, "That was petty. Moment of weakness. Had a few." He flashes the backs of his hands at the camera, then catches himself in the viewfinder, and covers his mouth in a moment of genuine amusement, saying, "Oh god, I'm sorry, that looks awful. It was a wall, I swear to god, just a wall. I'm not a violent person, not ever. But…look, look, just…be ok, with this, please? I'm telling you, I tried *everything*. This battle's cost me half my life…and so much more, but I made it eleven years past the 27 club, and if you've heard my stories, you'll know how much I deserved to go down with that ship. For a junkie, I'm ancient… I know, more justifications. I'm the king of them."

He smiles, and at last it's genuine, open – startling. He looks like the weight of the world's just been lifted off his shoulders, and it's spooky as all hell. "*Was*," he says – I go cold all over. "I fucking *was…*" He shakes his head in amazement. "God, that feels good to say. Every bit of me, in the past tense. This lifetime, this hell, over and done with, all my mistakes and failures fading into dust and memory. What an *utter* relief…"

He smiles up at the sunlit window, and says, "Like I said – if you're seeing this, I'm gone. I was successful – I'm free. This is a scheduled upload – I'm coming to you from the past; there's no saving me now – don't try. I needed to get this off my chest, but it's time for me to go now.

"Keep fighting the good fight. Brownstown and Pacific addiction clinics, my death is on your hands. Tory government, my death is on your hands. This isn't a suicide – it's an assassination. Please remember that. Please don't hate me… I'm sorry."

He manages one last little smile, a wry wave, and that's that.

It's a long video – far longer than the one he made for us. I try not to be bitter about that. He's more honest, more open, talking to strangers than to his own friends.

We don't even find out about the video until it has a horrendous eighty thousand views, which happens within minutes of its unexpected release, and the figure's more than doubled by the time we've seen it through – Em's phone's blowing up; concerned relatives, every friend she's ever had, every YouTube clout-chaser she ever interacted with. Cindy forces her to turn it off, while we work out what the fuck to do. She wants the video removed, but Lucy won't hear of it; she's hell-bent on punishing those drug treatment agencies, getting the script for Zillah, if he ever does wake up. Em, seemingly eager to see *someone* burn for this, rapidly agrees, and an unlikely alliance is formed. Em's the only one with his passwords – the ultimate say has to be hers.

Cindy remains loudly in opposition, arguing that kids shouldn't be exposed to any of this, particularly not the graphic self-mutilation – Em rebuffs her; Zillah set the video to over-eighteens only, and he put a trigger warning on it. Cindy abruptly bursts into tears of fury – Zillah thought of *everything*, every tiny little fucking thing, apart from calling her – seeking help. It's painfully obvious she's still clinging to the belief that he acted on a whim, and nothing more. Em, nearly as gobby as Zillah at times, shatters that belief – he'd been on about suicide to her for nearly a year. I feel sickeningly guilty about how little time I've made for him lately, as Em tells us he took every antidepressant they could throw at him, dealt with numerous horrible side-effects, tried three therapists, and Em had to keep spying on his Amazon purchases after a pack of razorblades turned up in the mail – Zillah actually thanked her for getting rid of them.

"Don't you think he'd thank you for getting rid of this bloody awful video?" Cindy asks, wiping her eyes.

"You don't know him…" Em says quietly. "You know him, Cindy, but…you've been out of touch too long. The *only* thing he will thank us for, if he gets through this, is getting him that damn script, and right now, I'm not fighting him on that. If he never comes out of this…these are his final words – don't you get that?" Dabbing at her kohl-rung eyes, she says emphatically, "He told those doctors what he was planning, Cindy. Even if they never read that email, his worker knew exactly how bad things were getting, and I know that, because I had a go at the bloody man myself, over the phone, when Zill argued himself right into a panic attack – I took the phone, and tried myself – they weren't even giving him therapy at that sodding place, just phoning him up once a month, standing by as he got worse and worse, and when I begged them to *help him*, to see him more often, do *something,* all I got was this…this filibustering waffle about government cutbacks! I was so angry…I *am* so angry. I tried, and he tried, and *you* fucking tried – these doctors *cannot* claim ignorance, or innocence, in this! They all knew they held his life in their hands, and they didn't give a toss. I'm not cutting them any slack, Cindy. We're going to be in this awful hospital, waiting, and freaking out, and I want those drug centre *bastards* to feel one iota of the pain they've caused him, and us!"

Dissolving into fresh tears, she has Lucy save the video, in case YouTube delete it for being disturbing content – which it quite frankly is. Lucy saves it, then, rather unexpectedly, gives Em a hug, murmuring,

"Well said, lady…and I'm sorry. I know I've been a bitch… I needed someone to blame, but I was wrong. I didn't think you were good for him, but right now, I'm eating my words. And a lot of humble pie – ok? Tastes bloody awful. But someday, maybe, however this goes down, I hope I can call you a friend?"

Em frowns, but gives her a little nod – tentatively hugs her back. When they break apart, she says quietly, "We have to tell them something…" – there are rivulets of mascara-tears staining her cheeks like goth warpaint. She's gripping Zillah's limp hand, and the look on her face is fiercely protective. She's been in bits ever since she got here, blaming it all on herself, screaming down the phone at her mother, who apparently was the one pushing her towards the tough love approach, kicking him out of the house, in the first place. It's obvious, now, how much she does still care about him – I just hope it's not too little, too late… "We can't let these kids think he's dead, when he isn't."

"We don't know what he is…" I point out, and my voice sounds almost as flat and cynical as teenage Zillah's.

"No," says Cindy, frowning, "But that's why they need to know, Tom. He's made it sound like he's just slipping away, off to lala land, and they need to know that it is harsh, it's ugly, it's real and awful, and there are real people really suffering behind this shit, these bloody kids who've never even met him. Emma…take a picture. Please. If you're insisting on keeping that *revolting* video up, then take a picture of him, and put it up on your page. Show them. Or I swear to god, they will follow in his footsteps, and there will be a lawsuit, and I can't bear it!"

I agree with her. Zillah looked so scarily peaceful in that video. I mean, unhinged, obviously, with the blood all over him, but…something about his energy, the absolute peace he radiated…it's dangerous. In reality he was just high, and at the end of his tether, but like always, he managed to make it look like an advertisement for suicide. It's not ok… "Take the picture, Em. Leave his face out, please? Just show your hands or something, or the machines – whatever makes it look the fucking ugliest, without humiliating him completely. Do it, now – before anyone else sees this shit."

Em switches her phone back on, hands it to Lucy – Lucy gets a picture slanted across the bed – the ventilator and heart monitor, his prone form, chest bandaged, wires everywhere, Em's hand clutching Zillah's scuffed-up black and blue knuckles. I watch Em's trembling fingers as she goes to Instagram, and tells the world,

"PLEASE READ: Zillah isn't dead, but he's critical. We don't know anything more. Please don't blow up our phones – he needs to heal. I didn't know about that video – no one did. He scheduled it before he did the unthinkable. If you're struggling with these thoughts, please reach out. Get help. Everyone has someone who loves them – think of them, and reach out.

If there's any news, I'll update. Thoughts, wishes, prayers, all appreciated. I've never been so scared…"

She gives it the hashtag #ZillahMarsh for the sake of traction, copies the text, then posts it to both her own, and Zillah's account. Blowing out a shaky breath, she puts the phone down, folds herself around his limp arm, and bursts into tears.

YouTube take the video down half an hour later. Someone re-uploads it almost immediately, and we have the same fight about copyright-striking them. The video gets removed by YouTube anyway, though I have no doubt it'll continue to circulate on less scrupulous platforms. I borrow Lucy's phone, lock myself in the bathroom, and re-watch the saved version. I know the real Zillah's lying right there, in the next room, and the nurses even think there's a chance he might be able to hear us, but this whole place, along with his Schrodinger's Cat of a body, it creeps me out. I'm more comfortable with his recorded, fully functional presence – no matter what he's saying.

CHAPTER TWELVE

He's in a coma for the better part of five days. Honestly I've given up hope completely, as we all sit around, days blurring into nights, egg and cress sandwiches and vending machine crap. Em, however, absolutely comes through – apparently when she's not physically fighting him, she's fighting *for* him. She's even started shaving him, as well as she can with all the tubes, because she can't stand to see him growing a Depression Beard, as she's dubbed mine. She's got her cousin over a barrel about the whole Twitter thing; it wasn't really what sent him off the deep end, but it undoubtedly didn't help, so, Em guilt-trips the spiteful little twerp into becoming our personal lackey, running from house to house collecting clothes and bathroom essentials, and though we reach peak body odour on the third day, by the fourth we've actually started showering, and though morale is low, at least we don't reek, and the cousin's even brought us some homemade lasagne.

It's almost night-time, my least favourite time of day in this spooky bloody place, when the heart monitor goes erratic. At first it's only a little, just enough to set me on edge, but moments later his heartbeat shoots into overdrive, and we all launch into panic mode, hollering for the nurse. She arrives just as he starts twitching on the bed, choking on the tube in his throat, hands flailing uncoordinated at his sides – even Em's backed away in horror, but Cindy helps them get the tube out, which is awful to witness, Zillah gagging and wheezing on the thing, and even once it's out, it's like he's still choking – the nurse has to help him sit up, sponging his mouth with water, and eventually we realise his throat's just so dry and damaged, it's all going wrong in there. When she holds out a plastic cup of water with a straw stuck in it, I think grimly, *Here we go. Acid test. Has he got any grey matter left? Does he even remember how to feed himself?* His hands are beyond clumsy – he's trying to grasp the straw, or the cup, but he just keeps missing, nearly knocking it everywhere – it's as though he's gone blind, or become severely handicapped, failing hopelessly at this simplest of tasks, and it goes on and on until I think with a sickening lurch – *he's gone*. Everything I've ever known as Zillah, since we were both teenagers – this struggling mess in a hospital bed is all that's left.

I have to turn away – I can't even watch.

A moment later, Lucy tugs on my shirt. When I turn back he's got the straw in his mouth, and he's actually drinking. This goes on for quite some time – the nurse won't give him too much at once, he clearly wants more, she keeps shushing him every time he tries to open his mouth, so he's just gesticulating clumsily and irritably at the water, ignoring us all – it's like nothing exists for him except that fucking water, and I still don't know if it's a bad sign, or just completely understandable, after five days with a tube rammed down his throat.

Finally Em creeps back to the bed, takes his hand, says his name…and his reaction nearly gives me a fucking heart attack. His voice is shot, all he's got is this rusty squeak of a whisper, but he goes, *"Em?"* looking baffled, but overjoyed, like she's his favourite person on the planet. I'm so relieved it makes me dizzy; his words, his intellect – maybe they're not all gone. Em dives straight in for a hug, tears pouring down her cheeks, and he clumsily hugs her back, or tries to, then inhales sharply as the rib I broke twinges, and she leaps back, apologising. He makes an attempt at taking her hand – there really is something way, way off with his coordination, or his vision, but they get there eventually, then he just sits there, holding her hand, looking

Copyright Dorian Bridges 2024

pleased, but confused – especially when he stares round at all of us, gawping back at him like he's the puppy-dog in the window, and we're all waiting for him to do a trick.

"Why?" he whisper-croaks, about an hour later, then reaches for more water. Cindy grabs it and holds it for him before he can knock it across the room. He drinks, then tries again, whispering, "Why?" He looks at Em, looks at me, at Cindy, then frowns bemusedly for several seconds, before adding, "Alright?"

None of us normal, non-medical folk know what to tell him, but Cindy's in there, reassuring him,

"We're fine, everyone's fine, Zill, it's just you we're worried about. What do you remember?"

He frowns, shakes his head, and immediately groans, clutching his temple like his brain's splitting in half. He's gone several shades paler, sinking back on the bed – Cindy calls the nurse for pain relief, and we promptly get a bollocking for overtiring him – essentially he was starving his entire body of oxygen while he was dying on our bathroom floor, most critically his brain. Now he's trying to think again, those oxygen-starved brain-cells are getting back to work, and it's pretty clear it hurts like hell. No one knows yet what his capabilities are – what faculties he may have lost; even those scant few words have left him in agony, and his lack of coordination isn't exactly reassuring. My mind goes to some dark fucking places, wondering how many braincells he's fried – what the long-term damage is going to look like…

CHAPTER THIRTEEN

It's slow progress, after Zillah's initial Lazarus act. The headaches are killing him – almost literally; they get so bad he's too nauseous to eat, can barely keep water down at times. He looks utterly done in – cheeks hollow, dark shadows under his eyes, too tired to talk much without it kicking off another crippling headache, but we slowly manage to establish the very basic basics:

First off, Em makes him unconditionally happy. Whether it's due to oxygen deprivation, the coma, his escalating benzo habit, or simply a trauma response, the last thing he remembers with any real clarity is being with her, driving back from the park a few days before it all happened – that's why he asked if we were ok; he thought he must've crashed the car. It's a bit awkward – no one's got the heart to tell him Em actually dumped him, and she refuses to say it herself, 'cause after five days in here, facing up to the possibility of him being gone forever, she's clearly desperate to make another go of it. I'm glad…probably. I know Zillah loves her, but I also realise the emotionally charged nightmare world of a hospital is no place for making solid future plans; who knows if what she's feeling will last. For now though, Em's the sole thing that seems to bring him any joy in the depths of this, and I'm not ruining that by sharing my doubts with anyone but Lucy. The other awkward thing, of course, is that Zillah doesn't even know he tried to kill himself, much less that he announced it to over half a million people, then invited them all to his post-funeral knees-up. We shield him from that as best we can, feeding him the pre-agreed line that he did it on a whim, after a tiff with the drug treatment agency.

Copyright Dorian Bridges 2024

"That…script?" he says, after a long moment's thought, and from the look in his eyes, I reckon he's seen straight through our bullshit. It was never a *whim,* was it; he'd been thinking about suicide for months. "They didn't…uhh…?" He trails off, wincing slightly, one fist pressed to the side of his head.

"No," says Cindy. "That's why you did it."

"Hell…" he mutters. We can't get anything else out of him after that. I'm worried – I've watched his suicide notes more times than all the others put together, and maybe that's ghoulish, but…I needed to understand. I remember him saying he had a checklist, things to stay alive for, and now I have this awful feeling we've just wiped out the only thing left on it, all over again.

Lucy leans over the bed, tells him,

"We know what this means to you, Zill – it's not over 'til the fat lady sings. We *will* get through to those drug treatment fuckers – you're not alone in the fight now, you got it?"

He blinks that he understands – it's become his low energy, minimal head-movement version of a nod. He's clearly in pain, and the nurses hustle us out for him to rest – he's zonked out most of the day, every day, his brain still healing. The coordination in his left hand is officially shot, likely due to the way he landed when he crashed out – we're all hoping physio will help, but it clearly worries him, and us. Between his endless sleeping, and the sickness-inducing pain in his head, he's been essentially bedridden, and a big question mark still hangs over his physical capabilities – if this lack of coordination extends to his lower body, it could mean months – or forever – in a wheelchair. More pressingly though, his memory's become a concern – conversations have to be repeated, and during the brief periods he's alert and comfortable enough to talk, we realise how much he's struggling to find words. I hope like hell that'll improve: Zillah's obnoxiously unstoppable debate-club eloquence means everything to him, and watching him struggle with words now, getting more frustrated and emotional by the second, it's painful. He doesn't even remember the first overdose, so all the friction with Em is wiped clean, tabula rasa, which is precisely the way she seems to want it.

Pretty soon he wants to use the internet – he asks about social media, how long it's been since he posted; he's worried about the money, worried about worrying people. We tell him his phone needs charging, to get some rest, and convene outside for an emergency meeting.

"We have to tell him about that video sometime," says Lucy. "He'll only find out from some bloody kid…"

"His brain's still healing," Cindy says, "He won't handle it."

I agree with her. "You know what he's like with online drama – he'll have a fucking aneurism if we tell him there was a public note…"

There's a long silence. Then Em says,

"He needs to see the video he posted, Tom. No – I'm telling you, whenever there's drama, the only thing that settles him down is watching back what he posted, and knowing he spoke his mind clearly. If we just tell him there was a video, he's going to dwell on it, imagine the worst, and worry himself sick, but when he sees it, he'll know he spoke perfectly, and that most people have nothing but sympathy for him. We can't keep putting this off – he already knows something's up, can't you tell?"

Copyright Dorian Bridges 2024

"D'you think he'll manage it?" I ask Cindy. "It's a long video…"

She thinks about it, then digs her sunglasses out of her bag, saying, "I'll turn the brightness down, he can wear these – I think he'll be alright in that respect, but…god, you'd better be right about this, Emma…"

"I am," she says. "And I'll be right there with him – we all will."

So that's that. We break the news – he broadcast his suicide note. The heart monitor bleeps into instant overdrive – he looks horrified, but somehow, again, not entirely surprised. Em starts massaging his shoulders, whispering something in his ear – the minute the screen's in front of him, his own likeness talking unhinged bollocks, he seems, oddly, calmer. The cuts on his chest are news to him though – he could feel some stinging there, but he didn't know he was marked forever with 'DRUG WAR MARTYR'.

"Fucking *backwards*," he sighs.

He gets through the video, though in places he's clearly mortified, heart monitor bleeping wildly as his anxiety peaks, but for most of it he just stares in a sort of spacey amazement. When it's over he says, "God, that was…" – he trails off, eyebrows raised, apparently unable to even find the words. In the end he sighs, and just gestures his bemusement. "I was…so calm. So, so calm… Really thought I was about to die, didn't I?"

"You really nearly did…" I say. "Mate, you took—"

"That doesn't matter," Cindy cuts in.

"It does," he says. "Tom, that's your…*toilet*, isn't it? I killed myself, in your…umm…" He trails off, looking blank, then exasperated. It's becoming a familiar expression. The silence stretches on until I fill in,

"Bathroom?"

"Oh, hell," he mutters, despairingly. "Yeah. I killed myself, in your bathroom? I'm sorry. That was…horrible of me…"

"No, it wasn't. If you'd done it anywhere else you'd actually be dead."

"So," Lucy begins. "How do you feel now? About everything, I mean – still being here?"

He glances awkwardly up at Em. Even that movement makes him wince.

"Just tell us the truth," Em says. "No more lies, about anything. What you said, in the video, about us breaking up? It…sort of happened, just days before this. You overdosed – accidentally – and I lost my shit. I was so afraid of losing you, I pushed you away. I thought I could control how much losing you would hurt me. Turned out it made no difference – it hurt like hell, for five days, and four nights…until you came back." She smiles tentatively – takes his hand. "Zill…I know there are problems here, and maybe we can't get through them, but I am not…*capable* of letting this go. Not until we've tried every single thing there is to try. I've had a lot of time to think, and research…and if you're still hellbent on this sodding script, then…I'm willing to see how it goes – ok?"

He's smiling, but when he moves to kiss her, she places a finger against his lips, adding, "But I *cannot* live with the fear of this

Copyright Dorian Bridges 2024

happening again – can you understand that? I have to set that boundary, for my own frazzled sanity. If there is *any* part of you, right now, that thinks you might try again…I need to know. Not to walk away, but to help you. So, just tell us, please? Are you…here to stay, or have you got other ideas?"

Zillah frowns, hesitates – glances towards Cindy.

"No one's sending you back to that terrible facility," she says, guilt weighing heavy in her voice. "If you need to go inpatient, we'll find somewhere better, or monitor you at home – I'm happy to assist with the latter. We just need you to be honest with us, Zillah."

He closes his eyes for so long I'd think he was asleep, if not for the stressed-out bleeping of the heart monitor. Then he says softly,

"I died for that script, Cindy. My hand's all…fucked up, it probably always will be. My head feels like a…?" He trails off, jaw clenched – it's a good twenty seconds before he manages to carry on with, "Christ, I can't…remember the word – a…bashed up…*fruit?* I can't *think* right, I don't remember anything Em just— I mean…we broke up? For real? That's why I was in Tom's…thingie?"

Em lays a hand on his shoulder. "I never wanted it to be over, Zill – I just didn't know what else to do. Please don't stress about something that barely happened?"

"I don't *remember*," he repeats, with clear frustration. "It's like I've woken up in a…? In…umm…" He trails off, visibly at a loss. Rubbing his temple, he attempts to plough on, asking, "You know? Where it's like, this is all…? Oh *shit*, I mean—"

"A nightmare?" I guess.

"*No,*" he says, irritably, "I know I'm *awake,* Tom – it hurts too bloody much to be a…a nightmare. It's like I'm…? *Fuck,* there's a…word…?" He loses his thread again, wincing and rubbing the side of his head. He's getting paler and more exasperated-looking by the second, but by now we all know there's little point telling him to get some rest; if Zillah's got something to say, he's damn well going to try and say it, no matter how lengthy and painful the process. "Oh, shit it, man, what am I even trying to say? I know this is…*real,* but nothing feels…*trust*…*able?* Like, it's all—"

"A parallel universe?" Em suggests.

"*Yes!*" he exclaims, *"Thank you!* You keep telling me things I don't remb—*remember,* my brain's…fried*,* and every time I try to…to explain, my words just ev…? Evep—? Oh *Christ,* Em, I can't stand this!" He rakes his hand through his hair, repeating shakily, "I *died* for that script. I don't even know if I can walk or…or fuck again, the whole *world* saw me do it, and it wasn't a…? An…? Whateverthewordis? You know? A…? An…attention…plea for…atte—" He breaks off with an exasperated growl, erupting, "*Bloody hell, Tom, d'you get what I am trying to…to say here?!*" He's staring at me, pale and tense, looking like the fate of the entire universe rests on my answer.

"Cry for help?" I say quietly.

"*Fuck!*" he half sobs, burying his head in his hands, the bleeping of the heart monitor growing more hectic by the second.

"Hey, you're still healing," Em intervenes, rubbing his shoulders. "Don't get impatient with yourself."

"I *died* for that script," he mumbles doggedly through his fingers. "It wasn't a…a 'cry for help', I meant it, but…aren't things meant to get…*better,* afterwards? Am I getting this…y'know? Umm, this…*script,* or is…is all of this for nothing? Because…if it is, if my brain is…is…*mush, forever,* and they're still…saying *no,* I—I just *can't—*" His voice cracks, and he takes a shuddering breath, then whispers, "Why didn't you…let me go, Tom? You should've just *let me—*" Em moves to hug him, but he flinches away, begging,

"Get out, all…*all* of you, *please!* My head's shut—*shattering,* and I can't…*do this* right now!"

He slumps back against the bed, white as a sheet, tears in his eyes – whether it's the pain in his head, or the stress of that conversation, we barely make it out of the room before we hear him chucking his guts up into the cardboard bowl that sits eternally by his side. Em runs back in to pass the mouthwash and call for more pain relief, Cindy bringing up the rear. Lucy and I are out in the bleak white corridor, wondering what to do with the awful realisation that nothing's changed – not for Zillah.

So what the hell are we meant to do with him now?

CHAPTER FOURTEEN

The next morning is a much-needed upswing: Zillah's legs, his balance, they're in full working order – it's a huge moment. Out comes the catheter, and then he's really just in hospital because no one trusts him not to top himself again. He's only allowed social media when accompanied by Em – so far he's just posting pictures of revolting hospital food, with captions like, "Mmm. More slop that tastes like donuts and gravy all at once. It's ok – everything I eat gets thrown up within an hour anyway, the pain in my head's that bad. (Pro-tip, kids – don't kill yourself. If this is the afterlife, it's fucking shambolic.) Yes, I'm miserable, no, I'm not THAT miserable. Em's with me – always. She's shockingly perfect. Is there a word for 'luckiest guy in the world' and also 'stupidest bastard on the planet'? I need that word in my vocabulary.". These captions require the assistance of both Em, and a thesaurus, to assist in plastering over the holes in his memory. How he's going to cope when he gets back to actually speaking to a camera, no one knows: it's increasingly obvious he wants no one outside this hospital room to know about his memory issues. Numerous friends have offered to visit, only to be told, via Em, that he doesn't want to see anyone at all, for the foreseeable future.

The irrational world of social media hasn't gone easy on Em, despite Zillah's suicide-video plea to leave her alone – it all happened so fast; they saw his dumped-and-homeless video, the Twitter rumours about his using causing her to 'evict him' from the house, and then it was, 'Surprise, kids, I'm killing myself!' – now there are drama channels and Zillah's most psychotically rabid fans trying to get Em cancelled for kicking him out 'onto the streets' when he was already struggling, calling her 'The self-help guru who pushed her boyfriend to the brink', or 'Emma Lee – Clout Chasing 'Girlfriend' From Hell'. Admittedly there's a decent amount of shit being thrown at Zillah too, that he's a scheming, manipulative junkie scumbag who tried to kill himself to get back at Em, or 'just to get free drugs off the NHS', and if that's someone's goal in life, they're better left to fucking die anyway. There are some nasty, nasty words flying at both of them, but Zillah's is, by and large, a sprinkling compared to the dumper-truck of hate landing on Em's head – she's understandably in bits. Much as we weren't always her biggest fans, the way she's cared for him throughout this whole mess has cracked even Lucy's shell of wariness. Watching the world put her through the wringer now is bloody awful.

We do our utmost to shield Zillah from the ugliness, but even in his current state of hapless forgetfulness, he's not an idiot. When he sees a comment telling him to 'guard his heart' against 'that narcissistic murderess', he rapidly discovers the ongoing drama, and nearly blows a gasket, insisting on making a post informing the world that it can shut up or fuck off on the subject of his love life – "I cannot believe anyone with half a brain would misconstrue me so completely. Say what you like about me, I deserve it, I'm a goddamn imbecile, but Em? Em is fucking blameless here, and she's the ONLY thing keeping me afloat in this ghastly place. Don't even pretend you're pulling this crap in my name. Do you think this is what any of us need, right now? You make me quite literally sick…" – he's not even exaggerating; his hands are shaking so badly he has to dictate the whole post for Em to type, repeatedly blanking on words and getting even more wound up – by the time it's done he's got such a hellish headache everyone gets sent home, leaving him quietly groaning in a darkened room, painkillers maxed out. It takes a few days, but his response quiets the worst of it, and his more understanding fans seem to cheer him up, thank god – not much else is doing the job. He's losing so much weight the nurses have started forcing him to drink meal replacement shakes, which are a nauseous battle he utterly despises, and with the ongoing memory issues, his mood's getting darker by the day. And then, when we get a rare, private five minutes, he admits the real thing that's getting him down – he's dying for some heroin.

"Why d'you think I'm so happy I can still…y'know…*walk?*" he hisses at me, when everyone else leaves for the cafeteria. "All I could think was *How am I going to…to score, if I can't even walk?* Tom, you've got to get me…out of here, I'm going uns—*insane!* It'll help the pain, for fuck's sake – I need it!"

I want to cry – I am officially in Groundhog Day hell, and I just want to fucking cry. If he didn't look so broken already I'd probably pull an Em and hit him. It's not fair, I know – he nearly killed himself over how much he hates being this way, but…Jesus. He reads it all in my face, and adds in an undertone,

"Tom, I am *not* going to…to OD – not ever again. I've learned that the…whatever-the-fuck sucks beyond all…bloody— I mean, the… Umm?" He rolls his eyes, frowns at the wall for a tense eternity, then growls in annoyance, and snaps, "Oh, *shit,* d'you know what I mean? The shit that happens after you do…dumb shit?" He stares at me, jaw clenched, looking increasingly frustrated and emotional. I quietly suggest,

"Consequences?"

"*Fuck!*" he explodes. "*Yes!* The fucking *consequences.* They're not…they aren't…the right…*size?* Oh flaming *hell*, Tom, can you hear me right now? Can you hear how…how fucking—How…*thick* I sound?" He buries his head in his hands, mumbling through his fingers, "I can't hack this, man. I couldn't do it before, and now – like *this?"* When he finally sits up, he looks close to an absolute screaming meltdown, pleading, "I need to…to get *out* of here! I need some…dope, and I need my bloody…*freedom*. What the fuck is the point surfin—*surviving* all that, if you're just going to lock me up in this shitty little…room forever, with no…with nothing to det— Umm…de…? Y'know? Dis…di—"

"Distract," I intervene, before he can start punching something. He snarls with annoyance –

"*Yes!* All of fucking *that*. Nothing to *distract me* from the fact I've prem…preg—Oh *fucking hell!* – permanently? – fried myself! Get me *out*, Tom!"

"You're impossible," I tell him, and I can't even look him in the eye – can't let him see how hopeless I feel, or how hopeless he bloody well seems. "You are *literally* impossible."

"'Literally', man? How much time've you been…taking with Em? Should I be worried?" I look up, and he's managing to force a wan smile. It lasts all of half a second, then I watch his fragile mask of humour disintegrate, his eyes growing tear-bright, his voice shaking as he says, "I can't hack this, man – I can't. Am I really…asking so much? Whole bloody host—*hospital* full of drugs, and I'm still not…allowed what I need? I'm ready to throw myself out the sodding…" The word eludes him – he flings both arms out in the direction of the windows. "Why do you *all* think I'm the…the mad one? The one in the wrong? I've fought through this shit for…for nearly four fucking ded—*decades,* Tom – I can't *do it* anymore! It's not me that's broken, man, it's the— It's—? Oh *flaming hell*, the fucking s…umm…*system?* The system is *fucked,* and—"

"Do you remember saying that?" I ask, frowning.

"Oh, what?" he says wearily, running his fingers over his eyes.

"About the sys—No…never mind. It's just, I think you said that, nearly word for word, the other day. Before everything…"

The déjà vu makes me feel faintly sick – how's he meant to not repeat history, if he doesn't even remember it?

CHAPTER FIFTEEN

The psychiatric consultant sees Zillah on his own, then with Cindy, and finally Em, Lucy and I join the group. We all know this appointment's pivotal: if he's stable enough to leave hospital at all – and frankly none of us think he is, but since when did the NHS put mental health before beds – the plan is that we all shack up together, form a commune at our place, given it's the biggest of our poky Millennial abodes, and apparently it takes a village to prevent a suicide. Zillah and Em will have to be on the sofa-bed, but that's better, we think – not putting him back in the room he nearly died in. We plan to take the locks off every bathroom in the house, and all sharp objects are to be ensconced in a newly purchased lockbox. Cindy'll be there as much as she can for medical advice, and to dispense all his meds, which'll also be securely locked up. It's not exactly house arrest, but it's not exactly *not*. Now getting discharged is just up to Zillah, and what he says to this shrink – if he puts a foot wrong, there's a very strong chance he'll be sectioned, and god only knows when they'll see fit to let him out…

By the time Em, Lucy and I get in there, Zillah looks artificially casual, and Cindy looks like she's munching a lemon. I get the strong whiff of *bullshit* in the air, and I'm not surprised – he made it pretty clear he was done being locked up, so god only knows what happy-clappy positivity crap he's come out with. He's been noticeably careful with his words these past few days, ensuring nothing can be directly quoted, used to section him, but I think we all know he's not ok. The fight to get him this diamorphine script is back on, at least, conversations going back and forth over email, but it still seems to be the sole perilous hope he's clinging onto.

We're greeted by a small, mind-mannered Indian shrink, who tells us, ambitiously, that all seems fine – he just wants our views on having Zillah out of hospital. Em says she's worried, but happy to be wherever he is. I ask,

"How dangerous would it be, right now, if he used heroin? With all the meds he's on, I mean, and the damage he's done to himself?"

"Are you planning to use heroin?" the shrink asks Zillah.

"Oh hell, Tom, you're the worst…friend ever! I just need that…that *script!*" Zillah groans, casting me a stink-eye of betrayal. "If I don't get it, what the bloody hell do you est—*expect* me to do? But I'm not going to…y'know…? Umm…fucking—" he stutters to a bemused halt, rakes his fingers through his hair in exasperation, and finally gets there – "*Overdose.* I'm not going to! I'll just…smoke the stuff, I swear, that's it, I—*Fuck*, man! You know I can't do this! I'm losing my *shit* having to…to quit in here, just like that!"

"It's not 'just like that'," Cindy disagrees, "You're on your script, and they're giving you codeine for the headaches. You've—"

"Codeine, Cindy – *seriously?* You think with my tele— Umm…? Tool—Oh *shit it,* man – whatevertheword! D'you think codeine even…touches the sides? I'm fucking *miserable!*"

"Of course you're miserable, hospitals do that to everyone, and you've been so sick. Just—"

"Exactly! I'd be less sick if I had heroin, for the…the *headaches!*"

I start laughing – it's awful, but I just can't help it. God, he's been so quiet and withdrawn and not himself these past few days – hearing the dope-monster justifications come rattling out again is gutting, but somehow almost a relief.

"What is funny?" asks the shrink. "This is funny, to you?"

"No, god no, it's so far from funny, it's just…I'm glad he's still in there, if that makes any sense…"

The shrink, clearly convinced I'm a monster of a human being, looks back to Zillah, and asks,

"Would you like stronger medication, for the headaches?"

"Fentanyl," says Zillah, without missing a beat – it's one of several words scribbled on the back of his hand.

"No. No fentanyl. Perhaps a short course of morphine. Orally only. Would that stop you buying heroin, for now?"

"It…might?" Zillah says, with uncertain optimism.

"He *needs* this diamorphine script," says Cindy, and I can see she's fully on-board Zillah's crazy-train on the subject now. "Can't you put a word in? Can't you talk to these bloody people for us?"

"The drug treatment team?"

"Yes," says Cindy, pulling out her phone, "I can give you their details."

"I can most certainly send them a copy of my recommendations, yes."

"And a cover letter, please, explaining that he's barely holding it together, even now. They know we're considering our legal options."

"Yes. Good luck to you. Now, Tom and…Lucy? You are happy to have all these people in your house? Very crowded?"

"Yeah," says Lucy. "It's fine. If you really, absolutely think he's ok, we'll have him."

"You are *positive?*" the shrink says to Zillah, "*Positive* you have no further thoughts of harming yourself? Not of suicide, not of cutting?"

Zillah states, "I'm…screwed up enough, thanks. Lesson learned."

"Ok. Home you go."

Zillah fist-pumps the air, and immediately curses and curls into a groaning ball with his hands clamped over his eye socket. Everyone else just looks tense.

"Morphine," Cindy reminds the shrink. "I think we're going to need it."

Half an hour later, we're out the door with most of a flipping pharmacy, from anti-emetics to combat the headache-induced sickness, to his methadone and anti-anxiety pills, to the morphine he's managed to wangle and is clearly rather excited about, plus antibiotics to ensure he doesn't get anything nasty from all the tubes that were in him, and several vile cans of Ensure meal replacement gunk. Zillah gets an anti-emetic before Em'll even let him in her car, then at long last, we're away from this hellish place.

Copyright Dorian Bridges 2024

CHAPTER SIXTEEN

Things feel like they're getting better, at first. His headaches, which are initially debilitating, the living room kept dark and silent for much of the day, start to lessen. Em's at his side every second – my fears of her fleeing the moment he gets back on his feet are abating, and all I can hope is that Em be, for now, that one vital thing on Zillah's 'checklist' that makes life worth sticking around for – even if he has to do it sober. He's still taking the morphine, even now his headaches aren't so frequent, and none of us put up a fight on that front – we know he's not exactly coping, even with that stuff. Em caught him sneaking out in the middle of the night, obvious where he was off to – he tried to do a fucking runner, but then he really did get a headache and could barely walk home even with Em's help. Christ, he was bitter about that – he's not accepting his limitations well, much as we keep telling him how lucky he is that he's not a bloody vegetable.

"You're not even meant to say that," he says, smiling slightly. "Just because they're…whatevertheword? Vege…tative? Doesn't mean they're a *vegetable,* Tom. A cabbage? A…carrot? Hardly…umm… evolution – don't be rude. Don't upset the braindead. We are *zombies,* and should never be under…uhh… Under….? *Underwear?* Oh, fuck it, brain – *underestimated.* Don't underestimate…undead… underwear. I'm putting that on merch!"

That was a rare moment of humour. His memory's a little improved, thank god, but it's still not all there, and the times his words abandon him until he can't form a coherent sentence, and feels "stupider" than he's ever been in his life, he loses his shit completely, storming off with tears in his eyes, visibly on the brink of trashing another wall. He also keeps trying to play guitar despite his hand, the coordination that's gone – he's getting physio, but he swings between going at it so hard he pisses himself off, and giving up completely, which pisses off his physio, and everyone else.

The drug treatment agencies are ducking and diving – no one wants to tell him 'no' again, outright, not after what he fucking did – Jesus, they're awful people. You can tell they don't give a shit that he nearly died, only that he did it so publicly. So now we keep getting these letters, from both of them – Brownstown and Pacific – saying they'll write back in a week, then in another week. Cindy, always a force of nature when rubbed the wrong way, is trying to lawyer up, talking to Zillah about his savings, how much they're both willing to blow on this. Zillah's in for every penny – Em's understandably upset; they were saving that cash for a house deposit, and while it's not a joint pot, as such, Zillah made her big promises. Now, in her eyes, he's willing to blow the price of a literal house on smack.

"Why don't you get it?" I hear him saying, miserably, when another money row blows up. "I love you, Em, you know how much I want this…place with you, but this is lit—literally life or…or death for me, I'm not just—"

"You said you weren't suicidal, Zill – you said you'd never do that to me again, so how's it life or death? *How?*"

That shuts him up, or it seems to. It's another week before we realise what he's doing. He's still not really been eating, just surviving on those tins of chocolate Ensure slop, but when one of Lucy's favourite plants dies, we realise its roots were swimming in brown ooze, and start to cotton on. He hasn't been eating those, either – he's living in oversized hoodies despite the weather, but that's nothing unusual since the hospital; apparently he actually did care about those looks-based compliments, now they've started to flip the other way. He'd come out looking so gaunt and awful, we never even noticed his weight was still dropping. When I get him alone, confront him about the chocolatey shit in that plant, he says,

"Do *not* tell Em this…but I'm doing a…a *thing*. Umm? Hunger striking? Just testing myself, right now, see if I can do it – don't want to make a…a fool of myself if I'm not up to it. But I think I can, you know. I'm not hungry anyway, all this…y'know, shit going on, and I already look like hell – that's got to…umm…stand in my favour, right, when we get to court? D'you reckon it'll put the wind up them? I do. I *really* do. I looked it up. I've probably only got…" He trails off, frowns, then lapses into the vague-but-frustrated expression that punctuates most conversations since the overdose. "Three…ish…weeks?" he says, at last, then his eyes are a-gleam with unhinged fervour, as he goes on, "That's all the…uhh…internet reckons I've got in me, at this weight, if I quit eating completely. They've *got* to cave. They've *got to!*"

"Mate, this is crazy – you're just going to get yourself sectioned, surely you realise that? You'll have another tube down your throat, too, it'll be bloody awful. Just…c'mon, man, you're home now – haven't you fucked yourself up enough for one lifetime?"

His eyes narrow slightly, then he flashes me this mocking, head-tilted smile, and the chocolate Ensure I'm trying to make him drink gets dumped into another pot-plant, right in front of me.

"Zillah…what the *fuck?*"

"Oh, *you* what the fuck! What do I have to do to make you realise it's…d…umm…*diamorphine*, heroin or…or death, for me? You're not leaving me any option but…death right now, are you! How clear have I got to…to make it, man? I do not want to be…*alive*, unless I am fucking…*medicated right!"*

I open my mouth, but he holds up an imperious finger, and shakes his head.

"No, Tom. No more of your bloody phol— Phisol…? Oh *fuck*, whatevertheword *bollocks* – you know what I mean! Don't *argue* with me, man. You've never been in…inside my head, meaning you have…zero right to speak on it. And I can't…argue with you, can I? Not anymore. Not like…*this* – no fucking…words left. So just leave it, alright? 'Cause if I was a…a dog, Tom, the state I'm in, you'd fucking see it. I'm not…eating, my brain, and my memory, and my…my fucking…my…*goddamnit!* – my…IQ? – all of it, down the *shitter,* you'd just let me go. Bullet to the…brain – that's all I'm good for. Don't you *dare* ask me what the fuck – *you* what the fuck! I wrote a…a *sign.* "Do not re…rejuv—?" He shakes his head, visibly fuming, then snaps, "*Why* would you bring me back like this, man, all…messed up and…and useless! I thought we were friends!"

"You remember that sign? When did you—"

"I *don't!* Lucy slipped up, told me about it. I thought of…of *everything,* Tom. I took a…cocktail to…bypass the bloody….Nalex…*whatever*, and I wrote that sign. Should've put a bag over my head, too. Idiot. Fucking *idiot."*

I just get up and walk away. I thought there was nothing he could throw at me that I hadn't already been through with him, but at this point, I just can't deal with him anymore. Even at uni he wasn't so completely fucking defeatist; I think that was one of the things I liked about him, honestly. He was this confused kid with ungodly issues, but in spite of all that, even at his worst, he still had hope that someday, somehow, things might get better. I don't know why he feels like he can confide in me about this shit, but he gives me it full whack the next day, everything he's been thinking – classic unfiltered Zillah. It's obvious how much he's been holding back, even before the suicide attempt; when he said that thing about 'every time I'm sober, I wish that I was dead', he truly meant it...and he wrote that lyric six years ago. The morphine isn't enough, he tells me, head in his hands, voice shaking with frustrated tears – he's trying, but it's just not *fucking enough* – practically writhing with shame, he admits that the oversized hoodies he's living in aren't just hiding how thin he's getting: he's been busting up safety razors, cutting himself with them, something he'd barely even thought about in over a decade.

"Tom, I can't even tell you how...*angry* I am, all the fucking time – I can't put it into words, because I can't...fucking...*make* words anymore, can I? I've still got the...y'know? The...ADHD...thought-speed, but now it's like my...like my brain's tied to this rusty fucking...trek—*tractor*. I'm angry with the...*system*, I'm angry with all of you for...for keeping me here, and I fucking dest—*detest* myself for what's happened to me! If I wasn't doing this, right now, I'd be ousid—*outright* killing myself – or *you*, honestly, and I'm not...over-speaking that. I love you, Tom, but I...I hate you enough to spill...*blood* right now. Better that it be...y'know...mine..."

"I've lost the plot," he concludes, finally meeting my gaze, and he doesn't even need to say it. It's all right there, in his eyes. They're flat, shut down, not like heroin grogginess, more like the disturbingly empty gaze of a fresh corpse. *Uncanny valley*. I'm not exactly surprised by what he's saying, but I am seriously fucking concerned. He's about the least physically violent guy I've ever known, outside of the awful shit he does to himself, but looking into his eyes right now, I don't even recognise him. His thousand-yard stare is beyond unsettling: I make a mental note to make sure all the knives are still safely locked up…even if I hate myself for thinking about him like this – as a legitimate threat to us.

"I'm trying not…not to kill myself again," he says, and sighs – "*Solely* because I don't want to do that to Em, but it's going to…happen, whether I like it or not – do you think I wanted to…to start doing *this*, after all this time? Em's going to fra—*freak* when she works it out! But…*fuck,* Tom, I've never been able to…cope with this s…umm…sobriety shit—shitshow, why does anyone think that's going to change? I mean, Christ, Lucy's on some…y'know…? Anti…misery pill? Isn't she? And it's been a…a miracle for her, right? Well what d'you think would happen if I fush—flushed it all away, then…locked her up in this…*place,* so she couldn't get more? D'you think she'd be ok? D'you think it would *help,* everyone telling her, 'Oh Lucy, I know you'd been…happy and…and…cess—*successful,* on that med, and now you're sobbing and…shrieking and…slicing yourself up, but I'm telling you, you're *so much better off* without that…that nasty dirty…*stupid-people drug!* One day at a time, Luce – isn't it better than being happily… properly…m…umm…medicated!' – do you *see* yet, Tom? Do you fucking *see* what's going on in my…in my *head* – what would go on in the head of anyone who needs a med to…to *function,* and can't fucking have it? And then you tell me I'm…*crazy* for…whatever-the-word-is? Umm? Fucking…*hunger striking?* – but Christ, man! I am only doing what I need to do to…to stay alive! Why doesn't anyone understand this!"

He rants himself right into a full-blown panic attack, and I have no idea what to do, or say. I just hug him, let him get it out of his system, but he never seems to feel any better – he just goes blank, mumbles an apology, then shuffles stiffly off to be alone – he hates it when anyone sees him getting this emotional; I know full well he won't look me in the eye for a week. The most tragic thing is, I can't deny there's at least some truth to his madness; those first forty minutes a day when the morphine hits, there's an improvement. He decides to do stuff – go outside, sit in the sunshine, take a ride to the park…but after that little window of time, it's back to the bleakness and the blankness, and more pot-plants are turning up with horrible chocolatey sludge in them, then he passes out on the stairs from lack of food, nearly breaks his bloody neck, *still* won't fucking eat, and at that point we have to admit that we can't cope with him. We aren't coping with him.

It's in the middle of the most dreaded discussion of all – where to send him now, what to do with him, whether it's back to the hospital, whether it's Cindy's place with a fucking feeding tube in his face – that's when the phone rings. Cindy answers it, dismally…but her expression rapidly shifts to shock, and she puts the thing on speaker.

It's a drug treatment agency – one we've never even heard of. Turns out they're not far away, and they've caught wind of his case, which is *not* hard, given the online shitstorm he's stirred up, the discussions going on all over gossip channels about 'The YouTuber who uploaded his own suicide', and ''Drug War Martyr' – The Tragic Case of Zillah Marsh' – whether he was right or wrong, whether prescription heroin should exist, whether it actually helps people, or is just state-sanctioned poison. Even with the headaches and his dodgy memory, the second he got out of hospital Zillah was fuelling the fires, spending every minute he physically could reading out pre-scripted inflammatory rants about Tory Britain, the dark truths of inpatient facilities here, the disease of the stiff upper lip, particularly when it comes to men and mental health, and the fact suicide's about the biggest killer of youngish blokes, and no one's even talking about it. He goes on endless scripted tirades about the disease of addiction, the depressing statistics and the necessity for a variety of treatment options, not just NA meetings, dismal methadone scripts or fuck off. He's got a good message, undeniably, but from the comments it's obvious every word he says is being overshadowed by the fact he's visibly dying in front of them – the internet only sees him every few days; his weight loss is even starker on screen, not to mention the fact he refuses to explain his ongoing memory issues, giving no reason whatsoever as to his sudden, post-hospital switch from improvisational ramblings to scripted essays, which has many people so confused there's a small but building conspiracy that he's being held hostage. And then Zillah, like the unstoppable motor-mouth he still is, cops in a moment of total exasperation to the fact he's hunger striking now – "Death or diamorphine – fuck these cunts, I'm not through with them. If they're going to kill me, I'm making them watch." He just drops it in a comment, like it's nothing, and though he deletes it five minutes later, it's already been screenshotted and uploaded to Twitter. The drama refuels – the pressure on Brownstown and Pacific redoubles.

So when this new place, Priority Healthcare, phone us up, it turns out they've had Brownstown in their ear. That place is *desperate* right now; they can't handle the influx of rude reviews, angry emails, kids turning up on the doorstep staging protests and throwing eggs – whipped up by Zillah's continued tirades, his most psychotically obsessed fans are getting more vitriolic – and organised – by the day, and are making their lives a misery: they just need it over. Unfortunately, they legitimately don't have space for him, nor do they feel it ethical to take him on as a patient after all this; it sets a precedent – top yourself on camera, and you'll get through the doors. So instead, they're leaning on this new place to clean up their mess.

Priority Healthcare provide diamorphine-assisted treatment, and wonder of all wonders, they're actually offering it to him, long-term, on the condition that he *shuts this shitstorm down,* before the 'cease and desist' letters start flying in all directions.

Em's Googling them as we speak, making sure they're for real, that it's not some kind of awful prank. The phone number checks out. It's kosher. They ask Cindy to call his current agency, give permission for his medical notes to be transferred, and say they want him there for an assessment tomorrow morning – if all goes well, they'll actually give him his first supervised dose. Their only condition is that he comes in without taking his methadone or morphine first. Cindy warns them about the headaches – they advise ibuprofen, paracetamol; nothing more.

"Holy shit!" Lucy erupts, the second Cindy hangs up the phone. She's shaking her head, grinning like she just shot her worst enemy in the balls. "Holy *fucking* shit. He did it. The lunatic actually did it!"

We go to break the news to Zillah – he's upstairs in the spare room, editing another video rant. When Cindy tells him what's going on, he can't even speak. He just walks over to her, gives her a hug, gets a bit tearful – I ask him if he'll please go and eat something now, and there's instant wariness in his eyes.

"Is this a trick?" he asks. "That…umm…blood test – was it bad? Was it bad, and now you're all…bullshitting me?"

"Zill, there's no bullshit," Em says, taking his hand, "I promise – no more lies, remember? If the blood test was bad, they'd be carting you off right now, and I wouldn't stop them. So what do you want to eat?"

"It's *tomorrow?*" he asks, still wary. "We're going to this place *tomorrow*, and you…you swear they're giving me a shot, if they like me?"

"They don't have to like you," Cindy says, smiling slightly, "Thank god. They just have to know you're there without taking any drugs first. It's 11am. You can do it."

He nods, smiles out of the window for a minute, then says,

"Wow. I guess we're going for a…umm…McDonalds then, if that's ok?"

Cindy gives him an ecstatic hug, then we're out the door for some much-needed grease. But when we get there, it's like he just can't do it – he picks three chips to pieces and drinks his Coke, but he still won't fucking eat. Em's having an increasingly loud freak-out, right in the middle of the restaurant, telling him he looks like death, that his bones are jabbing her in the night, that she's shit scared again, until he hisses at her,

"Dear god, will you stop…embarrassing me, *please!* I don't want to…to *explain* this to you!"

"Explain what? You've got everything you need, and you still won't bloody eat! I don't get you! Do you really want to die that badly? *Why?* Why are you doing this to me!"

"I'm not doing it to…to anyone – I don't want it! I'm not hungry!"

"You have to be, Zill, it's been—"

"I won't believe it, until it…*happens* – why don't you get that? These people are…are such slimy, lying…*bastards* – I don't trust them as far as…as…oh, *whatever!* It's too much, too fucking…hectic. I feel sick. Take me home."

Cindy sighs, and starts bagging up the food, telling him, "You're bloody well eating some of this on the way back, Zillah – if this goes on one more day, I'm having you tubed. And you will *hate it.*"

He rolls his eyes, takes the tiniest bite of a chip, chews it with a grimace, and eventually has to swallow it with a swig of Coke like it's a pill. He physically shudders, and shoves the rest back to Cindy. It's obvious he's not faking – he was exactly the same at uni before his exams, and now he's got himself this twizzled up about tomorrow, being on the very verge of 'death or diamorphine', his stomach's flat-out not having it.

When we get home though, I have another crack at it, showing him everything online about the place he's going. I tell him about the merry hell his fans are unleashing on Brownstown; the fact that place is pleading with every drug agency in the county to medicate him into submission. At last I get a genuine smile out of him, and after a bit of a debate, he gets an Ensure out of the kitchen, and drinks it.

Copyright Dorian Bridges 2024

CHAPTER SEVENTEEN

We get the train into the city centre the next morning – Priority Healthcare's only a stone's throw from the station, and thank god, 'cause apparently he'll have to be supervised for quite some time, meaning multiple daily trips up here, but for what they're offering, Zillah doesn't mind too much. He does, however, mind the fact he isn't allowed any opioids beforehand. Lately he's been waking up between 6 and 7am to hassle us for his methadone, then by eight it's the morphine, irrespective of headache status. Without any of that, it's obvious he's feeling it. He's practically on his knees to Cindy to let him have *something*, one of them – she has to explain literally five times over that he *will* be piss tested for freshly imbibed methadone, that she will not lie for him on the morphine front, and that he's an inch away from ruining everything he fought so hard for. I can't even tell if he's having a particularly bad day with his memory, or if he's just that freaked out by the first jitters of withdrawal, but it's all going in one ear and directly out the other – the argument goes round and round all morning, getting uglier and uglier. Cindy is a miraculously tolerant woman.

By the time we're ready to leave, he's shivering in an oversized hoodie, and has been in and out of the bathroom at least five times. He claims he's getting a headache, too – no one believes him, but when he gets that whiter-shade-of-pale thing going on, we realise he actually is in pain. Cindy hands him two ibuprofen and an Ensure to take it with, and the look on his face is just priceless; you couldn't insult him more if you tried – "Not even…codeine? Not even *fucking codeine?!*" He gets so upset we all have to leave the kitchen while he has a minor breakdown at the table. We just about get him out of the

Copyright Dorian Bridges 2024

house on time though, and after he spends the majority of the train journey locked in the bathroom, you can see he's given himself a pep-talk – he's determined. Shivering in the depths of his jacket, he grabs Em's hand, and just starts powerwalking in the direction of the clinic.

The interior of Priority Healthcare's a bit swankier than your average NHS waiting room, but somehow it's still got that grim feeling about it – the plasticky chairs, the fliers stacked against the wall, the smell of disinfectant. Zillah's rubbing his temple with one fist, eyes squeezed shut behind oversized sunglasses, occasionally whispering, "This was a…a terrible idea, man… Why didn't you just let me get some gear? Why do they make it all so…*impossible?* This is fucking…*torture!*"

"It's only this once," Cindy tells him, yet again, with the patience of a saint. "Once they've got your dose figured out, everything'll be easier."

And then, at last, they let him in for his assessment. We watch him disappear through the locking doors, one arm wrapped tight around his bony frame, the other still clutching his head like his brain's about to fall out. All in all, he reminds me of how we'd all be on a Sunday morning towards the end of our rave career; running on empty, rocking the comedown from hell – he's been a nightmare this morning, but I feel for him.

All we can do now is cross our fingers, and pray he doesn't say, or do, anything stupid enough to get himself blacklisted by this agency too. Em's tapping away on her phone, getting ready to tell the world he's got his meds, and that – as per Zillah's agreement – it's time to stop the abuse of Brownstown and Pacific drug treatment centres. Zillah's calling it the 'Troops Stand Down' speech.

Copyright Dorian Bridges 2024

As I sit holding Lucy's hand in that disinfectant-smelling room, I think how bloody amazing it is what you can achieve, when enough mad people band together behind quite possibly the maddest one on Earth. What Cindy said in that café was true – we've all thought, over the years, that Zillah chucked his potential away on the most vacuous of 'jobs'…but if it saves his life, I swear I will never mock his career choice again…

CHAPTER EIGHTEEN

ONE MONTH LATER

It's been a few days since I heard from Zillah, when he wakes me up at 5am on a Sunday, with an oddly manic, whispery phone-call, summoning me off to the local woods – *"Now?"* I groan, incredulous. *"Now!"* he whispers, and before I can say anything else, he hangs up on me. For anyone else, this 5am demand would get an instant 'Fuck off', but when it comes from Zillah, it could mean literally anything, from 'He's found something big and dead in those woods, and cannot rest until he's made me look at it too', to 'There's internet drama kicking off, and he's seconds away from hanging himself on a tree' – with all that creepy whispering, and the general air of highly-strung paranoia, he really did sound a bit off: I groan my way out of bed, and start getting dressed.

Things have, overall, been pretty miraculous since the Great Diamorphine Victory…though it has been a slow-rolling, and not always smooth process. Turns out the preconceived notions I – along with Em and Lucy – had about the diamorphine script were way off. Even Zillah didn't entirely know what he was getting himself into; it's not a soft option, at all – he's getting clean, safe, dose-measured stuff, but new Tory legislation is making life for diamorphine script recipients harder and harder. For the foreseeable future, Zillah will not be allowed to take any of the stuff home with him, meaning he *only* gets supervised, pre-arranged doses, at Priority Healthcare…and they're only open from nine 'til six. That means, if he's craving, or anxious, or something goes wrong, outside of those hours, self-medication is no longer an option. He's been struggling with that quite a bit, but the support they're giving him at Priority is genuinely bloody impressive – particularly in contrast to his experiences at Pacific. Though they're not open all hours, Priority have a 24-hour crisis line, where, instead of chatting to a random Samaritan who can do nothing but nod and sympathise, there's a trained member of staff, who can access his notes, give genuinely useful advice, and so far – touch wood – they've managed to talk him off the relapse ledge every time.

On the less positive side, however, they were cautious to a fault with titrating his dose – it meant nearly a week of him waking up the whole house at 7am with his withdrawal-induced panic attacks and general flip-outs; by the fifth day he'd *really* had enough – between the withdrawal, and the heightened anxiety it always gives him, he'd been up all night, had thrown up twice, and at that point, Kamikaze Mode was unleashed. He stated that the whole diamorphine plan had been a 'stupid fucking waste of time', that this 'shitty world' wasn't 'built for him anyway', that he was getting straight back on street gear, and 'if it kills me, GOOD!' – and then he tried to storm out of the house, which, obviously, none of us were about to let him do – not in that state of mind.

The whole thing broke down into a pretty ugly tussle – he even threw a punch at me, but given I did a few years kickboxing in my youth, and Zillah's Fight Total stands at precisely zero, it didn't land…but it did piss me off enough to get him in a headlock in the middle of my front garden, shortly followed by jamming my thumbnail into a few particularly painful pressure points until he'd stopped struggling, and conceded to wait 'til he was dosed and stable, before making any rash decisions. He wasn't exactly chuffed with me though – another hole got punched through my bathroom wall, and after that, Priority conceded to give him a small dose of methadone every evening, so he wouldn't wake up certifiably insane each day: a sigh of relief was breathed by all.

Once he was stable on his meds though, there were still…*quibbles.* It turned out Zillah had basically signed his life away that first day, meekly agreeing, in a haze of dope-fiend desperation, to all sorts of things he vehemently disagreed with after the fact. For one thing, they were insisting he see a therapist there weekly, which sounded ideal to the rest of us, but Zillah was *seriously* against it, saying therapy had only ever made him worse in the past, and now he straight up wasn't doing it. Their second request, was that after making his obligatory video to settle down the online drama, he was to take a full month's break from his furious video shitposting – just one month off, to 'get some perspective, and let things cool down'. Again, reasonable, but Zillah was *fuming*, his justifications ranging from financial obligation to 'freedom of speech' to 'no one else gets forced to quit their fucking jobs, do they?', to which I pointed out that nobody else's 'fucking job' involved riling up teenagers into throwing eggs at drug workers. All in all, I think Priority Healthcare were starting to seriously regret taking on Motor-Mouth as a client at all, and in the end, they put the boot in; it was comply, or be downgraded to the same miserable methadone script he'd been on prior to the overdose – no more diamorphine, not from them – not ever again. That got him where it hurt – he'd had a few tastes of their perfectly pure, legal, safe and stress-free dope by then, and he wasn't giving it up easily – he grumbled, but conceded to do as he was told.

The new therapist, despite Zillah's initial shock and repulsion at being 'preached to by an infant', has turned out to be one of the best things that ever happened to him. She may be young, but youth brings new ideas, and an open mind – rather than digging through the distant past, making him talk over his traumas, and generally sending him into an emotional tizzy of self-destruction, like all his previous therapists had, she's been focusing solely on the here and now; coping strategies, healthy alternatives, harm reduction. She got his prescribed benzos increased, to stop him buying them off the street, and Em's been keeping the majority of the things in a combination-lock safe, to stop him bingeing – if he has a Big Emotion, these days, the rule is, he has to wait. Ideally it's five minutes before he takes anything, but even if he only makes it to twenty seconds, it's still a victory – a small but vital bit of evidence that he's more capable than he thinks. Combined with walking meditations and grounding exercises, her plan is that, little by little, he shifts his freakout coping mechanism from drugs, into learning how to 'self-soothe'.

Another big revelation was that she's got him queued up for an autism assessment, given this therapist thinks he's a bit *more* than just the particularly 'extra' case of ADHD we'd always assumed – apparently it's only been in the last eleven years that you could be diagnosed with both, and in typical Zillah fashion, it now seems he hit every branch on the neurodiversity and dysfunction tree on his way into this world…and autism would explain a lot. These days I regularly find myself wishing like hell this therapist had been around while we were at uni – it's a bitter pill to swallow, the knowledge that he could have been helped, and that so many of his problems today might've been nipped in the bud, or dodged completely, if only we'd known what those problems really *were*. I find the 'what if' of it all an acutely depressing brain-spiral, but Zillah, who generally prefers vengeance over brooding, is already scripting fresh cannon fodder on the subject, for when his Online Shitposting Ban expires.

The new therapist's other impact on his life is – I suspect – the reason he's currently in the woods at 5am, doing god knows what. He goes up there nearly every morning now, though he's oddly cagey on what he *does there*, beyond, 'It gets a bit…weird, Tom, alright? Don't be nosy. It's helping. That's all you need to know.' Whatever mad business his therapist's got him doing though, he's been noticeably more chill since he started these pre-dawn excursions.

A milestone moment came after two weeks on the script, when he and Em moved out of our living room, and went back home…which was probably timely; they seem – tentatively – to have stopped going at each other's throats, and there was *a lot* of sex going on. Loud, joyous, celebratory sex – I don't know how much more our creaky old sofa-bed, or Lucy's sanity, could've taken. Zillah seemed happy to have his own space back, though he was depressed by seeing his car gathering dust on the driveway; he only bought the thing – his first really decent motor – a few months prior to the suicide attempt, and now he's got a hand that may never be able to reliably shift gears, and a brain that may or may not be too 'glitchy' to be trusted behind a wheel ever again.

We'd all gotten used to his dodgy memory, and the occasional 'brain glitch' that came along with it – those times when, for a brief period, his memory seems to get worse than ever, he goes a bit strange and blank, loses all his words, then freaks out about it; we'd frankly just accepted it as part of the New Zillah Package…but it's starting to look like the hospital overlooked rather a lot, with him – most likely assuming he was a lifelong drugs casualty, and not worth investigating too hard – until now:

Twelve days ago, some *absolute* scumsack of a troll released the most vile video, which has gone depressingly viral, and the fallout has been a *shitshow*. It was gleefully entitled 'Zillah Marsh Is A Trainwreck Now!' and was nothing more than an eleven-minute-long compilation of him, in the background of Em's livestreams, the one place he's felt comfortable enough to appear unscripted, blanking on words, blank-staring, and generally glitching out, the highlight being the point he got so confused he tried to walk into the fucking broom closet. The little psychopath who uploaded that thing must have filmed *hours* of footage; the editing made the whole thing look far, far worse – and more constant – than it really is, bringing floods of morbidly curious bastards to Em's livestreams, all salivating to witness Zillah's brain going wrong. When *he* saw the thing, he was so bloody mortified, he immediately clambered out of an upstairs window and ran off in a blind panic to get obliterated…though it seems a guardian angel got in his way; he managed to eat a few handfuls of illicit benzos, but he was shaking so much, all the heroin got spilled on the carpet, which was, in his eyes, he later told me, a 'rock bottom' even bleaker than the bloody overdose.

It took us days to scrape him off the ceiling about the whole thing – his phone was blowing up, the internet nasties were calling him 'brain damaged', 'intellectually crippled', and basically every slur and insult that has always been his greatest insecurity – he spent the better part of three days with his head down the toilet. The upshot, however, was that the video gave Em something to show his doctor, regarding these mysterious 'glitches', and now he's meant to be booking himself in for more scans at the hospital. The doctor Em spoke to suspected a mild type of seizure, and if he's right, medication might mute the whole thing considerably. Whether it'll be enough to get him back behind the wheel though, only time will tell.

And that, more or less, covers it – today marks 90 days since the suicide attempt, which makes him 89 days clean, as far as ingesting street heroin…and even though much of that time was due to the hospital stay, then our 'house arrest', it's still a huge deal – even when

Copyright Dorian Bridges 2024

he was 'sober', it was rare for him to manage this long without a single minor slip-up. We've all agreed we're doing a big meal out for his hundredth day, and he seems pretty determined not to blow it. If this strange whispery phone-call means he's fallen off the wagon with an undignified thump, something must've gone really, strikingly wrong…

As I reach the woods, it's 5.48am, and the sun's risen just enough to make the gloom between the trees only faintly foreboding. I try Zillah's phone – he doesn't answer. Cursing under my breath, I get out of the car, and start following the track into the semi-darkness of the trees.

The path is damp, mud squelching underfoot, leaves dripping on my head, but despite my extreme reluctance in the matter of being out here at this hour, I have to admit there's something magical about it, the mingling freshness of camphor and petrichor and ozone – it smells like the whole world's brand new…

As I get further into the woods, mostly looking down at my phone, typing out a *Where the fuck are you?* text, I start to hear screaming. It sounds like someone is seriously losing their shit, and that 'someone' sounds a lot like Zillah.

"*FUUUUUUCKKK!*" he goes, "*YOU FUUUCKKING CUUUUNT!*" – shortly followed by, "*GOD* I HATE YOU SO MUCH! YES, YOU, YOU FUCKING...FUCKING BUMBAG! RUUUUUN! RUN AWAYYYY! YOU BASTARDS ARE...ARE...*FREAKS OF NATURE!*"

"Oh bloody hell…" I mutter, wondering what on Earth I'm walking into. I can hear no voices bar Zillah's – if he's relapsing, it's clearly on something weirder – and livelier – than the usual… I round a large oak tree, and there he is, completely alone, literally leaping up and down in a triumphantly deranged war-dance, in a small clearing, waving a large stick about and, I rapidly realise, cussing out every squirrel in a five-mile radius.

"Uhh, Zill?" I say, and he spins on the spot, his expression a horrified mirror of my own, until he realises it's only me, and he starts laughing, dropping his stick and bounding over to give me a hug.

"Nearly gave me a fucking…heart attack!" he says, as we break apart. He sounds a bit hoarse – god knows how long he'd been screaming at squirrels – and he looks rather manic, but otherwise he seems surprisingly compos mentis, all things considered. "Don't…sneak up on me, next time!"

"I don't think I was sneaking, mate – you were *very* loud. Are you…? I mean, is this…*normal* woodland behaviour, or should I be concerned, right now?"

"No?" he says, looking confused, as though I didn't just witness the most batshit spectacle I've encountered in years. "This is what I *do*, in the…y'know? Umm…tree-place? – I thought I told you that…didn't I?"

"You told me your new therapist makes you come here every morning, and that it 'gets a bit weird'? I knew you were being cagey about something, but…*this?* Really? The way you've been dodging the subject, I thought you'd be singing Kumbaya…or having a wank. Possibly both..."

He laughs, shaking his head, then he leans closer, and stage-whispers, *"Not…out here. Not on a…a Sunday."* Drawing back, he grins, then adds, "Nearly fucking…shat myself, when you said my name. If anyone ever sees me, out here, doing…*this*, I'm bate—blatantly getting s…uhh…*sectioned?* You didn't… y'know…film me, did you?"

I shake my head. "Don't be paranoid. You know I never remember to film anything worth filming."

"'Just because you're paranoid,'" he sombrely quotes, "'don't mean they're…?' Uhh… Not a… *Umm?"* He rolls his eyes – "Bollock it."

"Poignantly spoken."

"Don't be an arse, man."

"Sorry, Zill. It's just…I'm still trying to work out if you're…you know? Actually *ok*, right now?"

"Oh, what the fuck is that supposed to mean?" he demands. "I told you, *she* makes me—"

"Cuss out squirrels at maximum decibels, at 6am on a Sunday, waving a massive phallic stick around like you're summoning sexual gremlins? *Really* – you're going with that?"

"Oh *god,* Tom – don't be so bloody n…umm…narrow-minded! I'm meant to let out my…y'know…emotions, somewhere I won't get…arrested. I just put my own…*icing*, on the…the recovery ritual, a little bit. Screaming's good for the soul. Squirrels don't fucking care, not really. Anyway, it's…working, isn't it?"

"That's what I'm trying to observe and decipher, to be honest…"

He side-eyes me. "Are you just…tossing big words out, to be a…a cunt, right now?"

"Jesus, Zill – you phoned me at 5am, all whispery and strange – I don't know if I'm coming or going, let alone using big words to bedevil you…"

"Bedevil! Fuck off. You *are* doing it on prep—on purpose!"

"Mate, *are you high* – yes or no? Answer that, and I'll stop being so weird with you, alright?"

He watches me with a frown, then says, a touch too innocently, "On life? Ab…absolutely. Every morning!"

I keep watching him. After a moment of squirming, he glances awkwardly at his right hand, just for a split second, and I realise for the first time, undistracted by flailing sticks and yelling, that there's a clumsy bandage protruding from his coat sleeve.

"Ah, hell. What the fuck have you done to yourself now? Is this why you called me?"

"*Umm*… Would you…believe me, if I said it was a…uhh…? Fuck. I've got no words except 'punting'. A punting…accident?"

"Right – of course. Zillah Marsh, infamous punting champion. C'mon, man, what really happened?"

He throws his head back, flings out his arms, and groans dramatically at the sky. "They…*fucked with me,* man! They *fucked* with me, and I got…fucked off, and some…shit got fucked up. End of…umm…thingie."

"I didn't ask for the sweary cliff-notes, Zill. Do you need a hospital, or just a better bandager?"

He scowls at the mud for a moment, sighs heavily, and slouches off to the side of the path, dumping himself down on a fallen tree, and digging in his pocket for his new Health-Upgrade weed vape, which produces no smoke, and minimal stink, while also packing a punch like weed got reinvented by the Devil himself. I follow after him, sitting down and asking,

"Who's fucking with you? Is this about that bloody video again?"

He visibly shudders, wincing slightly at the mention of That Video. I inwardly curse myself for bringing it up; I have no intention of even telling him how many mutual friends have phoned me this week, wanting to know exactly how bad the 'brain damage' is, and whether he's even capable of coherent conversations anymore – *that's* how bad that bloody video made it look…

"*Fuck,*" Zillah mutters, throwing me a jittery glance. "Don't even…mention that shit, man. Not right now…"

I apologise, and wait for him to finish vaping himself into a gentler dimension. Finally, he says,

"I…punched the safe."

"The safe? With the drugs in?"

He nods, regarding his bandaged hand with a grimace.

"Did you get in?"

He scowls – "Do I *look* like the sort of…of superthug who can take down a reinvent—*reinforced* steel door?"

"I'm dodging that question for the sake of your ego. So you *didn't* get into the safe?"

He shakes his head, and takes a vast drag on the vape.

"Ok? So, all this…flaily-demented, squirrel-bellowing shit – this is just the New You, enjoying his time out in the woods? *Wholly sober?"*

"Uhh…*sort of"* – he pulls a face. "You might be getting a…a slightly esc—*elevated version,* right now." He frowns, sighs, then glumly confesses, "I punched the safe….and when that didn't work, I…delved down the…the sofa-cracks, generally…umm…ransacked the house, and found a couple of pills. Didn't…y'know, recognise them, but thought they must be mine. No. Bollocks. Fucking…*Pro-Plus*, wasn't it?" He shudders, giving me a wide-eyed stare of profoundly unwarranted horror.

"You mean…*caffeine? You* phoned me, at 5am, all whispery and demented, because you accidentally took two caffeine pills? Jesus, Zill – I thought you could handle your shit on the most extreme of substances!"

He rolls his eyes – "Tom, you *know* I've been avoiding strim—*stimulants* like the…you know, like…bumboils, for years! You'd be all…'whispery and demented' if you'd just popped two…super-strength…caffeine pills, after decades of absolut—Umm…*abstinence.* In fact, fuck abstinence, if this is where it gets you! It took me two…two Ubers to get here, man! I literally…puked

Copyright Dorian Bridges 2024

while waiting for the first one, and it drove off without me. I am *not having fun!*"

I just start laughing. He rolls his eyes again, and passes me the vape. I hit it a couple of times, then ask,

"So…what started this mad rampage, that's led you down a life of violent crime and caffeine-addled squirrel-abuse?"

He scowls, saying darkly, "Prot—umm…Priority fucking…Healthcare. They *really* fucked me over. It—"

"Ah *hell*, mate – you haven't dug your grave with them too, have you? Look, if you get blacklisted by three agencies in one county, that's starting to look like a *you* problem, so what the fuck did you—"

"I did *nothing!* Well…besides forget. Which is more or less a…y'know? Pre…existing medical…*thing*, in my case, isn't it? You'd think they'd be a bit frog—forgiving, but instead, they….they—"

"You *forgot?* As in, to turn up – for *dope?* Since when—"

"Oh god, Tom, please *fucking*…shut up and let me…finish! I had a bit of a…a forgetful…benzo snafu, on…umm…Wednesday? Double-dosed myself. Maybe more? Who knows. All I *know* is, I was a bit…sleepy? So I got there, fell asleep on the…the counter, for probably… half a second, I don't know, but they s— They fucking s—! *Ugh, hell,* man, I'm so…*pissed* I can't even find my words." He blows out a long breath, shakes his head, and groans, "Christ…this *caffeine!* My heart's beating like it's playing black…black metal!"

I slap him on the back – "I don't think you're about to die. Come on – what horrors have Priority unleashed on you? They can't have kicked you out, just for that, surely?"

He shakes his head. "No...thank god. But I did get a...a whacking great...*lecture* about being an...'overdose risk', and after that? No drugs. None. They wouldn't doze—*dose* me. I thought they meant, like, *at all*, you know? Fuck off 'til...t...umm...tomorrow? Instant panic attack. Wasn't pretty. Finally they told me I could wait, and...umm...'sober up'" – he curls his lip in disgust, "I *wasn't even...high!* I was just a bit...sleepy! But I had to *sit,* on their...grotty fucking sofa that smells like...like dopefiend-feet and old...ashtrays, and just...y'know, fiddle with myself for the next three hours, until I seemed—"

"'Fiddle with—?'"

"Oh, you *know* I'm being...met...metamorph...*whatever* – I had to *sit there*, on that stinking fucking...couch, for three hours, getting all...goosebumpy and shev—shivery, before they'd let me at my dose, and now? Well...now I'm on a sodding *taper.*"

"Wow," I say, passing back the vape, my brains already half scrambled – "Spoken like congealed doom. I think I'm a bit stoned for this – are they tapering your diamorphine, or—"

"Oh, keep up, man – it's the...umm...the benzos, *obviously!* You know full well this wouldn't be a...a polite little...*grumble* if it was anything else. Full on Grot—Godzilla moment, I'd be having, if it was the diamorph they were taking away. But—"

"So it's not as bad as it could be?"

"Urgh, *Tom*, you really are the...the *worst!* I'm complaining here – don't pact—*placate* me with...bullshit! I don't want to go back to buying...benzos off the street, but I bloody *will* if they take them all away from me!"

"Or," I intervene, "Just a suggestion – you see how it goes, and actually try out these new coping skills you're learning?"

"*Hmm,*" he says, sounding intensely dubious. "I prefer these…coping skills when they come with a…a trusted backup plan…"

"Yelling at squirrels isn't trustworthy enough?"

He pulls a face.

"Oh mate, you'll be fine. You know how careful they were with the diamorphine dose, not ODing you – they'll be the same with tapering the benzos – it'll be slow. Might even do your memory some good, taking a few less. *Trust in the universe,* and all that shit."

"Christ," he mutters, raking his fingers through his hair, "You're as bad as Em. Just 'cause I'm…y'know…*behaving myself* these days, doesn't mean I find it…*easy.* I'm fucking…*stressed* about this! Did I tell you I punched the safe?"

"Yes – reluctantly. Was that this morning?"

He runs his fingers over his eyes. "Last night, this morning – same…samesy. Look, Tom, I've…umm… I've got something I need to say." He frowns at me for a moment, then adds, "I did, actually… drag you out here for a reason – it just…fell out of my head, so…I'm sorry you had to witness my…y'know, squirrel…caffeine, demt— Uhh, dementia. But…umm…the real thing?" He watches me for a moment, chewing his lip with a worried frown, then he says, "You know this whole…hundred-day…meal idea, right?"

"Yeah? I think you're still allowed it, mate; caffeine's not exactly—"

"I'm not *saying* that, Tom. What I'm saying is, it's—I mean, the whole—Ah *hell*, man, it's just…weighing round my neck like a…m…umm…millstone! I don't want the *stress* anymore, I can't take it!"

"Mate, that's fine; no one's forcing you to eat with us if it feels like too much pressure, being the centre of proceedings – we can do that bit without you, then—"

"Oh, fuck *off,* Tom! You're not slel—*celebrating* without me – it's my thing! I did most of it! What I'm saying is, I want it for…umm… *ninety* days, instead. I think I can make ninety."

I watch him with a frown. "Uhh, you think you can 'make it' 'til tomorrow? Tomorrow's fine, but ten more days is impossible? *That's* what you're saying? Am I wrong to be a bit worried by that statement?"

He frowns. "It's tomorrow? You sure?"

"Yup. 90 days tomorrow."

He leans back, blows out a long sigh of relief, and says, "Ok. Phew. That's…that's good. Great, actually. Let's do it tomorrow. And after that, no more…counting days, alright? No more of that…that shit. It's too…y'know…stressful."

I watch him for a moment. "Are you planning to fuck up spectacularly the minute we've celebrated this, like a crap dieter celebrating losing a stone by eating a whole gateaux? 'Cause you've *really* got that vibe about you, right now…"

"Oh, piss off, man. I'm clef—*caffeinated*. I'm not planning to…fucking relapse. I just sort of…*promised myself something*, if I got to the cell…uhh…*celery?* Oh, fuck it, umm…*celebration*."

I wait for him to enlighten me. He doesn't. He's smirking about it though.

"What's the big—"

"No!" he says, immediately, "Can't tell you, not now, not…*yet*, not until we're at…*at the meal*. Or it won't come true. So, can we? Can I book this fucking…y'know…restaurant, for tomorrow?"

"If you reckon you can get a table this late, and it'll make you happy, then you know we'll be there. With bells on."

He smiles, looking heartily relieved, then he gets to his feet, and starts demanding a lift home.

Copyright Dorian Bridges 2024

CHAPTER NINETEEN

This place isn't bad, actually – I can see why Zillah chose it. It's admittedly bizarre for a restaurant, all neon-lit gloom, tanks of weird, hypnotically glowing jellyfish, and a mirrored ceiling, but the array of American-style junk food looks good, and it feels more like a nightclub than a restaurant. He's been missing nightclubs, since the overdose – he doesn't get too many of those blinding headaches anymore, but strobe lighting, it seems, is a pretty reliable way to set him off. He's taken to phoning up venues before he attends, and doing all he can to bribe, flatter or otherwise coerce the DJ into leaving the strobe button alone all night. Sometimes they even go for it, and, decked out in twattish-looking sunglasses, just to be sure, he gets a night out – he's even made himself a rhinestone-covered t-shirt with 'Not as much of a nob as I look' spraypainted across the front, specifically for these rare and glorious occasions.

Lucy's taking a picture of the jellyfish, when something grabs me by the hair – I turn around, and it's Zillah.

"Bloody hell – you're nearly on time? Is the apocalypse nigh?"

"Always," he says, and gives me an enthusiastic hug – his studded jacket feels like being tackled by a disgruntled hedgehog. Some things never change. His purple hair's had a white streak bleached into it for the past few weeks – a visual representation, he says, of going grey with stress. He looks the opposite of stressed tonight though – as does Em, who's hugging Lucy with a smile. The girls' truce has blossomed into a surprisingly solid friendship, since Lucy accepted that Em isn't an insufferable social media airhead, and Em, as a consequence, realised Lucy isn't all spiky exterior. They're even starting a reading group at our place, with three other friends, all bonding over their mutual love of smutty fantasy novels. I was rather looking forward to eavesdropping on the sexual fantasies of five horny women, but Lucy, knowing the paper-thickness of our downstairs walls, has barred me from all meetings…giving me the perfect weekly slot to get stoned and blow up pixels with Zillah.

As we take our seats, they're already deep into an incomprehensible, sniggering discussion about the sex life and penile attributes of 'dark elves'. Zillah's telling me he spent the day recording his Triumphant Return video – the great Internet Shitposting Ban expires in two more days, and he's enormously keen to get back to ranting at a camera.

"Guess what?" he says, beaming all over his face. I'm pretty sure I could, but I don't. I just smile, and gesture for him to go ahead.

"I did the *whole* damn thing un…umm…unscripted," he says, practically aglow with pride. "Had to cover the whole sodding…table in…in post-it notes, with big words on them, or whole…sentences, and it wasn't thoughtle—*flawless*, or fast – it's going to take a lot of editing to get rid of all my…umm… Oh fuck –" he rolls his eyes, "You know. Word-blanks. But it's ok. I mean, it's…tangential…word-vomit, really, and my head hurt like a bloody…*bastard* by the end, but, whatever – *I did it.*"

I come round the table to give him another hug. "That's huge, Zill – seriously. Did you address the *dreaded video* in this thing, or would you rather not talk about all that tonight?"

He frowns. "Oh, I addressed it. I mean I…well, I tried. Got a bit…stressed out, started…ranting, and this *fucking* benzo taper, man – I took all the…wotsit? Umm…*pills* I'm allowed, and Em wouldn't give me extra." He pulls a face. "Had to knock off the…ranting, before I literally…yacked over the camera." He sighs, chews his lip for a moment, then admits, "Had to be rather more…honest about my *brain* than I'd have liked, given the whole…*video situation*, but…fuck. I think they'll only stop dice…uhh? Dissecting me? – once they know all the…gory details anyway, you know?"

"Sadly so… Oh, did you wear yellow?"

"Huh? Why would I—"

"Oh, you know, that fucking conspiracy bullshit, everyone thinking you'd been held hostage – haven't you seen them telling you to wear yellow in your next video, if you need rescuing?"

He laughs. "Ah, shit, yeah – I did…umm…touch on that madness. Forgot about the yellow though. *Bollocks!* That could've been funny. I mean, if I actually…owned anything yellow? Hmm…" He trails off, doubtless plotting some bizarre act of trolling – and the waitress arrives with the drinks Lucy and I ordered, assuming the others wouldn't turn up for at least another fifteen minutes. Zillah groans with envy as an Old Fashioned and an Amaretto Sour get placed on the table in front of him, demanding,

"Did you *literally* just order my…favourite drinks, on prep—on purpose? Is this a test?" He eyes them contemplatively, then grins – "Fuck it. Can I have a swig?"

Lucy laughs. "Which one?"

"*Both…*"

I take my Old Fashioned off the tray, and ask, "Is that really a great idea?"

He pulls a face – "You know I've never stood by the…uhh…NA, AA model, man. I had half a glass of wine the other night – the rest's still in the…thingie. It's fine – I'm fine. I've got my…drug of choice, haven't I? I don't need to fuck about with your rop—rotten slop. Wouldn't risk a whole one, but let me have a *taste*…"

Lucy gives Em a questioning glance.

"*One* sip," says Em – "No more."

"Living on the edge!" says Lucy, and hands over the Amaretto Sour – I roll my eyes. Zillah's sense of self-preservation is still non-existent. We're going to have to watch him like a hawk – probably forever.

He holds it up, and declares,

"To my…umm…ninety days, and to all of you…wonderful…lunatics who fished me out of the…death-bin and…tolerated me this long. Thank you. And I mean that – a lot. You're…y'know…amazing. But I am never, *ever* counting days – not ever again."

Without waiting for clinked glasses or disagreement, he takes a sip, moans in bliss, snatches my drink, does the same, then reluctantly hands them back. Lucy applauds his little toast – Em's already flagging the waitress down, and rapidly distracts Zillah with food choices, before he can decide that ten sips are no worse than two.

He drags me off to the disabled stall the minute we've ordered, on the pretence of topping up his weed high, using the dreaded new vape. He warns me that it's freshly loaded – the thing's practically a psychedelic when packing a full wallop; Zillah loves it. It's obvious he hasn't hauled me in here just for this though. He has me sit on the closed toilet seat, while he takes the reasonably spotless-looking floor.

"Tom..." he says, vape still hissing away in his hand. "I sort of...promised myself something, if I made it this far..." He pauses, frowning, then says, "I need to pick your...umm...head, man, about proposals? You did alright with Lucy, didn't you? She said yes, I mean – first time, like, no...grand hoolim—*humiliation*? It's—"

"Whaaat! You're trying to get *married*? You?" I'm awestruck.

He laughs – shakes his head. "Christ, Tom, you don't have to...to say it like that – we've had this conserv— Concen—? Oh, fucking hell – this *talk*. We've had it before, haven't we?"

"Well...yeah, but honestly, you were wasted at the time – I wasn't taking anything you said seriously."

He shrugs. "Another life, another toilet, another...chemical. At least we haven't got a puking mate in the...uhh...the backdrop this time around, eh? I know it wasn't the most...charming, umm...whatevertheword, and I might not have been exactly...*on form,* but that doesn't mean I didn't mean it."

"Do you mean it now, or are you just being weird?"

"I *mean it,*" he says, frowning. "A lot. This whole...proposal plan's got me through a lot of...of bullshit sober days. I knew I couldn't ask her unless I...y'know...earned it..." He frowns, chews his lip for a moment, then sighs and says, "I know it's...*odd*, Tom, having me on track with life, after...38 dest—disastrous years – sometimes I feel like you don't know what to do with me anymore. You've got to upgrade your whole phig—Phys...? Uhh...phren—Oh shit it, man – word?"

"Philosophy?" I say, smiling.

Copyright Dorian Bridges 2024

He rolls his eyes – "Yeah. Slippery little bastard. *Philosophy:* I've…y'know…*graduated*. More or less. Doesn't mean I don't still need you – I always fucking will. We're just into the…the *adult arena,* now – I reckon it's time to talk proposals." He grins. "What I'm—"

"Hold up, mate – can I just confirm that you guys are *genuinely* steady enough for all this? I know you seem good on the surface, but then you always did…until I witnessed the infamous Diamorphine Smackdown in my fucking living room – I've told you the gory details; it wasn't pretty. Do you two ever…get like that still, behind closed doors?"

He glances up at me, grinning, and shakes his head in despair.

"You mean does she still…slap me round the face, right? And do I still dom—uhh…demolish bathrooms? Not lately, no. I even admitted to the…y'know, safe-punching, and we didn't *fight* about it – I was honest, I didn't make any…any snide remarks, and Em was…surprisingly understanding – we worked through it." He smiles, then winces, adding awkwardly, "Tom, I'm…*ugh.* I'm sorry I brought my…end-stage-insanity…*whirly-storm* into your house, man. I hate that I don't remember the ugly details. My brain chases itself in so many vile…circles about what I must've said, how…nuts I must've been, just…Christ. Those were nearly your fry—final memories of me, and there's so many nights I feel like running away to…to Mexico, just so I never have to look any of you in the eye ever again…"

"Give yourself a break, mate. I promise no one judges you anything like as harshly as your little Satan Brain. The Bathroom Incident is firmly in the past – now the sodding workmen have cleared off, at least. We've got the nicest bathroom we've ever had, and Lucy's over the moon with it; all is *more* than forgiven. And your 'whirly-storm' of crazy has been buzzing round me for over half my life – I'd be lost without it. Returning to this proposal though, are you both…fully ready for it – marriage?"

Zillah's beaming at his boots, unable to even meet my gaze as he says,

"Yeah…we are. You know how *I* feel, and it turns out she never stopped…loving me either – even when I was being… y'know…*impossible*. She's amazing. Probably a re…umm… re…*constituted*? No, fuck, sorry. Re…? Rehydrat—"

"Are you shooting for 'reincarnated', mate?"

He sighs. "Thanks. She's a reincarnated saint – she's got to be. You *know* what I was like, before…*everything* – I couldn't disagree…politely, I had to get all inte…umm…*intellectual* and…preachy about things. Not so much now, huh? Not capable of it, am I?" He grimaces. "Much as I hate my…dented fucking brain, I'm pretty sure I'm easier to live with. And after all the…ghastly crap that went down in that revolting host—hospital, what else could I do? I had to let her in, completely, no more…y'know, umm…debate-teaming and…info-dumping my way round things. Once I stopped all that…*shit*, and just told her how I was actually…feeling, it turned out she was listening all along – I was just coming at her like…well. Like a twat, frankly."

He gives me a wry smile – "Maybe almost dying got me a…free pass, or maybe she's just…*amazing*. Once I got the…the script, and she got the 'old me' back – *and* realised it wasn't just a…y'know…junkie…free-for-all – she actually got behind it. No

Copyright Dorian Bridges 2024

more m…umm…medication fights – none! We're back on the same team, and I could *not* be happier about that." He beams, then grimaces, adding, "Even though she's been writing a bloody…*brutally* honest blog piece about this year, and how glad she is to see the back of…? Uhh…oh hell, what did she call me?" He frowns at the wall, lapsing into a protracted silence that I've learned better than to interrupt. "'Zombie Boy Zillah…and his…? His…methadone…*mumblings?*'" he says, at last. "Was that it? Somewhere close? *Ghastly*, but at this point, I reckon she's earned the right to…to call me any damn…name she likes." He shakes his head, grinning. "Anyway…I'm going nowhere – she's going nowhere. I want to sleb—celebrate that." Beaming, he passes me the vape.

"I'm happy for you, Zill – really."

He sighs, prompting, "But…?"

"No – no 'buts', it's great, just –" I take another drag on the vape, trying to formulate my words. "All I'm saying is, are you *positive* you're steady enough in recovery to go shaking the whole applecart about like this?"

He smiles. "Oh, it's not going to be like that. We're never going the…umm…traditional route. No big scary weed—wedding. Aside from the fact I'd…undoubtedly…stress-puke all over the…vicar, Em doesn't want all that fuss anyway. All she cares about is the…dress. That's a…wotsit? Umm…*rite of passage*? – that needs to be done – but she doesn't want a big hectic…*awfulness* of a day, all that…hellish planning, being the centre of attention, everyone staring at her walking down—"

"My *god* you two are weird," I say, laughing as I hand him back the vape. "You both put yourselves out there for millions of strangers to stare at, even though you had a panic attack doing a presentation to nine people at uni, and now Em doesn't even want to walk down the aisle? You're mad!"

He laughs under his breath. "That much has been…whateverthewood by mutt—*multiple* doctors, Tom. It's just different, doing it over the internet, no…no staring faces. So—"

"What's the point of a big white dress if no one's going to stare at it?"

"Tom, you're drunk, will you just…shut up and…and listen to me, please?"

I start laughing. "I'm in the Twilight Zone! Zillah's getting married, Em's a wallflower, and now we're hiding in a bathroom and *you're* telling *me* I'm too wasted. Ahh! I was right – the world's ending!"

He shakes his head in mock despair – takes another drag off his vape. "I'm never letting you at this thing again, man – you can't handle it. But I need your…y'know…*advice*, so can you keep your shit together for five minutes?"

I'm howling. It's beyond backwards. He's right though, it's that bloody vape – four drags on top of a strong cocktail, and now I feel like we're twenty-one again, mischievously hiding out in Zillah's room with Cypress Hill playing and a towel up against the door to keep the smoke in. Zillah reaches out to pat me on the head, and keeps inhaling. Finally he says,

"Ok…ok, I'm catching up. I'm resigned to sub…umm…sub-optimal? – advice, but all the same, I'm asking."

"You're not even on one knee – I won't marry you unless you get on one knee."

He humours me, shifting on the floor, then he says,

"Tom, I need to ask how the hell I go about— Oh, *fuck, ouch!* No, nope, I'm too old and…bony for your…*shit…nanigans?* man – note to self, don't propose in a public…loo." He gets off his knee, which clicks loudly in protest, then says, "Right, so… Em – like me – cares most about the…uhh…honeymoon? Like…travelling? But the thing is, I don't know if I *can?* With my…y'know…script, I mean? I could go with…methadone, done that before – obviously we couldn't touch anywhere strict, like Thai—"

"I thought this was about proposals? Wouldn't she rather have a say in the honeymoon, or foreign wedding, or whatever you're thinking here? Why not just pop the question, then work on it as a team? That's my advice."

"*No,*" he says firmly, frowning. "No…she needs to know what she's…getting into. She misses travelling, after this year. I miss it too… All the…the little things. Walking down those long…tubey-things to the plane, the *smell* of the plane, getting off at the other end being…blasted by the heat of a whole other crom—Uhh, continent? – it's magic. But I don't know about the…*med situation…*" He trails off, frowning at the floor, chewing his nails.

"Going back on methadone, you mean? Even for a week or two?"

He nods, not looking up.

I sigh. "I don't think I can answer that one for you, mate. Personally, I'd be worried. I know you'll be on holiday, you'll be distracted, which—"

"I know, I know, being somewhere…different's going to help with the…cravings, but I wasn't exactly…*great*, on…on methadone, was I? I mean, I hated myself, and now it's pretty clear that wasn't entirely… un…un-rational? I may not remember Em…dumping me, but it wasn't really a shock. Not when she explained what…y'know…did us in. All the…nodding out, the sleeping all day, my fucking…'dead zombie' eyes? What's the point me…forcing myself back on that crap, for Em's sake, trying to give her a decent…honeymoon, then just becoming this bloody zoom—zombie she can't stand?" He watches me anxiously. Just looking him in the eye, I know what he means. He just *looks* different these days. Even with the side-effects of the overdose doing a number on his brain, he still seems clearer, most of the time, than he's been in so long.

"Shit, Zill… I don't know. Honestly I'd be more worried about you doing something stupid to yourself. You were self-destructive as all hell, that last week you don't remember."

"I was self-destructive as all hell my whole…*life* before getting the script, Tom – I don't think you can blame the…uhh…methadone…"

"No, but it's essentially you, unregulated, isn't it? I just don't think you should rock the boat – certainly not yet. Wherever you go, you're going to be able to score street gear, you know that, you've got killer junkie-dar – and it'd hardly be the first time, would it? Not to bring up bad memories or anything, but need I mention the great Barcelona fiasco? It's going to be tempting. We've all seen the news stories about fentanyl these days, and that's only *one* potential—"

"Oh fucking *hell*, man. You think I can't…handle it, you think—" He growls under his breath and runs his hands through his hair, muttering, "Barcelona for *shit's* sake! You've got the memory of a…a twisted ol—*elephant…*"

"I'm sorry, Zill, but am I wrong? You were barely a year into using on that trip, you had your methadone, and you still couldn't stay away from it for five days. I'm just—"

"Oh *god* Tom, I get it, ok? Wherever we go, I'm going to…to fuck things up. As ever, you're right, you're right, and I fucking…hate you for it – I've got the…*willpower* of a pissed-up lo…umm…*lemming,* drugs are everywhere, and that's that. It's never going to happen, is it? Great. Fucking great. Now what?"

"Oh Jesus, Zillah. C'mon – just look at the flipside. It only sounds terrible because things are so good for you now. You're like this blissful *entity* these days, floating about the place all level-headed and chill. Think about the fact you got Em back – I didn't think that would stick, when we were in the hospital with you. All your problems were still there – I thought she was sticking around out of pure pit—*sympathy*. But then you got the script, and the therapy, started going for your mad mornings in the woods, and you really mellowed out – there's no way I ever see her leaving you. It's a good thing."

He sighs. "True…I guess. But what am I meant to *do* about this? Can you stop bret—*berating* me, and just…just tell me what to *do?"*

"I repeat – pop the question, give Em a say in the matter. This isn't the Victorian era, mate – I know you think sweeping romantic gestures are great, but Em's more of a control freak than you've got her pegged. And when it comes to you and meds, or mental health, she's got a lot to say. So let her say it. Worry is not a good wedding gift."

"*Shit*," he says, slumping back against the wall and staring up at the ceiling. "Fair points... Horrible, but fair... So if I'm just...jumping into...y'know, umm...proposing, how do I do it? When?"

"Well, have you got a ring yet?"

He smiles slightly, and shifts so he can dig in his pocket.

"Oh fuck – no way! You fucking *brought it here?* Are you planning to—"

"*Hell* no, I just wanted to show you – is that so...*weird?* Be warned, man, it's a piece of shit – that's the whole...umm...thing. There's no way I'm choosing the ring, no way she'd ever want me to, so I've bought her an...an absolute...piece of shit, just so there's *no* point at which she can ever think it's...serious – the ring part, at least..."

He produces what looks to me like a very, very standard engagement ring, and holds it out.

"What...umm...where's the joke? It's boring, sure, but—"

"Read the...stuff, round the sides."

I peer closer, and realise the gold band is engraved with, "*I love laughing at livers.*" I start laughing, asking, "What the fuck? Is this some...anti-alcohol joke of yours?"

"No!" he says, head in his hands, laughing, "Jesus, Tom – *Live, Laugh...Love?* You know, that cheesy fucking...whatever-the-word-is? Em can't *stand* it – I mean, no one can, anymore – and she...she hates rings like this, the single...stone on a solid gold...thingie type; they were super...y'know, trendy about a decade ago, then *everyone* got one, and now the only difference between them is how big a…wotsit? Uhh…diamond? – your bloke could afford. It's just a…a pissing contest, for dull people, you know, the…*live, laugh, love* kind of people? I thought she'd get a…kick out of this bloody men—*monstrosity*. I went for the most…medium stone I could find, too, just to make it even worse. Though yeah, actually – I *do* like laughing at people's…y'know…livers, when they're…hungover, and I'm not."

I keep my opinions to myself, as far as liver damage goes, instead saying,

"I've *got* to play devil's advocate here, Zill…'cause maybe I'm just stoned, but, what's stopping you jumping right in? Why *not* do it tonight? All I'm saying is, if you start overthinking this proposal shit, you know you'll only get so stressed out you bail on the whole idea. So why not just *do it,* here – *tonight?"*

He blinks at me, going wide-eyed with horror as he repeats, *"Here? Now?!"*

"Well, I can think of a million better times and places, but I also know you'll work yourself up into an unbelievable tizzy if we try and make it perfect, then I leave you to go it alone. I reckon there's no time like the present!"

He blows out a shaky breath, staring at the ring in his hand, and saying nothing at all. When the silence stretches on for several more seconds, I ask,

"Have you got any better ideas?"

He glances up at me, looking anxious, and oddly vague. The silence, and his bemused expression, continue. From the look on his face, you'd think he was figuring out the meaning of life, realising he'd left the gas on, and being threatened with an especially disquieting method of execution, all at the same time. It's become a familiar look. I sigh –

"Ah, hell… Have you lost all your words, or have I stressed you into a full-on BSOD?"

He stares straight through me, and when he opens his mouth to speak, nothing comes out. He looks increasingly panicky. Blue Screen Of Death it is, then. I get off the closed toilet seat, and sit down next to him, saying quietly,

"Mate, it's fine. I'm right here, Em and Lucy are outside. Just breathe."

I have no idea if he even understands words when he's deep into one of his bloody brain-glitches, but regardless, he lets out a shaky breath, and curls up in a ball, forehead on his knees, fingers tangled into his hair. I lay a hand on his shoulder, and wait it out.

It takes the better part of two minutes before his anxious breathing slows, and he tentatively raises his head. He looks mildly awkward as he meets my gaze, and begins,

"It's… I'm…?" He sighs in irritation, rolls his eyes, and just points a finger at his head. *"Glitch,"* he manages, at last, stating the patently obvious, then, "S…umm…sorry?" He shivers slightly, and the automatic pocket pat-down begins. I can see the dawning horror in his eyes as he finds himself bereft of benzos, and I intervene,

"Em's got them, mate. Five minutes wait, remember?"

I'm expecting a total meltdown, frankly, and it's nothing short of miraculous when he just mutters an emphatic *"Fuck!",* closes his

Copyright Dorian Bridges 2024

eyes, takes a few slow, deep breaths, then checks his watch. After that, he just sits there, frowning, and breathing. He's visibly freaked out, but nonetheless, he's holding it together. I'm bloody impressed; god bless the new therapist – he's getting better at dealing with this shit every time I see him.

A few moments later, he forces a smile, nods decisively, and says,

"Umm. Yeah… I've re…umm…? Re…configured? Sorry for the…*weird*. What were you saying?"

I watch him for a moment, then suggest,

"Let's go and eat, mate – it wasn't important."

He looks disapproving –

"Tom, I'm not…*stupid* – you were looking all…all meaningful a minute ago. Now you're just being…" he trails off, frowning at the wall. "Oh, fuck it, man, don't make me…work for it right now – you know the word. Talking down to me? Dickishly? Word, please?"

"Patronising?" I suggest, smiling slightly.

"*Indeed*. You're being patronising as…as all hell. Tell me what you…y'know, said – I'm ok."

"Might be a bit stressf—"

"*Tom*, you are…stressing me out far more by keeping it from me! I've lost enough m…umm…memories, haven't I? It pisses me *off* when you use my glitches to rob me even more. *What* did you *say?*"

"Alright…" I concede, "I'm sorry – won't happen again. This may have been a really stupid, stoned thought anyway…but what I was saying, was that you should, maybe, get this proposal over with, before you can terrify yourself out of the idea completely. You've got the ring, she's getting drunk, and I'm here for moral support – why not just—?"

"Here?" he says again, wide-eyed. "Now?! *Propose,* to Em?"

I nod.

He blows out a shaky breath, pockets the ring, and says firmly,

"No. No fucking way. Not here, not…tonight, I can't, I'm all…glitchy and you've…wigged me out. I need to prepare."

"You've got the ring, you prat! How much more prepared d'you need to be?"

He frowns at the floor, and lapses into silence for so long I have to ask if he's glitching again – he tells me to fuck off; he's thinking – that takes a while these days…

"Thinking what?" I whisper, when the silence stretches on. *"Can I help?"*

He glances up, and a mischievous grin spreads slowly across his face. "I'm getting…*ideas,*" he says, eyes a-glitter with increasingly manic glee – "You're right…as usual. It's now or…or never. Let's just fucking…*do it!*"

I slap him on the back, asking,

"D'you need help planning, or are you just going to wing it?"

"Plan," he says emphatically. "So…the theme of the ring is just…awfulness, right? Like…y'know, umm…cornball, dull people,

awful shit? Can you think of a *really terrible* way to…to propose to her?"

I burst out laughing – "I don't know that we're headed down the best track here, mate!"

"Look, you said it yourself – I'm too fucking…anxious to do it well, so why not s—umm, screw it up completely?"

"That's basically been your life motto, 'til this year, hasn't it?"

"Got me this far," he says, with a slightly manic grin. "C'mon, ideas – teb—terrible stuff! What would she *hate?*"

"Well…you said she didn't want to be the centre of attention, right? So what *if—*"

"Ah, not that, Tom – she'll…hate me forever if I do anything really…y'know…showy. *No,* you arsehole! Don't look at me like that, I mean it – it's not…not happening. What else?"

"Well, how awful d'you wanna go?"

He grins. "How awful are you thinking?"

"For starters, you should get *plastered*, Zill, like really, really—I mean, shit, no, you don't actually *do it* – get a vodka bottle, fill—"

"Wait!" he interrupts, wide eyed. "Shit…I'm slow, I'm fucking slow, but I think I've got it! Drunk is an…an idea, but not on its own – on its own I'm just being a…y'know, a…nob, but what if…" He trails off, then says, "Crap, it's in my…umm, thing? Jacket? Get me that vodka bottle, and my…my jacket. Just tell her I'm…I dunno, taking a dump. That's a…a good start."

"Then what?"

"Meet me back here. Quick, before it all…y'know, falls out of my head!"

I sneak back to the table – it must be bloody obvious how stoned I am, I can't stop grinning, literally face paralysed in a grin like a total nutter. When I grab Zillah's jacket off the chair, Em asks,

"Where is he? You've been gone ages. Food's here."

"Oh…he's, umm… Yeah. *Bathroom issues.*" I pull a 'things are unfortunate' sort of grimace, but it doesn't go the way any normal person would lean.

"Oh hell," she says, instantly alert, "What's he done? What's he taken?"

"Oh god, no, no – he's fine! Not dying, just…*busy in the bottom department*. I'll fetch him. *Don't worry!*" I add, in my most jovial-arsehole voice. Not waiting for a response, I nip back through the corridor to the bathrooms, head out the other end, and bemoan to the bartender my need for an empty vodka bottle –

"Engagement prank," I explain, "Don't worry. Nothing can go wrong!"

He smiles blandly – guy looks at least as stoned as me – and produces an empty bottle of posh vodka.

"Oh, *perfect*, mate – thank you. He's not just drunk, he's blown a fortune on it. *Beautiful!*"

Copyright Dorian Bridges 2024

I leg it back to the bathrooms, and find Zillah lying on the floor of the disabled stall, sniggering at the ceiling.

"What's so funny?" I ask.

"Germs!" he says. "Just...*germs!*"

I never get to hear why they're so hilarious – the minute I remind him of what we're doing, it startles him straight into another wide-eyed, blankly staring glitch-out – he's back with me in little more than twenty seconds this time, but now he hasn't got a clue why *I'm* banging on about germs – *"What?* Shut up, Tom, ubv—obviously there are...germs, piss germs, shit germs, probably...sexual ones to boot. Have I been *lying* in this? Eurgh, hell. I shouldn't do this tonight, man, it's too much, I need—"

"To psyche yourself up and prepare, I know. Tough shit – not happening. Here – start slurping this down."

I've filled the vodka bottle with water, after rinsing it thoroughly – I hold it out to him.

"Nice," he concedes, grudgingly. "This cost...five hundred...quid, you know?"

"You're taking the piss! Seriously? *Vodka?"*

"Yup. I like looking at how much I'm not...spending on that shit sometimes. The...umm...Harrods? – *they* fucking stock this. Wonder if Em knows..."

"No time for wondering, she's already stressing about you, I—"

"What the fuck did you say!"

"Nothing! ...but I think she, possibly, read it as 'He's overdosed in the bog again' – not what I was going for, but—"

"Urgh *hell*, man – will you people never let me...live it down? Look, just hold the...thingie when I give it to you, it's already filming, and don't forget to be an...arsehole...vlogger, 'til I say the...the *code word*. Which is...umm...'crawfish'?"

"Are you gonna remember that?"

"Uhh...no. Hang on." He fishes in his jacket, finds a pen, and scribbles *'CRAWFISH?'* on the back of his hand. Then he curses, getting that pissed-off expression that comes on whenever he runs into one of his limitations, and says, "You're gonna have to keep thirst—thrusting that thing in my face the whole way, man. I can't...drink and film all at once – not with this sodding hand. So just help me be ub— uhh, obnoxious?"

"Can do. Absolutely."

Someone starts banging on the door. Zillah hides behind me.

"Zill?" says Em's voice. "Are you in there?"

"No!" he says, "Sit down, I'm fine, I'm coming! I'm just...doing what people *do,* in...umm...in...*these bloody places!*"

A brief pause, then, "Zill? You *actually ok?*"

"*Yes!*" we groan, in unison.

"Oh, why the fuck are you in the loo with him, Tom! Get out here! It's his ninetieth day, and if you're in there doing what I—"

"I solemnly swear," I tell her, "There is nothing illicit in this toilet. Have a *little* faith in him…or me, at the very least. He's a bit glitchy, that's all – everything's fine, we'll be with you in no time."

"Ok…?" she says, still sounding thoroughly dubious, "Well, if you're sure you don't need me…hurry up – the food's getting cold."

As her heels click away from the bathroom, Zillah nervously appears from behind me, still clutching his camera. "Got that on film," he says, "Apparently. Not sure I needed or…or wanted it, but…alright. Hold this?"

He hands me the camera, picks up the vodka bottle, and I open the door.

As we walk towards the table, I'm going backwards, camera held dramatically aloft. Zillah's coming at me, swigging his pseudo-vodka, and telling the camera at maximum volume,

"Hello, world! There's something very…special I wanted to do today, and I don't just mean getting royally ru— umm, *rat-arsed!* But I did that too, 'cause what else d'you do on your…y'know, sober birthday? I'm at this swanky…ish…restaurant-place, celebrating being off street gear for…umm…ninety days? …and I just blew *five hundred fucking quid* on a bottle of the most esp—*expensive*, legal v…umm…vodka out there – now I'm drinking *all of it!* Eurgh, it's bloody disgusting!" He violently spits a large mouthful up the wall – the girls are in sight, both standing up, looking aptly horrified. "But it is!" he continues, "It's all about the bloody ligatur—*legality* in this dump of a...a Tory...wasteland, and this stuff is LEGAL!" He thrusts his bottle in the air, and actually gets a whoop and some applause out of a plastered-looking table to the right of ours. "I mean, it's...poison, it makes you violent, or...y'know...violently...suicidal, it's *way* more toxic than smack, it's not even a fun drug, but n...umm...norm...alising? – this filth, it makes all the sense in the world! The Tory party won't know what's hit it, now the Infamous Bren—*Braindead Boy's* back on the LEGAL STUFF!"

"Zillah..." Em begins, eyes like saucers, "What the *fuck* are you—"

"I got somethin' *for you!*" he announces, in a rather overdone slur, and I thrust the camera into Em's face, Zillah hollering, "We're gettin' it on video, 'cause iss...iss *important*. Iss our big...umm...moment! Wave to the camera, babe!"

"What the— *Babe?*" She frowns at his eyes, and I can see she might be cottoning on. Maybe it's the lack of booze smell. Should've drenched him in the stuff. I draw back, getting both of them in shot, and bellow,

"Making memories, Em! *Memories!*"

Zillah drops to his knees, both of them, pulls the ring out, then starts doing a 'we are not worthy' bow until she takes the thing, at which point he sits up expectantly, stage-whispering, "*Read it, please!*"

"I love...laughing...at livers?" – she is, too. Laughing, that is.

"Look how...how *medium* it is!" Zillah giggles, back on his feet – "It's so...so *medium!* Em, baby, will you please m...umm...marry me in a medium way, get...medium...fat, and have exactly the…uhh…per clap—*capita*…average of…*of*…? Oh, *shit it,* I've forgotten! – one-point…something kids, with me?"

"Please, *please* tell me you're not actually drunk?" she says, in a nervous undertone.

"Of course I'm bloody not," he replies, frowning. "Stoned out my box, but that's it."

"Is all this…for real?"

"The ring…isn't. The babies most certainly aren't. But umm… Yeah? The…*asking,* is…is real? Very real?"

He watches her anxiously, then gives up on all pretence, and starts babbling, "I'm sorry for this…this godforsaken…stupidity, Em, I am, seriously, but I was never gonna get it right without hive—hyperventilating, and…throwing up – probably all over you – you know I'm the least r…umm…romantic mess you can possibly imagine when I get…nervous, so this was…uhh, Tom's idea. Totally, totally Tom's idea. I know – it's terrible. I'm sorry. He got me stoned. But will you just…marry me, Em? Please? If it's…it's what you want, too, of course? It's just, after everything we've…survived this year, there's no one else in the glal— Umm…galaxy? – that I want beside me, whatever the world throws at us next. You're the most…beautiful…surprising woman I've ever met, and if you didn't…kick me in your sleep, and have a really dis…uhh…disturbing thing for bad… Umm…? Oh, whatstheword? All your bloody dead things? The ones you think are…*hilarious*, but I keeping having…scary-dreams about? Word?"

"Taxidermy?" says Em, laughing.

"*Yes!* It's a good thing you keep sneaking those un…unspeakable… horrors into our bedroom, 'cause if you didn't, you'd be *too* fl…umm…flawless. I'd run…screaming from your…y'know? Too-perfect…*ness?*" He sighs, shaking his head in despair as he says, "Oh hell, Em, I'm…mangling this – you're more amazing than my…bashed-in brains can vlerb—*verbalise*. But you know me – who I really was, as well as the sub…umm…sub…standard, thrift-store…*thing* I am now, and somehow, you still seem to love me, in spite of my many…dents, bruises and…cata…catroph? Oh fuck – pretty bad…flailings?" He runs a hand through his hair, rolls his eyes, and mutters, "Christ, this is a mess. Stupid un…unscripted video – too much…talking today. Head's gone spaghetti. I'm sorry, Em, I'll write you something when we get home – I will. It'll be…brilliant. Might take me a few days, but it'll do you je—umm…it'll be…good? Hopefully? So I'm…I'm sorry this sounds so…*ugh,* but, would you…*maybe,* consider doing me the…*brain-melting honour* of becoming—"

"Uhh, guys?" Lucy interjects, with such atrocious timing I kick the leg of her chair, "I think that table's filming us?"

"Oh, fuck me…" Zillah mutters, turning to stare – the drunk table are indeed filming us, on multiple phones. They've definitely recognised him, or Em, or both, and now his imitation piss-up is being beamed around the globe. He's about to go running over there, but Em grabs his arm, saying,

"Look, fuck them. Are you *positively* for real?"

"I am?" he says, sounding about as certain as a sunny day in Wales, and fiddling awkwardly with his hair. "I *really* am? Would I have spent so much time…shopping for such a…a godawful piece of…shit if I wasn't? Seriously, look at it – I'm proud of that. But, no – I mean it, I'm…serious – will you? Marry me, I mean? You know I don't want a massive, crazy…umm…wedding, no—"

"Neither do I. *Ever*. No scary weddings, but there'd better be a—"

"A huge crazy white…dress, I know – I haven't forgotten that bit. We'll do it. Absolutely. As many crazy white…dress shops as you like – any time. Does that mean you're…you're saying…*yes?*"

Em smiles at him, and holds up her weird little in-joke of a ring. After the slightest hesitation, she slips it on. "It means yes," she says, and takes his hand. "This is the worst and weirdest proposal on planet Earth, Zill – you literally *spat* up the wall – but honestly it's still better than the three years I was banking on it taking you to ask me at all. Of course it's a yes. I tried out the world with no you for five days, and four nights, and it was my own personal trip to hell. You asking to be my permanent sidekick – *and* not choosing the ring? Flawless execution, fiancé." She grins, but when he moves to kiss her, she holds up a finger, adding, "But I do have conditions. You *keep* going to therapy, for as long as it takes, and we are *not* worrying about this wedding for at least another six months. I'm not putting any more stress on you, or us, right now, so…can you handle me staying at the fiancée stage for a while, before we double-upgrade to husband and wife?"

Zillah's beaming like a lottery winner – "*Fiancée…*" he whispers, visibly delighted. "It's a lovely word – especially on you. Wear it as…as long as you like – I'll be…umm…obedient?" He grins, until a flicker of doubt crosses his face, and he quietly adds, "I hope I don't…fuck it all up. I mean, I really, *really* don't want to…lose you over my…stupid—"

"Hey – we've talked about this. There's only *one* thing I'd walk directly the fuck away from, and that's you trying to jump off the sodding planet again. So, *you* don't go leaving Earth, and *I* don't walk away. It's not that hard, is it?"

He smiles, but he still looks uncertain – "Your job's harder than mine…"

"Oh, Zill, you are *not* intolerable. Come on – you know all the snarky jealous chicks in my DMs are even more obnoxious than the dick pics, right? If I ever need reminding how lucky I am to have you, believe me, I get clobbered over the head with it daily."

He laughs, then they're lost in a very gropey kiss, until the weed gets the better of me, and I butt in, "But where are you *wearing* this crazy white dress to, without a real wedding?"

Em pulls away from Zillah, but stays entwined in his arms. She shrugs – "Garden party, maybe? At my folks' place. We'll do a little registry office thing, then fuck off there. And afterwards, I'll probably wear it to goth clubs, 'cause why not?"

"Wow," says Zillah, clearly taken aback, "You've…thought about this more than me!"

Em looks sheepish. "You…umm, write a lot of post-its these days. Might have found one stuck to my sock. Knew you were thinking about it…but I wasn't expecting *this*. Please god tell me that bottle never had vodka in it?"

"Define 'never'?" I say, and Zillah cuffs me round the ear, rather harder than intended. That hand is bloody lethal.

"I swear," he says, smiling – "I don't even like vodka." Turning back to me, he hastily adds, "Tom, since I'm…blaming this on you, will you *please* just…bribe that table before Cindy's…y'know, umm, wayward…sibling…*thing* goes off? She'll be distend—*descending* on this restaurant with a…a crazy-jacket in seconds!" He thrusts a handful of cash at me, and I hurry off to rein in the chaos.

When I glance back, they're happily entwined, and I find myself wondering whether, just occasionally, there *is* such a thing as a happy ending. Zillah's got his eternity of legal drugs, and though they've come at the price of everything he once valued in himself, I can see him coming round, little by little, to the fact that his newfound peace of mind is far more priceless. Em's clearly happy with her more-or-less functional Zillah, and Lucy's visibly delighted amidst an entire tableful of abandoned junk food. It's a tableau of dysfunctional bliss, all captured in the upheld cameras of four pissed-up, gawping strangers. I stand back for a moment, just to take it in: *utopia…*

And then, one of these drunken prats drops an *absolutely* revolting comment about Zillah's intellectual capabilities since the overdose, and I plummet back down to this shittily flawed Earth, wondering whether Em'd mind too much if I knocked someone's teeth down their throat at her engagement dinner…

Copyright Dorian Bridges 2024

Copyright Dorian Bridges 2024

More From This Author:

Millennium Gothic: an autobiographical tale of growing up on the early 2000s goth scene, interwoven with the twisted allure of the early 'pro ana' communities, first loves, first drugs, and heavy secrets...

The Putrescent Vein: a collection of dark porno-gore short stories, featuring everything from multiple vampires, to the sexual fantasies of a boy traumatised by vaginas, a seductively corrupt modern spin on *The Picture of Dorian Gray,* and the confessions of a used car salesman, in lust with your automobile...

Both books are available on Amazon.

Printed in Great Britain
by Amazon